"CHILLING AND THRILLING!"
—Best Sellers

"MIND-BOGGLING!" *—Nashville Tennessean*

"HIGH SUSPENSE THAT RIVALS *DAY OF THE JACKAL!*" *—Oregon Journal*

> *This is the voice of Armageddon. You can see how close I was able to get to the Vice President of the United States and how easy it would be for me to have killed him. In fact, the pistol was in my pocket. But the man was not sufficient to my purpose. For mine must be an act so vast it will become the yardstick against which all assassinations, past and future, will be measured. . . .*

"A countdown to disaster, with built-in tension and bizarre sex . . . a must for all suspense fans!"
—Library Journal

"Tension mounts to fever pitch, right to the edge-of-your-seat climax!"*—Beaumont Journal*

"THIS IS THE ULTIMATE ONE!"
—Kirkus Reviews

Bestsellers from SIGNET You'll Enjoy

The Voice of Armageddon

by DAVID LIPPINCOTT

A SIGNET BOOK from
NEW AMERICAN LIBRARY
TIMES MIRROR

Published by
THE NEW AMERICAN LIBRARY
OF CANADA LIMITED

TO J.E.B.

"The trouble with assassination is that most of the interest and sympathy goes to the victim, while the assassin winds up a mere footnote to history. I had to do better than that.

Skyjacking—particularly with all the new rules—always gets good news coverage and seemed like a real challenge. But tell me honestly: does anybody remember the name of even a single skyjacker? Hell, no.

That was the beauty of the Armageddon plan. As I finally worked it out, it was designed so that all of the world's interest and attention would be focused on me, and me alone. Which was only right. After all, I'm the guy the world forgot."

—Opening lines from the
journal of Lars Colonius. The
document was not discovered until
some hours after the matter had been
concluded.

Chapter One

There's no sign on the house where I grew up in Buffalo.
I don't guess there ever will be. But I bet taxi-drivers will
point the house out to strangers anyway and tell them
who used to live there and they'll talk about what kind
of person I was and wonder why I did it and maybe
feel a little shudder of fear just looking at the place.

And, hell, that's better than a damned sign any day.
—*Extract from the*
journal of Lars Colonius

Wednesday, April 29—Armageddon minus eighty-
five.

LARS COLONIUS stood waiting, bareheaded in the sun,
on the edge of the crowd outside the All-Rite Shopping
Center, off U.S. 75 into Macon. Although it was not yet
midmorning, the suffocating damp of an early Georgia
spring brought a lacework of sweat to his unhealthily pale
forehead, and Colonius twice had to touch a handkerchief
to the roots of his thinning hair. This he did almost fur-
tively, since it made him feel self-conscious; at twenty-
five, it was not right that a man's hair should already be
going.

Carefully, he stuffed the grayish handkerchief back
into his trouser pocket with his left hand. It was an
awkward movement for him, but necessary; the right
hand was in his other trouser pocket, endlessly fingering
the cheap, blunt-nosed thirty-eight, stroking it, massaging
it, drawing power from it. Occasionally, he shifted its
position in his pocket completely to feel the sudden cool

1

of it through the pocket's thin lining, shoving it hard against the damp skin of his upper thigh or pressing it into the warmth of his genitals.

The crowd cheered suddenly and loudly, punctuating their applause with strident Rebel yells. Lars Colonius cheered too, although he later couldn't remember a word of what the speaker had said.

Quickly, Jimmy Eggans, the candidate for governor, held up his hand in a promise to the crowd that his remarks were almost over. Behind him on the platform, the Vice President tried not to look relieved. His speech of endorsement for Eggans was already delivered, although, since Georgia hadn't had a Republican governor since Reconstruction, the reasons for his being here were politically obscure.

Involuntarily, the fingers of Colonius' hand tightened around the pistol grip as his eyes narrowed to study him. The Vice President was staring fixedly at the back of Eggans' head, nodding occasionally in approval, his mouth set in the half-smile of unqualified, partisan endorsement. But the vacant look in the man's eyes showed that, like Colonius, he was hearing nothing of what Eggans said and that his mind was absorbed in thoughts of things far from the All-Rite Shopping Center: his family, his future, the state of the nation, possibly. Colonius tensed and stared so hard at him that the Vice President seemed suddenly to feel it; the politician's eyes swung slowly from the back of Eggans' head to stare directly back into Colonius'. For a second, they remained locked to his, then moved suddenly away, as if embarrassed.

The crowd was cheering again as Jimmy Eggans stepped far back from the microphone to show his speech was over. Beside him, the Vice President applauded vigorously and leaned over to Eggans with some secret word of assurance. To one side of the platform, the small Dixieland band found its brass throat as Jimmy Eggans and the Vice President started down the short half-flight of wooden steps into the crowd, which surged forward to surround them.

State troopers grabbed hands and began pushing Jimmy Eggans through; Secret Service men quickly formed a series of solid eccentric rings around the Vice President and began moving him toward the limousine sitting on the curb of the parking lot. Lars Colonius shoved hard and brought himself to the edge of the outer ring. With his left hand, he pushed aside obstructing arms and shoulders; his right remained in his pocket, tensed around the automatic.

Then it happened. A reporter in the crowd called to the Vice President, who paused to find the source of the familiar voice. Colonius lunged forward, shoving his right arm between two Secret Service men and thrusting it directly at the Vice President. There was a small cry from somewhere, the Vice President's mouth dropped open and his eyes widened to stare unbelievingly at Colonius. Not very far off to his left, a flashbulb popped.

With a sudden, twisted smile, Lars Colonius seized the Vice President's half-raised limp hand in his and shook it vigorously. There was a stunned pause, and it was over. A sigh seemed to come from the crowd. The Secret Service men glared at Colonius angrily. The Vice President's face relaxed into a relieved smile and he muttered something like, "Nice of you t'come. Be sure to vote right, son, hear?" Almost immediately, the eccentric rings closed around him again and swept him along toward the limousine, one of the agents still staring back at Colonius, resentful and annoyed that someone had managed to pierce their always-fragile defenses and somehow laid hands on their charge, if only to shake his hand and wish him well.

As the sirens of the motorcycles rose in an ascending wail, the motorcade pulled out onto Route 75 and swept the party on toward the heart of Macon and the luncheon. But Lars Colonius stood there staring at the picture frozen in his mind: the Vice President's half-open mouth, the unexpected flicker of the flashbulb in the bright sunlight. The scene was more charged in the reliving than it had been in the reality, and Colonius could feel himself swell with excitement against the cold, hard lump of the revolver in his pocket.

He stood there like that for some time, the crowd slowly drifting away, although virtually unnoticed by him. It would have been easy to do, so damned easy; but the man just wasn't right. He had been ready and willing to do it, but the man just wasn't right, dammit.

With a forward scrunch of his shoulders, Colonius kicked disappointedly at the hard red clay beneath his feet. Next time, the target would have to be chosen with greater care.

Thursday, April 30—Armageddon minus eighty-four.

Lying on his bed, Lars Colonius stared at the faded floral wallpaper of the Sweet Laurel Hotel & Apartments. It was a third-class hotel in a town where third class meant what it said. During the Second World War, when Camp Wheeler, slightly southeast of Macon, was swollen with hard-training infantry replacements, some attempt was made to redecorate the Sweet Laurel and it even conceived of itself as having a bright future; the same paper, when new and fresh, had been stared at by an endless succession of lovers, wives, and mothers in temporary residence until the Army should ship their men to be killed by the Japanese, via Fort Ord, California, or by the Germans, via Camp Kilmer, New Jersey. Three-quarters of the way through the war, Camp Wheeler, like many of the replacements trained in it, abruptly folded up and disappeared, their missions not so much accomplished as forgotten.

There was no particular reason for Lars Colonius to choose Macon as his new home; three months earlier, when his brother's GI life insurance—some $25,000 in today's peacetime Army—was paid him, Colonius simply moved out of the back room of his uncle's house in Buffalo and moved there. Macon was selected only because it sounded cheap, the air fare was low (night excursion rate), and Colonius vaguely remembered having heard someone talk about it once. It would make as good a base of operations for him as anyplace.

Rolling over on the thin mattress, which caused the wirelike network of steel stringers that served as a box spring to give a complaining groan, Colonius checked the balance in his passbook for the third time in two days:

$19,468.02. More than enough to finance the thing. Living in Macon was cheaper than he had dared hope and even with some of the high expenses the plan would run into later, it was going to work out fine.

But the victim would have to be selected with more care. Yesterday's encounter with the Vice President—Colonius had only learned he was even in town in yesterday's paper—could have been a disaster. Not only was the target wrong—he could feel that in the last few seconds before he translated the gunshot into a handshake—but the plan itself was wrong. The realization of this jolted Colonius badly, but there was no escaping the facts: The attention and interest, most of it anyway, would go to the man he killed, not to himself. And anybody really worth killing already had all the damned publicity he needed.

After the fact, of course, his own journal would be found and read, but in a clinical sort of way. Mostly, he suspected, by psychology students, lawyers, and judges. The essence of his philosophy, his thoughts and ideas, his life, his personal brilliance and what lay behind it, would not get a chance to come through, overwhelmed by general sympathy for the victim. The indifferent treatment given Oswald's notes and Bremer's diary—although the latter got published, he thought—proved how little impact was made by the documents of an assassin.

Colonius swore at himself for being so stupid as not to see this sooner and for letting himself even come close to acting at the All-Rite Shopping Center; after a frustrated pummeling of the iron bedstead, he began struggling to find a new master script where he would be the star, not a supporting player, in the drama.

A knock on the door made Colonius start. The savings bank passbook was hastily hidden beneath the thin, lumpy pillow. But then Colonius relaxed, reassured by the voice from the hall.

"Your paper, Mr. Colonius. And it's hot. Ain't it hot, Mr. Colonius?" The Sweet Laurel had long ago dispensed with any pretensions of staff; Colonius' newspapers—along with hamburgers, Cokes, and other items from the small, dingy store down the street—were de-

5

livered personally by Albert, a mentally retarded giant of twenty with the brain of an eight-year-old. The Sweet Laurel allowed poor Albert to earn nickels and dimes running errands for those of its tenants who wanted service; most of them, though, were a little terrified of dealing with a boy of so much size and so little mind. Colonius relished it.

Lars Colonius shook his head to clear it and stretched himself. "Yep, it's hot. Very hot. And bring in the paper, please."

The door opened slowly and the boy-giant shuffled in, the shapeless child's smile lighting up his face beneath the unkempt blond hair, and handed him the rolled-up newspaper. The gutted Brownie that invariably hung around his neck swung forward on its twine strap and made Colonius duck as he received the paper. That the camera had no insides didn't bother the kid at all; he would spend hours clicking away at things without benefit of film, lens, or shutter, oblivious to the fact that absolutely nothing was happening.

The paper delivered, Colonius watched him scratch himself, draw back, and wait for orders. It was one of the problems of having him around; he kept wanting to be so damned useful. Now, Colonius would have to pay the dues of a master to his slave and produce a snatch of conversation.

"Well, Einstein. Anything new and exciting in the papers today?"

Einstein giggled. He knew the question was a joke, even if one he didn't understand. It was like his name. He knew that was some sort of joke, too. But to him it was a term of endearment, a delicious private joke, proof of the only close relationship he had ever experienced. But it was a relationship that existed largely in his mind. For the nickname Colonius had saddled him with was to Colonius public proof of both his contempt for and control over Einstein. Some of the other tenants of the Sweet Laurel were distressed by the name and even more distressed to discover that Einstein appeared to enjoy the cruel joke, but since no one, including the boy, knew what his real name was beyond Albert, it was allowed to stand.

Einstein sucked his lip and pondered what answer would go best, conscious that whatever he said would be inadequate. "A rock got throwed through LeMar's window," he suggested hopefully.

Colonius fanned himself with the paper. "I see."

"It was a damn great big rock."

"Ummmm."

"Anything I can do you?" asked Einstein suddenly and desperately, panicked by Colonius' coolness.

Colonius smiled at the expected reaction, but pretended to have to think what he might want. He had been hungry for at least an hour. "Fritos. Bag of Fritos," he commanded finally.

Einstein nodded vigorously and shot out the door, the Brownie clanking against the buttons of his denim shirt. A command had been given, and he was back in an area he knew how to handle.

With a sigh, Colonius stretched back out on the thin mattress and unfolded the paper. Suddenly, he sat bolt upright again. He had expected the Vice President's unusual visit to Macon to be well covered, but it was the picture that stunned him. For reasons best known to the editors of the Macon *Telegraph,* the Vice President was shown in front of the All-Rite Shopping Center, and the picture gave Colonius an eerie sense of *déjà vu;* it was the same one frozen in his mind from the day before. The Vice President's half-open mouth, the widened eyes, the angry-looking Secret Service men. And there, to the left of the shot, immortalized by the thousand tiny dots of an engraver's plate, was Colonius himself, his own arm outstretched toward the Vice President, his own face clear against the crowd behind it.

At first the fact made him angry, although he couldn't have explained why. But slowly he felt an idea growing in himself. Destiny had delivered the Vice President to the All-Rite Shopping Center yesterday and destiny stayed his hand. Destiny had caused the photographer to press the shutter at that given second, and guided the City Desk into selecting that particular photograph out of the hundreds that must have been taken.

As a plan, killing the Vice President—or anybody like

7

him—might not be sufficient, but perhaps the picture had an unexpected value of its own. Possibly, the Vice President should be told he had been found wanting as a target, and the picture sent him to prove he was spared only because of this inadequacy.

The picture. Abruptly, a series of small, finely oiled tumblers fell into place. Pictures, a whole series of pictures. Colonius smiled thinly as he fleetingly glimpsed the outline of a plan that shattered his earlier worries about the assassin's usual obscurity. This thing with the pictures, if he could swing getting them taken, would only be the beginning of it.

He was still smiling when a knock on his door announced Einstein's return. Colonius let him in and stood there, studying him for a second, while Einstein became nervous, wondering what he'd done wrong.

"I think," said Colonius, "it's about time you got a new camera. One that works. I'll make it a gift to you."

Then, Colonius quickly buried himself back in the newspaper. Einstein was not used to receiving gifts, and Colonius was afraid this sudden gesture might cause him to cry.

And he had been right.

Chapter Two

Sometimes, that bastard Billy-Joe—he lives down the hall from me—reminds me so much of my kid brother, Nils, it's frightening. No real brains, either of them, but trickier than hell. Nils even had my mother fooled. She was always bragging what a nice boy he was, and shoving at me how he had so many friends, and crowing about all the presents he gave her. Those damned presents—swiped off the counter at Grant's, every last one of them.

Well, I guess maybe she liked him best because he was born late, just before they took all her tubes out. Too bad sweet little Nils couldn't pick her up a new set of those at Grant's.

—Extract from the
journal of Lars Colonius

Monday, May 11—Armageddon minus seventy-three.

THE CLIPPING from the Macon *Telegraph,* along with its curiously presented message, was received in the Justice Department's first mail of Friday the eighth. A date and time stamp on the corner of the clipping indicates it was opened at nine forty-seven of the same morning; the postmark of origin and the mailing date were also recorded, standard department practice with any questionable item.

Because there was no written message as such with the clipping, Colonius's first communication defied easy classification and came close to simply being discarded. Miss

9

Anna Salazar, the receiving clerk who handled it, remembers that it lay around for several days before anyone bothered to dig up a tape recorder and the message itself could be transcribed.

Even at this point, no one took it too seriously. In fact, as Miss Salazar was to recall later, the most excitement attached to the matter was a disagreement between her supervisor and the section chief as to whether it should be recorded as a crank note or a threatening letter.

Eventually, both clipping and transcript were sent upstairs and wound up in the hands of a young government attorney, Chasen Calder. Calder found the transcript "highly disturbing," but had been criticized earlier in the year for overreacting to crank mail and wasn't about to get caught doing it again. Still, he went strictly by the book and sent copies of the material, without comment, to both the FBI and the Secret Service.

There, for the first time, the message was given serious consideration. The Secret Service had learned, over the years, that people who ramble on about assassination, even ones with nothing particular in mind at the time, can all be potentially dangerous and have to be taken seriously. On the other hand, Colonius had given them very little to work with; they had nothing beyond a photograph purporting to be of himself, indications that the picture and tape were mailed from Chicago, and the fact that he was in Macon on the morning of March the third. The agent shown glaring angrily at Colonius in the clipping could barely remember the incident—and then only after being shown the picture. It was not surprising, he said. Several enthusiasts had pushed their way through the inner security ring during the course of the day's campaigning across Georgia, and, by now, all of their faces were badly blurred in his mind.

Accordingly, the best the Secret Service could do was to send an enlargement of the clipping to all of its field agents concerned, with a warning to take appropriate action if the man should turn up in a crowd again.

They did not communicate their concern to the FBI.

At the Bureau, the reaction was more relaxed, if occasionally laced with petulance. The material, they complained, had been handled by so many people that any fingerprint work was useless. The paper in which the package arrived had not been saved. Neither had the string. Further, they noted, although the United States mails had been used, no actual threat against any specific person was made and they questioned their jurisdiction in the matter.

The file they opened on the case is even more revealing. It consists of a single sheet of paper with the clipping pasted in its center. At the top is noted: *"Armageddon, First Name Unknown. Cross indx. Macon, Ga, 29 Apr, Eggans campaign. Other material (bulk) is filed under AR/337-09-C. ACTION: Hold for further communication from above named, if any."*

It is safe to guess that Lars Colonius would have been confused by the spectacular lack of reaction to his package. With no experience in the workings of government or even those of a large corporation, he would not have understood that any bureaucracy survives largely through some other bureaucracy's inertia, and would have been baffled by the fact that he was already buried in the files.

The lack of publicity, of course, did *not* surprise him. Tight security was to be expected in a matter such as this, and he delightedly imagined hundreds of undercover agents, each armed with his picture, combing the back streets of Chicago for people who might recognize him. In fact, because of the clipping, he wasn't entirely sure Macon itself might not be under heavy scrutiny, and remained indoors as much as possible.

There were, however, several items necessary to his plan he felt could not be entrusted to Einstein; he timed his shopping expedition for late in the afternoon, when it would be hottest and he felt most people would be indoors. Beyond this, he mapped his route to afford him minimum street exposure.

Around the corner from the Sweet Laurel, down Washington Avenue, was Appleby's, a store which sold radios and television sets, good luggage, and cameras of every description, from the cheapest to the best. This was Colonius's first stop. He quickly bought a Wollensak portable tape recorder, a folding leatherette traveling case, and a small supply of recording tape. (He originally planned to buy the Brownie for Einstein here as well but, deciding it would be wiser to purchase it separately, had picked one up at the Chichester's farther down Washington.) All of these purchases were paid for in cash, money he had withdrawn from his savings account the previous Friday.

The Wollensak was left at Appleby's to be picked up on the way back; Colonius had several other stops to make and didn't want to be burdened down by carrying it all over town. Crossing from Washington, Colonius then headed up Second Street, walked about halfway down it, and went into the Hobby Shop. There, he bought a simple home developing kit and the necessary chemicals, as well as a dozen more rolls of film for the Brownie. When the clerk smiled curiously, Colonius told him he was unfamiliar with home processing and needed that much film so he could make a lot of mistakes. This, of course, was untrue. When younger, Colonius had, after his mother died, set up a complete darkroom in the basement of his uncle's house in Buffalo, and considered himself something of an expert. His real concern was the amount of trial and error it would take teaching Einstein to use the camera. The dozen rolls he bought at the Hobby Shop, along with the six he'd already picked up at Chichester's might only be a beginning.

At the same store, he bought more recording tape for the Wollensak, as well as a splicing block; he'd learned from his experience with the machine he borrowed for his first message that a block would make the tedious work of endless splicing go that much faster.

Colonius counted his money. It felt clean and cool and good between his fingers—and even better when he realized how much he'd overestimated the cost of his purchases. Returning to Appleby's, he added a small, inexpensive radio to his pile; his room was rented to him complete with a television set, old but serviceable, and he had no real need of a radio. Still, it would provide him with one more source of voices and make his work with the Wollensak that much more flexible.

Back at the corner of Washington and Orange, Colonius flagged down a cab. Cruising taxis in Macon were a rarity—the cabs were radio-controlled and generally only arrived after a telephone call—but Colonius put down its unexpected appearance as a subtle signal from the destiny that guided him: Perhaps there was an agent riding on the bus he had planned to catch. For a moment, this thought even caused him to wonder if he shouldn't move from the Sweet Laurel to the Macon Hilton—they would be less likely to look for him in a first-class hotel and he could certainly afford it—but quickly abandoned the idea. The Hilton would never put up with Einstein's coming and going through their lobby, or the fact that Colonius now let him sleep on a floormat at the foot of his bed, as much a slave to his whims as a faithful pet or an Indian serving boy.

After trying unsuccessfully to haggle with the driver—Colonius used the argument that it was a long trip with a lot of waiting and he should be charged a flat rate—he gave the address and arrived at the travel agency near Shurling Drive some fifteen minutes later. There, Colonius picked up his airlines reservations for Detroit, one in the name of G. Hilton and the other in the name of S. Laurel. For the sake of tidiness, he would have preferred that these names matched those already on the stock certificates—W. Black and E. Ginger—as he had originally planned. But at the last moment—on his way up the stairs, in fact—he changed his mind and had invented the two new names. It was better to leave no leads that could be traced back if something should go wrong.

With the tickets securely tucked inside his shirt pocket, he had the cab take him back toward Washington, getting out about half a block down the street from Appleby's. He picked up the Wollensak and headed directly for the Sweet Laurel, bracing himself for the difficult job of teaching Einstein how to work a Brownie.

Sourly, he estimated it would probably take four or five days of highly concentrated, grinding effort.

Einstein was a complete surprise.

Colonius had no reservoir of information to tell him how long teaching a mentally retarded youth such a process would take; he had no way of knowing what to expect, or even if the training would be successful at all. But the progress was, to Colonius' amazement, fast and spectacular.

By the end of the first day, Einstein, sometimes trembling with eagerness, had completely mastered the Brownie—the aiming, the advancing of the film, even the operation of the simple flash attachment. The only part of the thing that gave him any trouble was loading the film, and he was beginning to get that.

Einstein would shoot away—Colonius varied the subjects to include objects in the room, lamps, tables, the bed, the doorway, but always included himself because he wanted to be sure that Einstein wouldn't get carried away under pressure and leave him out of the picture—and then Colonius would develop the negative and print the pictures in the bathroom.

The process left Einstein bugeyed. When the early, cloudy shadows of the picture began to show through the milky emulsion of the negative, he clapped his hands together and gave such a blood-curdling laugh of triumph that Colonius shivered. When the first roll of negatives was finally dry—getting Einstein to wait for this was not easy—and the positive image suddenly appeared on the first print, Einstein grabbed it from the tray of fixative and kissed it with excitement. Only the acrid taste of the fixing bath, Colonius suspected, stopped him from eating it whole.

They shot and they shot, that day, until all dozen and a half rolls of film were exposed and the floor was littered with their bright yellow empty boxes. But the excess of film that had caused the clerk at Chichester's to smile didn't go into the succession of trials and errors on the basics as Colonius had imagined; they went into making Einstein's picture-taking a completely automatic reflex to an order.

During the shooting of the last roll, Colonius moved them into the hall to see how his protégé would react to new surroundings and unexpected commands. Colonius suddenly sprinted down the hall and leaned against a doorway almost at its end. "Now, Einstein. Now!" he commanded. And was pleased to see Einstein slowly and carefully move the camera toward him, calmly readjust his aim to make sure Colonius was well within the frame, and press the button.

"Very pretty," came a sneering drawl from farther down the hall. "You fellas buckin' for *Photoplay* magazine or tryin' for the Macon po-lice mug files?"

Colonius spun around in the narrow hall; Einstein lowered the camera and looked confused. The voice, Colonius knew, belonged to Billy-Joe Armbruster, the floor's sole other resident. Billy-Joe was a youngish, blond drifter, mixed up in the minor-league rackets somehow, and the sort of born tormentor that only lower-class Southern white families can produce. He and Colonius disliked each other, and had from the moment they met.

Most of Billy-Joe's mistrust and dislike of Colonius came because he couldn't figure him out, and Billy-Joe sprang from a way of life where figuring people out was all-important. Here was this smart-assed Northerner who didn't talk to anyone, rarely was seen out of his room, lived on funds neither visible nor explained, and whose sole companion appeared to be a giant misfit no one else would pass the time of day with. For a while, Billy-Joe's dark, evil-cluttered mind had even toyed with the possibility that Albert was Colonius' lover, but the picture was so outlandish he dismissed it. Still, Billy-Joe had an instinct for profit that surpassed his nose for evil, and there was something shady enough about Colonius to convince him that eventually a way could be found to pick up a few bucks off him. There was that thing about the gun, for instance.

Colonius had bought the snub-nosed thirty-eight from him. Certainly, they were available enough around Macon, but the thought of walking into a gun store and buying one had seemed unwise. Around the Sweet Laurel, Billy-Joe's occupation was no secret, nor was the drawerful of handguns he kept in his room. It was the only time Colonius and Billy-Joe could be said to have had a conversation, and the only reason it finally got anywhere was that Billy-Joe's ferret mind could see where Colonius was heading long before the circuitous probing and parrying said it in so many words.

"You wanna buy a piece, why don' you just come out and say so?" Billy-Joe demanded suddenly.

It was a question Colonius was unprepared for. He wished now he'd just gone to the damned store and bought it himself. In fact, he told himself, it would still be much better to do that; buying a gun from Billy-Joe seemed easily as unwise as buying it from a store. Colonius shook his head to deny he was standing there to buy anything.

Billy-Joe ignored it. "This one, for instance. Not much to look at, maybe, but it can blow one hell of a hole through a fat nigger at twenty-thirty feet." He studied Colonius' face and took in the widening eyes; Billy-Joe was too sophisticated a form of white trash to use a term like "nigger" regularly, but he knew that Northerners expected it of him—along with the implication of having blown holes through a few himself. It didn't really matter; the biggest thing creepo-Colonius would probably blow a hole through was a tin can in some back alley. Still, he had to keep the fiction going, and rubbed the muzzle of the gun fondly with one finger. "Don' know what you is planning to use it for, 'course, but I should point out that the serial number on this one here has been filed off. No way of tracin' it back to nobody, casin' it should get left behind or some such."

Point, match, set. Colonius paid Billy-Joe forty-five dollars for the pistol, about thirty more than it was selling for on Vineville Avenue. A box of bullets—two cartridges missing—was thrown in as a friendly gesture. But possibly because the transaction had taken place at all, Colonius discovered he disliked Billy-Joe more than ever.

Now, he saw Billy-Joe stop leaning against the wall and start moving toward them in an aimless saunter. His hand reached out and examined the Brownie hanging from Einstein's neck. "My, my, Albert," his voice whis-

16

pered meanly, "a gen-u-ine Leica." He turned the small plastic camera over in his hand, his gray eyes flickering secretively toward Einstein's to suggest he might seize the camera and run.

Einstein's submissive nature was a staple belief of the Sweet Laurel, but as he watched Billy-Joe fondle the camera, the most precious object in the whole world to him, the usual good-natured, slightly silly grin was replaced by a twisted slash of anger. Abruptly, it turned into a cry of rage as Einstein grabbed the fingers Billy-Joe had clasped around the camera and roughly bent them back; then, the other hand sent Billy-Joe crashing against the far wall of the hall.

Fanning his aching fingers in the air, Billy-Joe stared at Einstein with a mixture of fear and injured fury. "You fuckin' moron. You god-damned ape-child. I'll come over there and—"

"Shut up," Colonius snapped at him.

"Don't *you* tell me what to do, you little creep," snarled Billy-Joe, turning around and moving across the hall toward him. Einstein's strength, apparently, made him a force to be reckoned with; Colonius was something else.

There was, standing alongside Einstein, shoved up against the wall, a cobalt-blue wrought-iron decorative urn, which, in the Sweet Laurel's better days, was probably filled with ferns or a rubber plant. Currently, it held a mixture of soiled sand and festering cigar butts. Picking this up with one hand—it must have weighed seventy-five pounds—Einstein raised it easily over his head and advanced on Billy-Joe, rocking from side to side, giving a series of animallike moans that flattened Billy-Joe back against his side of the hall with terror.

"Einstein!" Colonius yelled. But Einstein kept on moving across the hall toward Billy-Joe. "Einstein! *Einstein!*" cried Colonius again, and reached out one hand to touch his arm.

Einstein paused and looked at Colonius dimly, then shook his head as if wakened from a dream. Slowly, he lowered the urn and blinked his eyes in wonder. "I was scared he was to hurt you, Mr. Colonius," Einstein mum-

17

bled in the voice of a scolded child. He blinked his eyes again and stared at Colonius. "I was scared."

Colonius felt oddly. It gave him a strange sense of warmth to be protected like this, a sensation he didn't remember ever having felt before. But the incident also illustrated to Colonius a danger in the use of Einstein. If something outraged him, he could blow the whole carefully worked out plan; the camera made Einstein vulnerable and Billy-Joe knew it.

What Billy-Joe didn't see—he wasn't really very smart —was that the camera also made *him* very vulnerable.

Wordlessly, Colonius walked back toward his room, followed silently down the long hall by a shuffling Einstein.

Wednesday, May 13—Armageddon minus seventy-one.

During the next two days, Lars Colonius made a good deal of progress in getting himself and Einstein ready for their departure by plane. Their trial run. Their first mission.

And Billy-Joe Armbruster made a serious mistake.

There was very little to recommend Billy-Joe as a person. Women were vaguely attracted by his lithe, animal looks, but beyond that, Billy-Joe was a liar, a cheat, a small-time hood, a whiner, a bigot, and an incurable snoop. His antennae told him something was up with Colonius, something that involved Einstein, something that involved the camera, and something that possibly went back as far as involving the snub-nosed thirty-eight. Because his instincts in these things were rarely wrong, and because the situation smelled of profit, he began following Colonius in his sorties outside the Sweet Laurel to see if he could scent what was in the wind.

Shadowing him—and recently he was inevitably paired with Einstein—around Macon was a cinch. They traveled mostly on foot and only occasionally resorted to taxis. Billy-Joe watched with curiosity as Colonius bought Einstein a soft leather tote bag; as he bought two dozen rolls of film for the Brownie and placed them in the tote

18

bag; and finally as he carefully put the plastic camera in the tote bag along with them, Einstein watching as if they were packing a rare jewel. That damned camera again, thought Billy-Joe. It had almost gotten him brained with an urn, and he patted the pistol he'd gone back to carrying in his pocket after the ruckus with Einstein at the Sweet Laurel.

From outside a store window, he watched Colonius buy Einstein a suit of clothes—nothing fancy, but better clothes than he had probably ever had. Farther down the street, he saw Colonius buy him shirts, shoes, and a raincoat to go with the suit. It was all very strange; Billy-Joe could make no pattern emerge from it, unless it was that Colonius was plain crazy. He knew better than that.

But the two really bewildering things came the next day. When Colonius and Einstein came out of the Sweet Laurel for their early-morning session of picture-taking (always of Colonius and someone or something, Billy-Joe noticed, which was bewildering in itself), Einstein was walking, deliberately it seemed, some considerable distance in front of Colonius. Twice they paused on a corner, and Einstein stood there while Colonius leaned against a building and pretended not to know him. Then, to the first stranger that came along, Einstein pantomimed being deaf and dumb, and handed him a note. The face of the accosted stranger changed quickly from suspicious to helpful as he read the note, and then, again entirely by signs and signals with his hands, he gave Einstein explicit instructions of some sort, apparently showing him how to get someplace. During the second of these meetings, the sign language with which Einstein responded to the help was so effusive he forgot to retrieve the note from the stranger before taking off. The man, after chasing Einstein a bit, grew hot and tired and gave up, finally tossing it helplessly into a street trash basket.

Billy-Joe waited a second or two to make sure Einstein and Colonius were gone, then retrieved the note himself. It was self-explanatory, except for one point—what it was supposed to accomplish:

To Whom It May Concern:
The bearer, George Germaine, is a patient of mine and
is a deaf-mute. Because of this, he is sometimes thought
by strangers to be mentally retarded, which is not the
case. However, since the condition does render travel for
him extremely difficult, I would appreciate any help you
could give him in reaching his destination.

/s/ WALTER KRAUS, MD

Below the typewritten part was Colonius' spidery handwriting: "Destination—590 Walnut Street, Macon, Ga.
Please direct.—W.K."

Billy-Joe studied the letter again. Walnut Street was
someplace even Einstein could have found with his eyes
closed. It was the goddamnedest thing. Starting back up
after the fast-vanishing pair, who seemed now to have
given up their game and were moving with more definite
purpose, Billy-Joe racked his memory for some confidence trick the deaf and dumb act might be part of, but
came up blank.

At the next corner, Einstein climbed on a bus and appeared to head back for the Sweet Laurel; Colonius continued on foot for a few blocks and went into the Third
Street post office. Billy-Joe watched as he strode across
the foyer of faded marble and opened a post office box,
withdrawing a single, badly folded, bulky manila envelope. This, Colonius studied for a second with visible satisfaction. Then, by the door, he ripped it open. From it, he
pulled out about three dozen sheets of paper, stared at
them for a second as if deciding what to do with them,
and finally tossed them into a receptacle by the door.
Torn neatly into four sections, the envelope quickly followed. Wearing a look of accomplishment, Lars Colonius
then strode out of the post office, out onto the street,
turned left and disappeared.

Billy-Joe's eyes remained on the day's second trash
basket, not liking the idea too much. But like many
devious minds before his, he knew you could frequently
find out more about a person by what he threw away
than by what he kept. And so, when he was sure that
Colonius was gone for good, Billy-Joe moved slowly over
to the receptacle, leaned casually against it, and reached

20

down with one hand to draw out both the discarded papers and the torn-up envelope. What he found confused him even more, and Billy-Joe swore at his own inability to figure it out. The paper, every page of it, was absolutely blank. The envelope was addressed to Colonius at the box number, but the address was in his own handwriting and the postmark was Denver. Goddamn.

The picture, Billy-Joe decided sourly, made no more sense than before. But more of the pieces were coming to light, and if he could fit them all together, he was convinced there was profit to be milked out of Colonius.

The next step was obvious. Among his other talents, Billy-Joe was not bad at picking locks—and the locks at the Sweet Laurel required no expert. Somewhere inside Colonius' room was the answer to the questions building up in Billy-Joe's mind: the camera, the deaf and dumb act, the phony note from the bogus doctor, Einstein's new clothes, and the envelope full of blank paper mailed from Colonius to Colonius, yet postmarked Denver. Inside the room were more pieces of the puzzle, the solution to the mystery, the key to some cash. Pérhaps a lot of cash.

In most people, driving curiosity is considered an admirable trait of character.

In Billy-Joe, it was to be a fatal flaw.

Chapter Three

Another thing that bugged me about Nils was all those dumb girls tagging around after him, begging him for it almost. Christ, he'd turn on that damned smile of his and they'd just about climb out of their panties where they stood. How my mother used to love that—sometimes I wonder if maybe she didn't sneak upstairs and watch them go to it through the crack in Nils' door. Big deal.

Well, I went to a whorehouse in Buffalo once to see what it was like, but the girl they gave me was so terrible-looking I paid her just to stay on her own side of the room. It wasn't that I was queer or anything; it's just that when you analyze it, sex is for animals. I can't believe anybody with a good brain does it except to get his glands off. And if you've got any sort of imagination, you can take care of yourself much better anyway. Hell, once I did it with soap ten times in a row without even stopping. Show me a girl who could do that for you.

—Extract from the
journal of Lars Colonius

Friday, May 15—Armageddon minus sixty-nine.

ATTORNEY CHASEN CALDER of the Justice Department finished reading the Secret Service report and allowed himself a quizzical eyebrow. He didn't want to be accused of overreacting again, and their sending of the photograph to all their field agents struck him as premature. There was no hard evidence indicating what they had to date was anything more than the work of a crank.

In the case of the FBI, the reply gave him nothing to

worry about. The clipping, it said, had been noted, but no action would be taken until further evidence, if any, was in.

A cool and practical assessment, Calder thought. For the moment, no more than that was indicated.

But Calder was still playing it by the book. Calling in his secretary, he forwarded the clipping, the message, the FBI and Secret Service reports up through the Department channels. To the pile, he added his own comment.

In his own experience, he noted firmly, nobody seriously contemplating criminal violence had ever written the Justice Department to tell them about it first, and sent along a picture of themselves to prove how easily it could be done. This, he added, would be self-defeating.

At the Sweet Laurel, criminal violence was being looked at in an entirely different frame of reference. Up until half an hour earlier, everything about Lars Colonius' plan had been proceeding nicely. A chart had been drawn with all the different possibilities for the ultimate target laid out on it, the advantages and disadvantages of each, and a simple scoring system devised to help him reach a decision. As far as the in-between steps, they were moving along well, too. Einstein had been drilled with the camera to the point where he operated like an automaton. His performance as a deaf-mute was beautifully convincing and should solve the problem of the airplanes. And, fortunately, Einstein delighted in this new game Mr. Colonius had invented for him to play.

Even the post office was cooperating. Colonius had guessed—and it turned out he was right—that if you mail an envelope addressed to the postmaster of one city, inside of which is another envelope addressed somewhere else, the outer envelope is automatically assumed to be the mistake of a mailing machine, postmarked again, and the inner envelope remailed to its destination. Particularly, if both envelopes carried full postage and there could be no suspicion at the post office that somebody was trying to get around postal regulations.

The mail waiting at the Third Street post office was proof that this part of the plan was workable, too; his base could continue to be Macon, while the messages to the Justice Department appeared to put him all over the country.

But a little while ago, on coming back to the Sweet Laurel, he'd found Billy-Joe waiting outside his door and the whole plan was suddenly in jeopardy.

"You take a right nice picture," drawled Billy-Joe, indicating with his thumb that he'd been inside Colonius's room. "Real nice. Funny, no one noticed you in the paper. You and Jimmy Eggans and the Vice President. Whoooo-eeee!"

Colonius stared at him. Everything depended on how much Billy-Joe had learned or guessed.

"I seed you and the crazy-boy playin' deaf and stupid around town. I also took occasion to read that pile of papers you threw away at the post office. Shame, throwing away all them nice blank pages. And after mailin' them to yourself all the way from Denver." Billy-Joe was watching Colonius's face, waiting to hit upon a subject that would bring a reaction.

"And that book you write all them words down in," added Billy-Joe, realizing by the twitch of a muscle around Colonius's jaw that he'd struck the sensitive area. "I don' understand what in the name of sweet Jesus they mean, you know, but then I never much understand you neither, Colonius. What I do understand is that you're up to some kind of no good—blackmail, maybe?—and I can be right handy with things like that. I reckon you'll need help." Billy-Joe paused and stared back at Colonius. "Sometimes for a guy to just keep his mouth shut can be a help, don' you agree there, Colonius?"

Colonius mumbled and turned away, trying to remember how specific the part of the journal already completed got.

Billy-Joe smiled and shrugged his shoulders. "What I suggest, Colonius, is that you set your mind to thinkin' about it for a bit, and then we can have a little talk and decide just how much help you'll be needin' from me, and how much you figure that help is worth in cash, and whether we can reach a figure that'll keep us both happy."

Tilting his blond head to one side, Billy-Joe smiled

again, this time inquiringly, to measure his impact. There still was not much on Colonius' face to go on, but Billy-Joe knew enough about extortion to know he had Colonius well on the hook; you could see the small beads of sweat breaking out on his forehead.

Billy-Joe stretched himself elaborately and yawned to indicate how firmly he was in the driver's seat, and moved toward the door. "I'll be waiting for you in my room about six for that little talk, Colonius. Meantimes, I'm going to take in a movie on account the theater is air-conditioned, and a day like today makes a man all sweaty, don't it?" He put one hand on the doorknob, then turned back toward Colonius. "And in case—just in case, you understand—you get any ideas about turning that ape-child of your'n loose on me again, remember old Billy-Joe don't go nowhere 'ceptin' with this"—and Billy-Joe patted the pocket of his pants to remind Colonius of the pistol he carried.

After Billy-Joe was gone, Colonius stood there for some time, staring at the closed door. The conclusion was inescapable. Billy-Joe had to be removed now. It wasn't part of the overall plan; it was a necessary step to allow the plan to survive. Sitting down, Colonius began searching for ways it could be done—and immediately; they left for Detroit the day after tomorrow so it could be nothing either complicated or time consuming. It was strange how these little details could be so bothersome.

Three hours later, Colonius was staring out the window dispiritedly, studying the faded yellow brick of the Logan Bank across the street from the Sweet Laurel. No plan had yet presented itself for the swift, easy disposition of Billy-Joe. He only grunted when he heard Einstein tapping on the door. Sensing Colonius's frame of mind, Einstein handed him the Coke and the Fritos silently and fanned himself in the breeze he could make by swinging the door back and forth.

Impatiently, Colonius signaled him to stop it; the motion was upsetting his train of thought. From farther down the hall, he could hear the water beating against the tin sides of the shower stall as Billy-Joe, back now from

25

the movies, luxuriated in the cooling jets. Getting himself ready for their meeting at six, thought Colonius grimly.

Suddenly, Colonius snapped his fingers and squeezed his legs together with excitement—the shower was one place where he didn't have to worry about Billy-Joe's pistol. With a wave of his hand, he beckoned Einstein closer to the door.

"Einstein," he whispered. "There's something we've got to do. Right now."

Einstein brightened. "Another game, Mr. Colonius?"

Solemnly, Colonius shook his head. "It's no game. It's Billy-Joe. Earlier, I found him here, in my room. He was trying to steal your camera."

The smile faded from Einstein's face, replaced by the terrible look Colonius had seen on it several days earlier. Quickly, Einstein raced over and unzipped the leather tote bag and checked to make sure the camera wasn't gone. Then, he turned back to Colonius in bewilderment. "My camera?"

"I got it away from him—*this* time," explained Colonius. "But he said he'll be back for it. And then it'll be no more camera. And no more games, either. He wants to hurt us—both of us."

The bewilderment disappeared and was again replaced by the terrible look. The simplicity of Einstein's emotions was almost terrifying to watch. "So we have to hurt him first," added Colonius, and looked up at Einstein. He was ready. "Okay, okay, Einstein. Just do what I tell you. Exactly what I tell you."

And pushing Einstein ahead of him, Colonius grabbed something from the floor of the closet and started them down the hall toward the bathroom.

It was over very quickly. On command, Einstein yanked back the plastic curtain of the shower stall, grabbed the dripping-wet Billy-Joe, and dragged him, still standing, out onto the cheap linoleum floor of the bathroom itself. Einstein twisted Billy-Joe's arms behind him and almost lifted him off the floor, poking his giant thumbs into the small of his back and holding him upright while Colonius darted in at Billy-Joe's wildly kicking feet and knotted them together with the sash of his seersucker bathrobe. (Billy-Joe's bathrobe had brought a smile to Colonius' face; in one pocket he could feel the pistol Billy-Joe kept to defend himself against Einstein.) Partly from shock, partly from pain, Billy-Joe started to scream, but Einstein applied more pressure against his back, arching the slippery, lithe body of Billy-Joe so far out in front that he formed an almost perfect arc from his toes to his thrown-back head.

The screaming stopped as Colonius produced the plastic bag he'd picked up off the closet floor—Einstein's new suit had come packaged in it—and slid it down over Billy-Joe's head, closing the bottom opening a little around his neck, but letting the panicked breathing of Billy-Joe do the rest.

The bag was sucked hard against his face and through it you could clearly see Billy-Joe's terrified eyes widen as the full realization of what was happening hit him; the sinewy, glistening body thrashed and twisted to escape Einstein's grip, but could not free itself.

Taking a step back, Colonius watched the process of slow suffocation. Through the bag, he could see Billy-Joe's eyes bulge out farther and farther, out so far it seemed that Einstein's thumbs must be pushing on them from behind; a smear of frothy blood appeared on the inside of the plastic bag where Billy-Joe had bitten his own tongue, and the stain widened slowly; the vein on his neck, barely visible at first, now swelled large and pumped frantically; the muscles of his stomach heaved in and out like a man in orgasm, pressing up against the rib cage to force the last of the air from his lungs; the skin across his chest and shoulders quivered and convulsed and suddenly took on a mottled look, as if it were trying to suck in oxygen through the pores themselves. There was a series of violent shudders that ran the length of his body; the toes pointed stiffly, then relaxed, then pointed again, then went completely limp. A final spasm swept through him. It was over.

Colonius pondered how long it was necessary to remain like this to be sure of death. Another couple of minutes, he figured. He sighed. It wasn't entirely as he'd expected, although he couldn't have said what he imag-

27

ined. Except perhaps that it was less noisy than he would have thought, and quicker. Somewhere he'd read that men being hanged get erections while dying; Billy-Joe had not. But Colonius had. Perhaps the stories were wrong and it was the executioners who did. He would like to have asked Einstein about himself, but it was out of the question.

"Okay, that's enough," he commanded. Almost gently, Einstein lowered the body of his enemy to the floor. It was placed inside a brown plastic lawn bag scrounged from the back door of the Sweet Laurel, and the lawn bag was in turn stuffed into a large, canvas duffel bag. Einstein and he would shortly climb onto a bus—it was risky, but the thought of the other passengers' ignorance about the bag's contents delighted him—add stones, and dump the whole thing into the Ocmulgee River, which ran through Macon on its way to the sea.

"Good job," was all he said about the matter to Einstein, when they returned.

With his huge grin, Einstein accepted the praise and raced over to the tote bag to check on the camera, pulling it out and then sitting there stroking it, like a mother with a rescued child.

Colonius wasn't even sure Einstein realized what he'd done this afternoon. Or that the camera was safe forever from Billy-Joe now, because death is a very final thing.

He suspected not. For Einstein was already back talking excitedly about his first airplane ride. The day after tomorrow. To Detroit.

"What's Detroit, Mr. Colonius?"

Chapter Four

When I was a kid, people were always telling me how precocious I was—almost a genius, they said. Yet, I was always flunking things at school. And later, screwing up in jobs. How could this happen to a genius? How could somebody with a brain like mine do so badly and be hated so much at the same time? Jesus. I don't remember having a single friend, ever.

Well, the only explanation I had for it was that destiny was saving me for something special, saving all the genius for a single act that would suddenly make all the failures and the flunkouts and the rejections make sense.

And I now know what that something is.
> —*Extract from the*
> *journal of Lars Colonius*

Tuesday, May 19—Armageddon minus sixty-five.

WHEN CHASEN CALDER'S package of memos, observations, and other material finally made its way up to the Deputy Attorney General, Paul Goddard, it got an angry, not entirely rational, reception. Goddard stared at the neatly bound file of papers, carefully time-stamped and initialed, skimmed through the Secret Service and FBI reports, winced at the self-satisfied additions of Chasen Calder, and swore disgustedly.

This was unlike Goddard, an ordinarily carefully controlled person. He had only a gut feeling to make him feel the matter was being treated incredibly casually, but it was a feeling he couldn't shake, a sense of foreboding about the Armageddon file separating it quickly from the welter of crank mail that regularly wound up on his desk.

Spinning his leather chair around again, Goddard re-read the transcript of the message. Compared to a lot of the stuff he read, letters screaming at the President, the Vice President, and members of the Cabinet, this one was almost gentle. But there was a cold, ominous overtone to it that sent a shudder through Goddard, a carefully reasoned, logical intensity that made him feel the man meant what he said.

With a grunt, he buzzed his secretary and told her to get Chasen Calder up here on the double. Calder had left for lunch, he was told, and that fact only made him madder. Angrily, he sent hand-delivered directives to both the FBI and the Secret Service demanding to be informed immediately if anything further was heard from Armageddon. To underline his position, he also caustically informed the FBI they had, in his opinion as a lawyer, all the jurisdiction they needed, and bluntly ordered them and the Secret Service to start coordinating their efforts forthwith. For Christ's sake, hadn't they learned anything from Dallas?

Thursday, May 21—Armageddon minus sixty-three.

In spite of the air conditioning in the boarding lounge, Lars Colonius could feel himself sweating as the line inched slowly forward. He had no reason to be nervous—there was nothing in his luggage that the hijack detection devices would pick up—but he could feel his skin prickle anyway. The thirty-eight had been mailed ahead to the hotel so it wouldn't show up on the X-ray scanner, and the only metal things in his bag were his razor and the splicing block for the Wollensak. He guessed there might be a little curiosity about the tape machine itself, but they could tear the damned thing apart and not find anything suspicious. He was clean. It was the extra two days of waiting that bugged him, he supposed. At the last minute, he'd moved their reservations from Sunday to Tuesday, which was cutting things pretty close, but he didn't want

30

his own departure to follow too soon on Billy-Joe's disappearance.

This turned out to be a wasted precaution, since nobody even noticed Billy-Joe was gone. Almost all of the Sweet Laurel's guests were transients these days, and the landlady, old Mrs. Spiers, came out of her room only twice a day now—once to get her mail, once to receive her daily quota from the package store. Then, after peering glassily down the long, dim hall, she would sweep her faded kimono around herself with theatrical dignity and stumble back into her room.

Up ahead, Colonius could see Einstein pass through the inspection area easily and he heaved a sigh of relief. A travelers' representative from United had Einstein firmly in tow, and she waved the "doctor's" letter at the inspectors; they searched the tote bag anyway, but only glanced at the Brownie and then quickly passed him through. Einstein was nodding and bobbing and smiling at everybody, obviously enjoying this new game hugely, while the airlines people, from ticket takers to stewardesses, seemed as pleased to do small services for him as he was to receive them.

Colonius congratulated himself. The deaf and dumb act would work. Colonius had decided they should travel on the same flights, but separately. This raised the possibility of Einstein's talking to a passenger or a stewardess and saying something he shouldn't. But the note from Dr. Kraus that Einstein handed the ticket agent on arriving at the airport—and which was passed from hand to hand until it reached the stewardess at the top of the ramp—removed any need for him to talk at all, while the attention it got him made a game for Einstein out of keeping his mouth shut.

Colonius filed the deaf-mute act away for further study. Face to face with the physically handicapped, the average person, he decided, becomes so embarrassed by his own wholeness that he lets down the usual defenses and makes himself easy prey for manipulation. And this knowledge might have far more important applications than getting Einstein safely on and off airplanes.

31

The stockholders' meeting was like the All-Rite Shopping Center all over again—if you wanted to kill someone, they made it easy. The management of the company sat at one end of the vast hall, up on a sort of platform. Colonius could only count three or four guards—in plainclothes—and they stayed pretty well back from the platform, trying to look inconspicuous leaning against the side walls. The one time they took up position at the base of the platform was when some voices, from far in the rear of the room, began yelling about pollution or the environment or something; heads turned briefly to stare, but somebody in the back must have gotten to them because the voices died down pretty quickly and the meeting went back to listening to the treasurer's report.

Colonius was sitting in the fourth row, on the aisle, and he—or anybody else who wanted to—could easily have bounced right up onto the platform and shot the chairman and the whole damned management of the company before those guards got to him. Some security.

But Colonius was not here to kill anyone today; the plan that began with his picture in the *Telegraph* now made that approach obsolete. For a moment, he stared at the chairman and admitted to himself there would be an almost sensual satisfaction in wiping the bland smile off his complacent face with a bullet, but this man would be as wrong as the Vice President had been wrong, and Colonius had realized it long before he climbed onto the airplane.

For during his unexpected two-day wait in Macon, he had absorbed himself almost completely in roughing out the shape of the new plan, and he was in Detroit today to get another picture—nothing more. Painstakingly, he kept kneading and molding and refining the basic concept until it satisfied all his requirements; but the details of how to effect it, the selection of a precise target, and the limits of how high it could safely be allowed to soar remained shadowy and elusive, distant objects silhouetted against the sun which disappeared completely when stared at too hard. The pictures and the tapes and the killings—

possibly quite a number of them—were still a part of it, but now only as a means to an end. A small part of something far bigger that was crowding its way into the dark twistings of his brain.

The work with the Wollensak was exacting—and maddeningly slow. He was working longer stretches at a time than he probably should, but more stuff should have been on its way to the Justice Department already, and he kept at it doggedly. Colonius stared at the television set—the Wollensak's input was hooked to the set's receiver —and waited. In front of him was a rough chart with the key words on it, and each time one was said on the air, he'd check it off his list. It seemed to be taking forever. Occasionally, he would switch channels; there was no real purpose in this, but every now and then one channel would seem to start delivering more of the words he needed than another. And when that channel ran out of luck, he'd switch to yet another and try that for a while. Then, he played back what he had until he'd found where each word was on the tape, slapped it on the splicing block, and added it to his master reel, tightening the dead space between as he spliced.

Wearily, Colonius leaned forward and listened to the master tape again. It was complete now, except for one damned big hole at the opening. "This is the voice of. . . ." it played, and then there was silence, dead silence, as the space for the missing word, filled temporarily with blank white leader, passed over the play-back head.

Colonius swore so loudly Einstein woke up and looked at him blankly. With a disgusted wave of both hands, Colonius told him to go back to sleep; the last thing he needed right now was a conversation with Einstein. From his chair, Colonius switched channels again and turned the Wollensak back to "RECORD." That Goddamned word better turn up some place; constructing it out of syllables from other words—as he had on the first tape—sounded amateurish as hell.

On the flight to L.A., everything suddenly came together. Damned if he knew how, but there it was—the plan. Earlier, he'd been making a list of shows that were taped there—he was after another picture, himself and somebody big from TV—but none of the stars excited him too much and he'd thrown down the newspaper in disgust.

Then, it hit him. The whole plan. The real target. The way to do it—the works. It was crazy. Wild. One minute, he was staring moodily out the window at the pattern of toy farms and roadways six miles below, pretty depressed, wondering if maybe the project wasn't a complete bust, something else that had slipped through his fingers. The next, the whole damned thing was as clear in his head as if some evil god had leaned down and whispered it into his ear.

It was so obvious Colonius cursed himself for not thinking of it sooner. He pressed his legs together and squeezed his eyes to control his own excitement at the awesome simplicity of it, probing and pulling at the idea from different angles for signs of weakness, ripping it apart to find possible areas of risk or failure, tearing at it, torturing it, twisting and testing it to try to uncover some flaw he hadn't yet seen. He could fine none.

Yet, Colonius forced himself to stay cautious. Few things in life came to him easily, and he was suspicious of anything that did. It was only when the carnival lights of L.A. blinked up at him and the plane drifted down for a landing that he finally conceded the idea was not only foolproof, but stunning in its dimensions. All that lay ahead now was the detail work and the execution.

That last word, he decided, was so appropriate it was funny, and for the first time on the entire flight he smiled at the stewardess to show her he had as good a sense of humor as the next man.

Chapter Five

I had the craziest feeling the whole time I was in California. Every time I came around a corner, I kept expecting to run into my father. And he'd try to make a big fuss over me and say how sorry he was he had to skip on me, only I'd play it damned cool and just shake his hand and walk away. Now, that's a real crazy idea, you know, because nobody's seen or heard of my father since he walked out, when I was about ten, and he wouldn't recognize me if we had a head-on collision in a steam bath. The only way I even know he came out here was that every year on my birthday, for a while anyway, he used to send me a postcard of Hollywood Bowl. Then, they stopped.

Funny, the first time he'll know I'm still alive is when all this hits the papers. I wonder how he'll feel about it. Maybe he'll start sending me postcards of Hollywood Bowl again. Celebrities are always getting stuff like that in the mail.

—Extract from the
journal of Lars Colonius

Monday, June 8—Armageddon minus forty-five.

THE BOY lay on the couch staring hard at the ceiling. Dr. Ambrose let his eyes sweep the room, then the desk, then the desk clock, to check how much time was left in the hour. Four and a half minutes. He'd tried everything today short of punching his patient, Terry Ilvera, to get him to speak, but nothing seemed to work.

Now, the boy spoke suddenly and angrily. "You were

checking to see how much time, weren't you? You don't give a damn about me. It's just a job."

Carlton Ambrose sighed. For an analyst to get caught checking the time was considered very unprofessional; this was why patients so delighted in doing it. Ambrose forced a laugh out of himself. "Well, it got you to talk, anyway."

Trapped, the boy snapped his jaws shut. Ambrose let his mind do the same; the session was a wipeout, and he went back to being mad at himself for getting caught looking at that damned desk clock. It was the next appointment—last of the day—that had bugged him into being careless like that. A man from the Justice Department. Which the hell one of his former patients, released as cured, had blown it this time?

The question was of more than medical importance to him. Carlton Ambrose was chief of staff of the Living Clinic, a complex of bungalows and concrete-block treatment buildings incongruously set in the placid hills of southwestern Connecticut. He was also recognized as the top man in the difficult field of criminal psychopathology. Armed with these credentials, he had begun, about a year earlier, to appear in various courts in behalf of certain carefully chosen convicted persons; his plea, in effect, was that they be sentenced to the clinic for treatment rather than to prison for punishment. Originally, this angle had been reserved for people who could pay the clinic's stiff fees. But more recently, a large grant from the Ford Foundation had vastly expanded the clinic's staff and capacity, and Dr. Ambrose was appearing in court more and more frequently.

It was not a popular trend with either police departments or district attorneys, faced as they were with a public obsessed with law and order. Ambrose could be certain that any former patients who got into trouble after release from the clinic would be used against him the next time Ambrose appeared before a sentencing judge. And a former patient resourceful enough to call down the wrath of the Attorney General's office must have really pulled a corker.

The four and a half minutes were up and Ambrose

struggled to think of a pleasant note to end the session on; the boy preempted the pleasantness by striding over to Ambrose's desk and sweeping everything off it with an angry movement of his arm.

Dr. Ambrose shrugged as he watched him stalk out the door, then bent over and began picking up the debris from the floor. Wistfully, he discovered that the desk clock had not survived the patient. And it crystallized his discouragement. Any psychiatrist knows better than to expect thanks from a patient; but when the doctor was all that stood between the patient and the hard fact of prison, he could be forgiven for at least expecting civility. The damned bastards will do *anything* to get attention, he hastily reminded himself; that's why they sought out punishment. It was the core of the argument he used in court.

The nurse knocked and said Mr. Goddard was here and looked at the mess on the floor curiously. Ambrose dismissed it with a hollow smile and waited for the man to be shown in, hoping he would get to the point quickly. Ambrose couldn't stand legal bushbeating.

Mr. Goddard got to the point very quickly indeed. "We need you," he announced, after a minimal greeting. "We need you very badly, Dr. Ambrose. It's a matter of extreme urgency. You'll want to pack some things, of course, but there isn't a hell of a lot of time; we'd like to send a car for you at eight in the morning."

Ambrose was so startled he could only stare at the man. He found himself resorting to a nervous laugh, something he despised in his patients. And his response, when it finally came, was admittedly weak. "I don't believe I understand," he said lamely. The nervous laugh struggled to the fore again, but Ambrose squelched it; there was nothing on the face of the man from the Justice Department to suggest anything funny.

Mr. Goddard shook his head with apparent impatience and wandered over—he had refused the chair Ambrose offered him—toward the long row of windows at right angles to Ambrose's desk. The clinic was built on high ground and these windows overlooked a spectacular view of the rolling Connecticut valleys, caught now in the muted afternoon sun of early spring. Goddard appeared

37

to drink in the scene, studying the changing patterns of light and shadow on the soft hills, then suddenly spun around toward the doctor.

"Somewhere out there, doctor—*any*where out there; we don't even know what part of the country at the moment —is a man—a psychotic—bent on killing someone of great importance. I can't emphasize enough of how great an importance."

The eternal game of blindman's buff invariably played by government people annoyed Ambrose. He went straight to the point. "All right. He plans to kill somebody of great importance. *Who?*"

"That's precisely why we need you. We don't know who. In fact, he's indicated—there's some possibility, at least—it may be a whole series of people."

Reluctantly, Ambrose admitted to himself it was a fascinating premise. "This psychotic of yours. You say you don't know where he is. But, obviously, you know *who* he is. One should lead to the other—his past records must indicate a living pattern. A movement pattern of some sort. I should think the police—"

With a sigh somewhere between embarrassment and despair, Goddard finally sat down in the chair. He looked at Ambrose with tired eyes. "We don't know *who* he is, either. We don't know who he is, where he is, who he plans to kill, or why. The not knowing who he plans to kill is what is driving us up the wall. I don't even know whom to protect." Goddard massaged the back of his neck in weariness. "All we know is that he seems entirely capable of it—ingenious to the point of brilliance, I would say— and that he sounds as if he plans to go through with it, and that he must be stopped."

Lawyers and psychiatrists share, at least, one trait; they are experts at spotting seeming contradictions of statement. But from a lawyer the question Ambrose now posed would have seemed hostile; from him, it seemed almost gentle. "If you know so little about this man, if you don't even know who he is, how do you know he's psychotic, for instance? And how can you claim he's 'ingenious to the point of brilliance?' And that he plans to knock off somebody of—as you put it—'great importance'?"

"The messages. The pictures—" began Goddard.

"Pictures?"

"Pictures of himself." The answer was automatic, as if it had been given many times already today. Goddard got to his feet again, after glancing quickly at his watch. "I'll be going into the whole thing in detail at the task force meeting. I don't want to repeat myself."

A small fascination had been growing in Ambrose—a clinical interest in the unusual, a psychiatrist's instinctive involvement in any unfamiliar behavior pattern—but the peremptory tone Goddard used shattered it. "My going is out of the question. Forgetting the question of my responsibilities here, it seems to me you're attacking the matter backwards. You say an unknown psychotic is determined to kill an unknown victim. That's pretty damned vague. For one thing, you don't even know the man's psychotic. That's what I mean about attacking the thing backwards; a psychiatrist may be the last thing you need. Not all potential killers are psychotic. In fact, most aren't."

"He's psychotic," grunted Goddard firmly. "Several of your peers—Doctors Levy, Shumway, Haldemann—all agree to that." Goddard's eyes stared at Ambrose again. "It was they, incidentally, who suggested you. Unanimously."

With a laugh, Ambrose spread his hands in the air. "I'm flattered, of course. But possibly they're just trying to duck the job, too."

"They're still involved, all of them. Part of the task force."

"It's a job for the police. I don't usually say that, as you know. But I'm a doctor, not a detective."

"The police involved suggested you as well. I believe you know Evan Evans. He's in charge of the police part of this—on loan to us from Houston—and you were his first and only choice. He somewhat made it a condition of his joining the task force."

Ambrose was startled by this piece of news. He could hardly be said to know Evans, although they had met and he knew a lot about the man. Evans was chief of detectives of the Houston police, and not at all what he'd expected when they were first introduced. The man was brilliant. Not just as a policeman, but as a person. An MA, he thought, or it could possibly even be a PhD. In any case, something very unusual for a cop. His track record, he remembered, was spectacular. Houston seemed an odd place for him, but possibly as oil made the town rich, money made the town complicated. Ambrose stared for a second at the broken face of the desk clock. Levy, Shumway, Haldemann. And now Evans. The police were usually on the opposite side of things, but Evans he had to respect.

Across the desk, Goddard must have been reading what was going on in Ambrose's mind and decided it was the moment to press the advantage. "You see, doctor, the task force represents many different functions. Setting up something like it was necessary because this particular problem is so damned wide open. And so damned important. Christ, it's important. We tried the more conventional route. The FBI, for instance. I trust I can have your assurance of complete confidence on this statement, but we tried them and absolutely nothing happened. They didn't even know where to begin. It's no reflection on them, of course; this sort of thing doesn't usually fall in their territory. So a task force with people like you and Evans and others seemed the only solution, even at the risk of offending the Bureau. Evans, as the expert on tracking down psychopathic killers. You, the expert on what motivates them."

Painfully, Ambrose began building a resistance against a growing temptation. He turned the desk clock around in his hands, knowing it represented his frustrations with the clinic and the pressures being brought against it from the outside. The task force sounded like a fascinating, if temporary, relief from the tedium. But it was impossible. "I just don't see how I could, Mr. Goddard. Besides commitments to some of the patients here, I have legal responsibilities as well. Many are here under court orders."

Goddard seemed well prepared for this reaction. "Of course. But I plan to petition the court, *amicus curiae,* and, given the circumstances, I don't believe there'll be too much problem. I can't reveal to a judge as much as

40

I have here, of course; secrecy is vital to avoid any hint of panic. But I should think the pictures alone would convince any judge."

Those damned pictures again. Of everything Goddard had said, Ambrose found himself most fascinated by that wrinkle. It was a compelling professional challenge, but a challenge he could not accept. Sadly, he shook his head. "You're a very persuasive man, Mr. Goddard. But I'm sure any of those other doctors you mentioned are more than capable of handling the job."

Goddard smiled. "Not this particular job. The task force. You're in charge of it."

"I'm sorry," Ambrose countered. "Regardless of how much I might want to—compelling professional challenge —terribly interesting problem—my responsibilities here, unfortunately—you understand, of course. . . ." Ambrose heard his own voice trail away, his eyes riveted on something Goddard was doing with his hands.

Leaning toward him across the desk, Goddard was putting slowly down, one after the other, like a cardsharp laying out the perfect poker hand, a blown-up newspaper clipping and four 8-by-10 photographs. His tired eyes studied Ambrose's face intently as he waited for a reaction to the final bait. Ambrose said nothing, but stared silently, hard and long, at the pictures.

Next morning, he was ready a full half-hour before the car arrived to pick him up.

Tuesday, June 9—Armageddon minus forty-four.

Almost from the outset, nothing about the task force turned out quite the way Goddard explained—or at least implied—it would be. It was not a case of his having overpromised; if anything, he had minimized the scale of the operation. And downplayed Ambrose's role in it.

The task force was set up in the Hotel Westbury in New York, smack in the most fashionable section of the city's East Side residential belt. The entire sixteenth floor had been taken over, both as offices and as sleeping quarters. Somehow, this sedate hotel seemed a curious place, with its slightly faded elegance, its old-world dining room set

41

hard by its smoky Polo Lounge, from which to run a manhunt, but Goddard had his reasons. Any such place in Washington, he explained, would make it difficult accounting for their activities; New York was a much better place for keeping secrets. For the same reason, a hotel was preferable to working out of government space or police offices. They could also sleep near their work.

Ambrose stared at the maze of special telex and telephone cables criss-crossing the Westbury's sixteenth-floor halls and wondered what the management had been told. When he asked Goddard, all he got was a tired shrug. By tomorrow Goddard promised, the full staff of the task force would be on hand and ready to go to work.

The statement annoyed Ambrose. After the rush to get him there, it was anticlimactic to discover nothing much would happen until then. The damned government again. "What about the briefing?" he complained. "I thought it was this morning."

"It is. I shall brief you this morning. Along with Evan Evans. Then, I have to take off for Washington. Tomorrow, you will brief the task force." Goddard seemed to be studying him and wondering if he had to explain further. Apparently, he decided he did. "A task force like this has some very strong personalities in it. People used to their own way. It isn't going to be easy to run it. And doing tomorrow's briefing puts you more in charge."

Ambrose decided it was time to open that matter up, too. "Look," he said. "Let's straighten that out right now. I don't want to be in charge. I'm not the guy to *put* in charge. You sort of threw that in last night and I didn't get to discussing it before you left. Now I am. I don't want it, I wouldn't be any good at it, and I won't accept it."

With a glance at his watch, Goddard shrugged and then smiled pleasantly. "There are a lot of reasons why it has to be that way. But we can go into it later, if you really want. Right now, there are some calls I have to get on before we get going. I told Evans the briefing would be around ten; that's half an hour from now. In the meeting room"—Goddard pointed vaguely down the long hall—"at the end, there. Sixteen zero six, I think it is."

He turned abruptly after a fast wave of his hand and disappeared into a room about halfway down the hall.

Stepping over the network of cables, Ambrose disconsolately made his way by the chattering telex machines back to his own room. Halfheartedly, he made a stab at unpacking, but gave it up and threw his long frame into a chair. That man Goddard. Charged with some sort of nervous electric energy—like the cables outside his door. Ambrose had no intention of becoming a platoon leader for him, dragging unwilling troops out of their foxholes to face an unseen enemy. Never. But the point would have to be settled before Goddard took off for Washington.

Stretching his long legs far out in front of him, Ambrose studied his shoes for a moment and decided he would make Goddard's remaining in charge a condition of his own staying on the task force. Evan Evans got away with something like that; he should be able to as well.

A decision made, he fished into his luggage and withdrew a package of Tijuana 12s—a mixture of regular tobacco and pot—lit one, slumped back into the chair again. At the Living Clinic, he was always very circumspect about this minor vice, never smoking it except in the privacy of his own cottage—and then only in the bedroom; it amused him that here, surrounded by police, Justice Department people, representatives of the FBI, and other visible agents of law and order, he should feel free to indulge himself so openly. This, he knew, was a small symbol of rebellion: Goddard and the government needed him more than he needed them. (Like many analysts, Ambrose suffered from ulcers, the result of constantly having to turn all hostilities inward. His own ulcers were particularly vicious—the bleeding kind —and he had taken to marijuana when alcohol was suddenly forbidden him. His own rationalization was that it was nowhere as addictive as alcohol, it relaxed him, and that, anyway, the laws were outrageously behind the times. The local police would not have concurred.)

A little later, a knock on the door produced Evan Evans. The sight of him shocked Ambrose as much as

43

the first time he'd met him; Evans defied the tradition of Texas lawmen by being painfully short and virtually round, wearing a dark, well-cut suit, and smoking an almost tiny, pencil-thin cigar. The only concession made to Houston was a discreet turquoise set in dull, hammered silver that served as a tie clip and the soft, Texas accent veiling his otherwise pristine English.

"Greetings," said Evans, shaking his hand warmly and coming into the room. His eyes rose to study Ambrose's height and then dropped as he compared it to his own short, round self. "We must look, you and I, a bit like the Trylon and Perisphere from the 1940 World's Fair. Or possibly, you're too young to remember it." Evans laughed lightly and shook Ambrose's hand again. Then, the smile disappeared. "I've looked forward to working with you for some years, Carlton. Although I could wish the circumstances weren't quite so grim. But greetings anyway."

"Oh, hell." Ambrose was glad to see Evans and as equally pleased to be working with him. But he was discouraged at the way the rest of it was working out. "That bastard Goddard. I can't figure him out."

"Goddard's all right. Bright. Hard-working. But this is a tough assignment for him—and, as you must know by now, an absolutely vital one."

Ambrose sank back into his chair and stretched out his legs again. "Agreed about it's being tough. But if it's so damned vital, why doesn't Goddard stay and run it himself?"

Evans tugged at a rounded earlobe that disappeared under his fringe of longish, salt-and-pepper hair. "Goddard's in charge of defense, so to speak. You're in charge of seek and destroy."

Ambrose found the term uncomfortable. Uncomfortable but accurate. Shifting himself in the chair, he stared at Evans. Earlier, he noticed Evans' nose give a suspicious twitch as the odor of the Tijuana 12s hit him; now, Ambrose could see that Evan Evans was sure his sense of smell hadn't failed him. The man, rocking back and forth on his small feet, looked on the verge of saying something about it, but apparently decided not to. Their conversation wandered into small talk and Ambrose made another stab at unpacking. Finally, Evans looked at his watch and pointed out it was about time to head for the briefing. With a resigned sigh, Ambrose nodded.

Together, they walked down the long hall toward the door of Suite 1607, an ominous black rectangle in the stark whiteness of the walls around it.

Chapter Six

But my real dream always was to be an actor. Or somebody on television. Particularly, the television thing. What a great feeling it must be, knowing all those people are seeing you and hearing you—like being born again, I guess. When I was younger, I studied some courses in it and later even went for a few auditions. Several stations wanted me to sign up. But then all that money came along and I had to give up the idea. People in show business are always suspicious of anybody with their own money.

—Extract from the
journal of Lars Colonius

THE PAPER was late that morning and it made Colonius irritable. Einstein kept running back to the store to see if it had come in yet, but it wasn't until almost ten thirty when it finally showed up. There was no real reason for Colonius to be this edgy, and he knew it; although the tapes and pictures had been sent by now, it was too early to expect anything yet.

Impatiently, Colonius seized the paper and scanned the front page. Nothing. Well, that was as he had figured. Einstein stood watching him, not understanding what all the fuss was about. Colonius calmed himself visibly and sat back down on the edge of the bed to show how unbothered he was, flipping through the pages further back as if he were looking for nothing in particular. Which by then, he wasn't. On page 12, however, something stopped him. It was a small story of little news value, and something only a paper like the *Telegraph*

46

would probably even bother to print. But it shook Colonius considerably.

They were going to start dredging the Ocmulgee. In about a month, it said. Every attempt would be made not to inconvenience motorists on Riverside, but some disruption was inevitable.

The possible discovery of Billy-Joe's body was about the biggest inconvenience Colonius could imagine, and he had to struggle to keep from panicking. He had no idea whether they would find the body, and even less if they could trace Billy-Joe back here from his fingerprints. Slowly, Colonius regained composure. Dredging wasn't due to start for a month, the paper said, so it wasn't anything too urgent. But there was one piece of mail due him whose address should be changed in case he did have to make a sudden departure.

Half an hour later, from the booth on the corner, Colonius called his aunt. She was startled, as she had been to get a letter from him the week before. The stuff he'd asked for—the snapshots of him as a child, the baby pictures, the home movies of him, the classbooks, the class picture and the birth certificate—all the things he'd written asking her to send him at the Sweet Laurel should now be mailed instead to his post office box. No, nothing was wrong, he told her. He just wanted to be sure it got here safely.

After he hung up, Colonius smiled to himself. When she had asked what he wanted all that stuff for, he told her it was for a girl. That made her happy as hell, of course; she was always pushing things like that.

There were four of them at the briefing: Ambrose, Evan Evans, Roger Elkins (an assistant of Goddard's, whose main function seemed to be to run the slide projector and tape machine), and Goddard himself. From the beginning, Goddard's presentation was factual, blunt, and totally without ornamentation; yet, by the time it was over, Ambrose found himself shaken—and just a little bit awestricken.

"Gentlemen," began Goddard, "I think the best way to give this to you is as we received it ourselves, with-

47

out any preamble or comment. You, doctor, have seen all the pictures, Evans only some. Neither of you is even aware of the tapes."

Goddard looked at Elkins in an unspoken question about the equipment, and then, after a quick glance at his notes, started off. "On Friday, the eighth of May, this newspaper clipping"—he nodded toward Elkins and the picture from the Macon *Telegraph* appeared on the screen —"was received at the Justice Department. The white circle drawn around the man's head—the man with the striped shirt and the dark glasses—was added by the sender, not us. The envelope was postmarked Chicago. Along with the clipping, the envelope contained the tape you will now hear."

With another nod at Elkins, the machine began playing the tape. The voice on it was disjointed, uneven, and distant, as if it had been recorded by a robot using a different trick voice for each word.

"This is the voice of Armageddon," boomed the tape machine in its hollow tones. "You can see how close I was able to get to the Vice President of the United States and how easy it would be for me to have killed him. In fact, the pistol was in my pocket. But the man was not sufficient to my purpose. For mine must be an act so vast it will become the yardstick against which all assassinations, past and future, will be measured. So I must keep looking. And so must you. Cheers."

There was a hollow click, the tape ran over a splice and onto white leader, and Elkins stopped the machine. Looking up, Ambrose could see Goddard brace himself for a reaction. There was none. There could be none. "The clipping," continued Goddard, letting a small flicker of displeasure cross his mouth, "is from the Macon *Telegraph*, dated the thirtieth of April. It was taken by their staff photographer the morning before. As for the strange sound of the tape, this tape, like all of them we received, is made up of words recorded off a television or radio set, then spliced together in sentences and re-recorded. In a way, it is the electronic version of the classic threatening letter or ransom note. You know the kind—made from words cut out of magazines and then pasted on a piece of paper."

Goddard paused again, still waiting for a reaction. Ambrose couldn't figure what he expected them to say. "Obviously," Goddard added, "fingerprints were checked for, but there were none that were usable. Frankly, for a while the whole thing was considered the work of an elaborate crank. That, of course, was before the three additional tapes and pictures of Armageddon with other possible victims were received. . . ."

As Goddard's voice wound down, a small sigh came from Evans. At first, the sound surprised Ambrose, but then he realized Evans had probably just finished measuring the size of the problem and was, like himself, suddenly feeling very inadequate. For a moment, the silence hung there heavily, broken abruptly by a question from Evans.

"Is there any way at all the source of anything on that tape can be located? That word 'Armageddon,' for instance; it can't be in very general use."

Goddard smiled weakly. "This guy apparently had difficulty finding it, too. The FBI reports that the same recording of the word is used on each of the tapes, except for the first one—they established that much through voice prints. On the first tape, though, the word is made up of syllables taken from other words. But to answer your entire question, I'd have to say no. The number of programs, local or national, any of the words could come from is staggering."

"But if it did turn out to come from a local program," insisted Evans, "it would give us a lead to where the man bases himself. One hell of a lead."

"Finding one word like that would be murder," answered Goddard briskly. He turned to Ambrose, apparently for support.

Evans' idea made some sense to Ambrose—he thought he had a possible way of making it easier—but he decided to pass for the moment. "Could we hear more?" he asked.

There was a startled pause; Goddard had almost entirely forgotten the other tapes for a minute, and the lapse, along with a general weariness, was written all over his face. They must, thought Ambrose, be working the poor guy to death on this.

"Good point," said Goddard, and picked up the notes again. "On Friday, May twenty-ninth, an eight-by-ten photograph arrived. With it was an additional tape." He nodded to Elkins and the slide appeared. "Again, the white circle around Armageddon's head." But Goddard had lost his audience; Evans and Ambrose were already discussing the slide. Henry Ford II stood to one side of an elaborate lectern, staring at Armageddon with bemusement. A man, blurred by the speed of his movement, seemed to be moving toward him, ready to pull down his outstretched hand. There were several other people in the picture behind Ford, but it was difficult to tell whether they were moving to protect him or advancing on Armageddon.

Goddard let the talk die down, then continued. "Although the envelope was postmarked Duluth, the picture was taken in Detroit. During a regular stockholders meeting. Mr. Ford doesn't remember the incident at all; Ford's head of security remembers only that a stockholder came up on the stage insisting on shaking Mr. Ford's hand. There had been considerable shouting from the back of the hall—these days, consumer protection groups, environmentalists, and special-interest committees buy a share or two of company stock and then come raise hell at these meetings—and Armageddon was pretty well forgotten in the shuffle. No one was particularly concerned with a man who just wanted to shake Mr. Ford's hand and say something nice."

Evan Evans spoke up quickly. "Did the security men remember anything about how the guy spoke? What he sounded like? What kind of voice?"

Goddard thought for a second. "They can't remember a damned thing about him. Nothing."

"So it's pretty safe to assume either that he didn't speak at all, or that if he did, it was in an entirely undistinguished voice," added Ambrose. He thought he'd caught the drift of where Evans was heading.

Ambrose was only partially right. "I was wondering,"

explained Evans. "It strikes me as odd that a man would send you pictures of what he looks like—granted, disguising your looks is pretty easy—but then go to one hell of a lot of trouble to hide what his voice sounds like. I don't know. Maybe there's something about his voice—a lisp, a stammer, an accent—so easy to spot he doesn't dare use it. Or, Christ, maybe the voice is so well known he doesn't dare use it because it's too recognizable. A voice, say, like that of an actor, or a movie star, or a—politician."

Goddard groaned. "Jesus."

But almost as quickly as he was stunned by Evans' idea, Ambrose saw the hole in its logic. "I don't think I'd worry about that, Evan. If Armageddon were already famous, he wouldn't be going through all of this. These days, assassinating a public figure, hijacking an airplane —they're massive bids for attention. Sure tickets to fame. Ways to break out of an anonymous society. That's why people—unbalanced people—are into them."

Elkins waited to see if the discussion was over, and then started the tape machine.

"This is the voice of Armageddon," began the machine again in its curious halting, up-and-down tones. "I assume, from your public silence, that you thought my first message was the work of a crank. It is not. Like all of those who have ignored me in the past, you underestimate my ability. I have an IQ of one hundred sixty-four and a Stanford-Binet of plus forty, if you want to know. Better than yours, probably. From this picture, you can see how easily I could have creamed poor old Henry, but I decided he was as unworthy a target as the Vice President. Killing him would make headlines, cause a big splash—but not a sensation. So the search goes on. Armageddon has plenty of time. You do not. Cheers." Again there was the hollow click, and the tape ran onto the white leader that separated the sections from one another.

Ambrose felt a small shudder run through him; it was as if Armageddon could read his mind and had known exactly what he would say a few minutes earlier and knew exactly what he would be thinking now after hear-

51

ing the tape. He struggled to shake it off. "Well, he certainly fits the pattern"—Ambrose glanced down at the pad where he'd jotted notes during the tape—"alternates between feeling ignored and persecuted. Conspiracy of silence. Abilities underestimated. Big splash to prove how wrong we are. There's a fancy word for it, but let's just say the guy is dying from a severe case of being unnoticed."

Evans waited until Ambrose was finished, but then turned impatiently to Goddard, waving the photograph. "Who took this picture?"

With a shake of his head, Goddard threw up his hands. "We don't know. All we know is that it was taken on a cheap camera. Probably a Brownie."

Evans was insistent. "But taken on a Brownie by whom? The newspaper shot could be an accident; this was a setup. In other words, Armageddon has an accomplice."

Goddard sighed heavily. "I suppose."

It was easy to see why Evan Evans wasn't popular with anyone in authority. "It's not a question of supposing anything, dammit," he snapped. "It's obvious."

Quickly, Ambrose cut in before Evans got himself in too deep. "What about the rest?" he asked.

The slide of Armageddon with Leonard Bernstein was shown. The picture and its tape were mailed in Minneapolis, where Bernstein assured the authorities he hadn't been for years. Neither could he remember where, when, or under what circumstances the picture was taken; he was surrounded by unfamiliar faces and the background was so bland as to be unidentifiable. His staff, Goddard promised, was trying to pin it down for them now.

The accompanying tape was much like the others, and the only new bit of information on it was a mention that Armageddon could have been a concert pianist, but had abandoned the project in discouragement. "There's no future in serious music," Armageddon explained. "Even Bernstein has to write musical comedies." This, apparently, was enough to dismiss him as a serious target; Armageddon was still looking.

In the picture of him with Johnny Carson, Armageddon's

clothes—the vividly striped shirt, the tight-fitting white pants, and the oversized sunglasses—for the first time looked in their own element. Although mailed from Austin, Texas, the shot had been taken outside the studio at Burbank, California, and Armageddon was one of a small crowd by the stage door waiting to cheer the star as he came out. The crowd was smiling, Carson was smiling, but Armageddon appeared to be smiling the hardest of all. Neither Carson nor his staff could date the picture; the scene outside the studio was a daily occurrence.

But it was the closing sentences of the accompanying tape that interested Ambrose the most. At the beginning of it, vague sympathetic reference to the difficulties of breaking into show business was made. Toward the end, though, Armageddon suddenly switched attitudes and used Carson as an example of how little talent it took to get ahead. "If I chose him as my target, all I would do is relieve millions of people of sheer boredom. But time has provided, gentlemen. Time, gentlemen, time." There was a long pause on the tape, then: "And the time is Armageddon minus forty-eight."

A frantic flapping sound came from the machine; the last of the tape had run through and its loose end beat emptily against the recording head until Elkins reached down and stopped the reel.

For the first time since the briefing began, Goddard sat down. He ran both hands across his face and stared at Ambrose. " 'Armageddon minus forty-eight.' I'm not sure I know what the hell that's supposed to mean."

A small, hard knot grew inside Ambrose, who was sure he did. "It's his timetable, I think. His schedule. His countdown." He stood up, hands shoved in his pockets, head slightly bowed as his eyes studied the carpet, but his tall, thin figure still towering over them all. "I don't know what happened to him between the rest of the tapes and this one. But it's all different now. He knows his target. He knows his date. And says so. Forty-eight days from now. Or from when he sent the tape."

"You're sure of that?" asked Goddard. His face had an unhappy look, a man whose worst suspicions have just been confirmed.

"From that one number?" asked Evan Evans.

Shaking his head, Ambrose took a few steps, hands still jammed into his back pockets. "The number, sure. But also because it's the first tape that doesn't mention he has further to look. 'Time has provided,' he says. And 'Time, gentlemen, time'—the call for closing time in English pubs. Pretty good imagery—closing time. And then 'The time is Armageddon minus forty-eight.' Pretty inescapable, I'm afraid. And I *am* afraid. Because I don't know how the hell we're going to figure out what he has in mind until he pulls it."

Leaning forward in his chair, Goddard began to press Ambrose in a worried voice. "Carlton, I know it's pretty early to ask this. But I take off for Washington in a few minutes, so I'm going to anyway. You must have some ideas about what he has in mind. Some guess as to what he's after. And I've got to know, even if it *is* only a guess."

With a turn, Ambrose stopped his pacing. "Armchair analyses are always unreliable. But what I can guess goes back to what I said earlier. The assassination—or whatever it is—will be planned to give him maximum exposure. All the attention he can milk it for." Ambrose took a couple more steps, then paused again. "Only in Armageddon's case, you're dealing with an ingenious mind. An extraordinary mind. So you can figure that however he goes about getting this maximum attention—the target he picks, the device he uses to destroy it—it will be equally ingenious, equally extraordinary. And frankly, at this point—I know it's not too much help—that's about all I can say."

Goddard finally asked what had obviously been worrying him from the beginning. His voice was so soft the question sprang at them unexpectedly. "Do you think it's the President?"

"Oddly enough, I don't," Ambrose said quickly. "I've thought about that, of course, and I'm not sure I could tell you why, but I just don't think so." Ambrose's hands rose in the air at his own inability to explain himself better.

Evan Evans wasn't so sanguine. "On the other hand, I

54

would certainly check out the entire time period around the date Armageddon gave us. And I mean check out. Hard."

Goddard nodded heavily. "Obviously."

"In fact," continued Evans, "all major events during that time period of *any* kind. Congress. The Senate. The U.N. International meetings of any sort—the Olympic mess at Munich is a good example of what I mean."

Almost involuntarily, Ambrose found he was shaking his head. "I wouldn't just limit it to quasigovernment things, Evan." There was no way for him to pin down what he was feeling, but he was bothered by a missing element of some kind. "I wish I could explain it better, but, dammit, I just feel that Armageddon has a surprise, a shock, for us—one built right into his target. Something we're not seeing. Everything I know or can guess about how the man's mind works, every instinct I have myself, tells me there's something we're just not getting. It's right in front of our noses and we're missing it. Goddamn, if we could only get him into some sort of dialogue, do something that would force him into more communication with us. Oh hell, I don't know."

For some minutes an aide had been waiting behind Elkins; now he stepped forward to remind Goddard of his plane. With a groan that showed how tired he really was, Goddard slowly picked up his suitcase and headed for the door. He paused and turned back to Ambrose. "Anything you want to try, Carlton, is OK by me. As long as it doesn't involve the public safety. Or publicity. All I ask is to be kept up to date. I'll be back in a couple of days, but, hell, we'll be talking anyway."

With an impatient nod toward the aide, Goddard disappeared out the door. Evan Evans settled into a chair beside Ambrose and gave him a long, inquisitive look. "What were you getting at back there, Carlton? About a shock for us built right into the target."

Ambrose stared at him and shook his head. "I don't know. I wish to hell I did, but I just don't know."

Chapter Seven

Sometimes I get a kick lying in bed thinking how many guys must be working on this thing. But every now and then, I get a spooky feeling—like I was playing chess with somebody in the dark. I move a pawn, they move a pawn. I move a rook, they move a knight. But we're playing blind. And one day someone's suddenly going to turn on all the lights and we'll know where all the pieces are. Christ, are they going to be surprised.

I wonder, can Bobby Fischer play chess in the dark?
—*Extract from the
journal of Lars Colonius*

Wednesday, June 10—Armageddon minus forty-three.

LARS COLONIUS riffled through the Macon *Telegraph* and could no longer escape it—something was wrong. By now the papers should be full of Armageddon. Blowups of the pictures, transcripts of the tapes, statements of concern from the authorities. There was nothing.

Even allowing for delay in rerouting by the various post offices, the material should have been in the hands of the Justice Department for days now. Yet there was nothing.

A shadow of some deeper anger passed across his face. Maybe it would never be made public, any of it, and the police and the FBI would move ahead silently and secretly until they caught him. And even after he was dead, not a word would be mentioned anywhere.

Colonius kicked the bed in his anger. Screw them. If he

kept the pressure up, they would have to act—if only to bring him out into the open. The thought made him feel better and he sat back down on the edge of the bed and tried to go back to reading the paper.

But in spite of the assurances to himself, Colonius felt edgy about the unexpectedly long silence; he needed publicity to make the final steps of the plan work. Reluctantly, he stood up and moved over to the writing table. From a drawer, he took a photograph and a reel of tape and put them on the corner of the desk. It was a set he hadn't planned to send until things were coming to a climax and the date was almost on top of him, but it was a set guaranteed to produce a fast reaction.

He glanced down the list of things to be done. To the top of the list he now added a reminder to himself to mail the new package that afternoon. Arrangements for some additional pictures and tapes—there were still more to be done—could be put off until tomorrow.

From the corner of the room came the sound of a cough. It was Einstein calling attention to himself now that Colonius had left the bed and was messing around at his desk instead of staring into space. Abruptly, Colonius drew a tape measure from the desk, called Einstein over, and began writing down the measurements of his sleeves, back, chest—like a tailor fitting him for a suit. In a way, that was precisely what he was doing.

The crazy smile lit up Einstein's face. "Ooooo-eeee, that feels funny." He giggled slightly as the tape measure, now stretched tight across his chest, tickled him under one armpit.

"I'm getting your size right," explained Colonius, although he knew the explanation was completely wasted on Einstein. Looking down at something on the writing table, Colonius compared the figures he'd taken with the figures printed opposite various size numbers in the catalog from The Compleat Angler, a sporting goods store in the best section of town. Size 40, extra large, he figured.

"You're going to buy this," Colonius said, showing Einstein the picture of a fishing vest, its canvas front, sides, and back covered with small pockets and loops to hold hooks, tackle, lines, flies, and other fishing equipment.

"For yourself, Einstein. You'll be wearing it on the big day."

Einstein stared at the picture and the smile grew wider. Anything with that many pockets had to be important. The "big day" remained a mystery to him, something distant, something wonderful, something of vastness that his God, Mr. Colonius, talked of constantly but never explained. God, Einstein supposed, was like that.

"And you'd better go pick it up this afternoon, I think," added Colonius. "Tomorrow, we take another trip. Chicago, and then back to L.A." Colonius appeared to be lost in thought, speaking as much to himself as to Einstein. "Maybe New York in between; I just don't know."

Einstein struggled with the happiness that was coming over him and nodded solemnly. "I like airplanes," he mumbled. That was one part of the thing he really thought he did understand now—the airplanes: You got on in one place, there was a lot of noise and people smiled at you a lot, and then when you got off you were in a different place. He understood neither why they went to the places nor what went on when they got there, except about the pictures. He liked the picture-taking part, of course; it was fun. And Mr. Colonius always told him how great he'd done afterwards. And how great he was about riding on the airplanes, pretending he couldn't hear or talk, except with his hands. That was fun, too. But it was all very strange.

Leaning over the catalog again, Einstein poked a giant finger at the picture of the fishing vest and raised his eyebrows, pointing to his ears and mouth to ask whether he was supposed to play that game at the store, too.

Colonius nodded and sat down at the typewriter. "Right. Damned right. I'll knock off the letter right now." He searched for the numbers again, and found them. "Size 40, extra large, I think."

Even with his labored hunt-and-peck system, Colonius finished the letter quickly. With a pen, he added the vest's catalog number and Einstein's size, as well as the doctor's initials, "W.K." Then, folding the note neatly, he handed it to him, standing up briefly to pull enough bills from his pocket to pay for it.

"OK, Einstein. You're on, kid. If they don't have the right size, well, just shrug your shoulders and walk out. We'll get one at the Army-Navy Surplus, or something."

Einstein took the note and the money, stuffed them in his pocket, and walked importantly to the door, a man with a mission. The effect was somewhat spoiled when he practiced shrugging his shoulders all the way across the room, but it didn't matter. With a wave, he disappeared.

Colonius sighed. Einstein was a chore. Yet Einstein and that damned fishing vest were a very important part of things. Ordering the vest today was probably premature—he still had forty-three days to go—but it might take several tries to get one that worked just the way he needed it to. And time for Einstein to get used to it. Leaning back over the writing table, Colonius checked the list again. A small but precise clock should be easy to turn up. Likewise, energy cells, fuses, switches, and resistors.

But the explosive posed a problem. It would be hard to come by in Macon without a lot of questions being asked. Of course, Billy-Joe, with his underworld contacts, could have picked it up easily enough, but Billy-Joe was packaged in plastic, weighted with stone, and resting silently somewhere on the mud-clay bottom of the Ocmulgee. Until the dredges came, anyway

Standing up, Lars Colonius carefully folded the list and slipped it between the pages of the journal; he would have plenty of time to figure out about the plastic on the long flights between Chicago, L.A., and possibly—he still hadn't decided—New York.

Anything Billy-Joe could do he could do better.

Saturday, June 13—Armageddon minus forty.

The almost tiny, fragile-looking professor stood in his workroom at the Westbury, surrounded by half a dozen tape machines and seemingly endless masses of tape. One entire wall was covered with acetate and on it was carefully printed each word from Armageddon's tapes, some underlined in red, some in blue, some in yellow. Other words had strange slash marks between their syllables, while arrows and circles joined any repeated usages from one sentence to another.

The man turned to peer at Ambrose through thick glasses, his serene Oriental eyes oddly in keeping with the aura of mystery that surrounded his work.

"First of all, doctor, I would have them go after the word 'Binet' in 'Stanford-Binet'," Dr. Sochi said in his soft voice. "These days it would only be used on some program concerning education—and even rarely there."

Dr. Sochi was a semanticist from the University of California and someone Ambrose had added to the task force on his own. The idea of getting him there had started with Evan Evans' comment about tracking down just one word on the tapes to a local program, something he said would give them a lead to Armageddon's home base.

This made sense to Ambrose, and a semanticist made sense in narrowing down the words to search for. Sochi had put together a list of all the words on the tapes and then ranked them in descending order of common usage. Apparently, 'Binet' came out at the bottom, and was therefore the easiest place to start.

" 'Armageddon'," Sochi continued, "only ties with the British salutation 'Cheers!' for second place, but I think I would go after it anyway."

Ambrose nodded and wrote them down. The two words would now be given to the FBI, which already had their local offices across the country standing by. Each office was to telephone every radio and television station in their area and try to find someone there who remembered using either word. It was a long shot, but it might pay off.

In addition, Dr. Sochi was tearing every inch of the tapes apart, probing the language of them word by word for any trace of regionalization, occupation, or background in the man who had put them together.

Ambrose looked at Sochi's lined face and was reluctant to go into this part of it, but felt he should. "How's the rest going?"

"Slowly. Very slowly. Nothing significant yet." Sochi

stared at the frantic confusion of arrows and colors on the acetate and shrugged. It wasn't an easy job.

With a football coach's smile, Ambrose touched his arm lightly. "You'll turn up something. And we can use anything you get."

Sochi smiled weakly as Ambrose left and turned slowly back toward the acetate, punching the button on one of the tape machines as he did.

Out in the hall, Ambrose carefully picked his way over the cables on the floor and walked slowly past the meeting room, where Evan Evans was locked up with the rest of the task force. It had taken longer for the whole group to assemble than Goddard had said, but they were all there now and in place. Their numbers alone made Ambrose uncomfortable; as a psychiatrist, he was used to dealing with people one at a time. So gradually he let Evans, who was more at home manipulating roomsful of people, handle not only the daily briefings, but the day to day operations. Only Doctors Levy, Haldemann, and Shumway—a psychological brain trust representing different facets of psychiatry—still reported directly to him.

The rest of the task force was organized according to function. Granger and Werther from the Secret Service—there because the Vice President's life had been threatened directly, and the President's by implication. Stuart and Zimmermann of the FBI—present since the mails had been used and state lines crossed in the threatening of other lives. Both of these two organizations to provide not only technical services, but an unlimited reservoir of manpower.

Ambrose was surprised to discover there were also representatives from key police departments across the country: Tiffin of New York, LeClair of New Orleans, Whalley of Chicago, Aslen of Denver, and Gerhardt of Los Angeles. Added to these were Hemslee of the Royal Canadian Police Force and Tantamara of the Mexican National Police. To Ambrose, it seemed too many.

"Politics," Evan Evans had explained. "Police politics. Say the target or the suspect turns out to have some connection with St. Louis. Well, you get more clout out of one phone call from Whalley of Chicago to his counterpart there than from a dozen by the Justice Department in Washington—or even from having the local FBI show up, right on their doorsteps. These guys are used to trading favors and information with each other. It's an informal, but damned effective, nationwide network. Don't knock it."

The network was already in full operation. Through the door of the meeting room, Ambrose could hear a constant ringing of phones and the low murmur of urgent voices; each man inside was either on a phone or waiting for someone to call back. Armageddon's picture was being circulated on a mythical federal want poster, but the word was going out through the network that the real charge in the caller's home state was child molestation. And for Christ's sake keep the newspapers off it because the victim had been a cop's eight-year-old daughter.

It was an effective way to get the local police across the country involved, Ambrose supposed, but the operation made him shudder. From inside the room, he heard someone moving toward the door, and Ambrose backed away quickly, almost tripped over the cables again, and fled down the hall to his own area.

Ambrose was spending most of his time with the brain trust. Shumway and Levy were pure psychiatrists, while Haldemann was more of a behavioral psychologist, but their talents meshed nicely with each other's and with Ambrose's, and they were making progress. Little by little, late on into the nights, the four of them had finally hammered out a plan. What Ambrose wanted was something that would force Armageddon out into the open a little, something that would give *them* the initiative for a change, something that would push Armageddon into departing, if only briefly, from his carefully worked out plan. The key to manipulating the man, Ambrose had decided, was his ego, and they concentrated on ways to use that as a psychological lever to move him.

Their early stabs at it Ambrose considered too dangerous to the public; there was always the chance of pushing Armageddon too far and having him explode in fury at whomever happened to be standing nearest him. But after considerable hauling and shoving, they were able to minimize this risk, even if Ambrose wound up cast in an oddly heroic role he didn't relish at all.

At lunchtime that day Ambrose was able to track Evan Evans down at his favorite restaurant and run the plan by him for the police point of view. The tiny cigar stopped suddenly, halfway to Evans' mouth, and his eyes widened with excitement. "Goddamn. It gives *us* the ball for once. I think it's great."

Ambrose nodded. "Goddard will be here in the morning. And he's not going to be so easy to convince. Can you cover the protection part of it?"

Evan Evans pushed back a plate with the remains of a *crème brûlée* and got the little cigar the rest of the way to his mouth. "Nobody can ever guarantee that sort of protection. For anybody. But I'll fake it to Goddard, if you want, and say I can."

"I'll give you the details this afternoon; let's get back." Ambrose watched as Evans paid his check, heaved himself out of his chair, and rose to join him.

There was no conversation until they'd walked several blocks. Then Evans stopped abruptly and looked up at him worriedly. "Do you think it'll work?"

"It better."

They stared at each other for a moment and then slowly started again walking back toward the hotel. Time, they both knew, was little by little beginning to run out on them.

Chapter Eight

Last night, I tried to watch every damned news show there was. Walter Cronkite bugs me the most, I think. That mustache of his, and the way he talks into space, like you weren't there. He reminds me of Mr. Fairleigh, the principal of William Howard Taft Vocational, and the reason I quit school. I was always in trouble so I saw him an awful lot, but he never got my name right once. Not one damned time. And no matter what I had to say, he just sat there and talked into space, like I didn't exist.

Well, that's one thing about Walter Cronkite; he'll get my name right.

—Extract from the
journal of Lars Colonius

Sunday, June 14—Armageddon minus thirty-nine.

"I DON'T like it," snapped Goddard. "I don't like it a bit."

To Ambrose, who'd barely gotten the first sentence of the proposal out before Goddard spoke, this seemed an unfair reaction. But he managed his most understanding smile for Goddard, who stood his ground bristling with hostility. "You're like some of my most interesting patients," he said lightly. "They start resisting before they even lie down."

Goddard stared at him balefully. He was not going to be charmed out of his position. "All I needed to hear was that one word, 'publicity.' Newspapers. Television. It's precisely what I made clear to you we *don't* want." Goddard paused for a second and apparently felt he'd overmade his case. With a shake of his head, he allowed one hand to rub his left temple and turned wearily to Ambrose again. "I'm sorry, Carlton. I'm just damned tired, that's all. This thing's got me on the ropes. I was hoping some more conventional method that didn't—"

There was a small, impolite snort from Evan Evans, who was leaning back, balancing his small chair against the wall. Given his weight, it seemed a precarious pose; but Evans, like many fat men, was surprisingly agile, almost graceful. "Conventional methods," he growled, "won't get us anywhere with an unconventional nut." Evans looked ready to say more but decided not to and clasped his hands behind his head, making his position look even more dangerous.

Impatiently, Ambrose tried to get things going again. "Look," he said to Goddard firmly, "I appreciate your fears about publicity, your concern about panic. But there is publicity and there is publicity. And one thing you've got to remember is that publicity—or attention, anyway —is part of what Armageddon is after. It's the usual syndrome. And if he doesn't get some soon, he'll pull something wild that will force you to give it to him. Then you'll really have your panic. That's point number one.

"Secondly, a little carefully controlled publicity—don't turn yourself off until you hear the whole idea—can put Armageddon's picture out where the public can help us find him. Right now, nobody knows what he looks like but us. Thirdly, if it's handled the way I see it, this publicity will force Armageddon to communicate with us, open a dialogue, respond to us. Even if only by mail or phone. But it will give us that much more help in finding him—and figuring out what his target is."

Ambrose had had his head down for the last sentence or two; now he raised it, looking Goddard squarely in the eye to underline what he was saying. "And finally—and really the heart of what we're about to propose to you—it gives Armageddon a target other than the one he has in mind now. Whatever it is. And one we can handle."

Finished for the moment, Ambrose looked away as if

65

embarrassed by the hard sell of his speech and studied the wall over Goddard's head. Goddard stared at him for a long time, then shrugged his shoulders and sat down. Ambrose suspected he'd won. As far as he'd gone anyway.

"I don't understand everything you're saying," Goddard said slowly. "Particularly about the target. But the rest makes some sense. Up to a point, of course. What are you *really* getting at?"

Ambrose began pacing the floor, his tall angular frame bent forward, his short gray head thrust out at an angle from it. "Dr. Haldemann has put together a psychological profile of the average nonpolitically oriented assassin. It's very like the profile for your psychopathic hijacker—it should be; their motivations are the same. But the point is Dr. Haldemann's profile gives a very bleak picture of a man. Desperately bleak. And one which jibes astonishingly little with what we know about Armageddon. In fact, the profile is just about the antithesis of everything Armageddon is—or, anyway, pretends to be. This profile would repel him, infuriate him, outrage him. And right there is why the idea will work."

Abruptly, Ambrose stopped his pacing directly in front of Goddard. "What I propose to do is present this profile—myself, personally, on television and later in the newspapers—playing up those parts we can guess will make him feel demeaned, eliminating the ones that might make him strike out at a stranger in anger. I believe by doing this I can goad him, anger him, force him into proving to me *personally* how wrong I am, how wrong the profile is. Force him into switching—even if only briefly—from whatever target he has in mind to me." He paused for a second, studying Goddard. It was hard to tell from the man's expression whether it expressed confusion or simply downright disapproval, but Ambrose plunged ahead. "Me. I become the target. The focus for his hate. The need to kill someone of importance to catch the world's attention translated into need to prove me and my damned profile of him wrong. By killing *me.*"

There was no response from Goddard, and Ambrose

66

decided it was time to break the tension a little. "I should add that Evan Evans assures me Armageddon won't succeed. This is a very important part of the plan, as far as I'm concerned."

Goddard looked baffled. He was trying to understand all that Ambrose had said, trying to absorb a great deal in a short time, trying to overcome his own closed mind to any sort of publicity for any reason, but obviously wasn't making it. Ambrose was planning to go into Haldemann's profile at some length; now, he decided it would be better to do nothing more than a skeleton. Quickly flipping the pages of Haldemann's report, Ambrose looked at Goddard, smiled encouragingly, and settled himself into a chair beside him.

"With me so far?" he asked.

Goddard tried hard not to look apologetic. "I think so. But some of this stuff is pretty far out of my line."

"I know. I'll keep it simple. Now, look. The psychological profile. It's a picture of a type of person. His usual background, his traits, his habits. In this case, it's a picture of a psychopathic assassin. But like anything built on averages, it's pretty grim. And in the case of someone unusual—like Armageddon—the average characteristics don't fit. They'll drive him straight up the wall. Just take what you and I know about him as a person. We know he's intelligent as hell, with an extraordinary mind and a high degree of imagination. That he's got ready cash for flying around the country and for buying supplies, so he either has or had a job that made good money. That he's reasonably literate. That he has an accomplice."

With a solid *thunk,* Ambrose hit the palm of his left hand with the rolled-up copy of Haldemann's profile. "But the averages say—the averages in this profile—that Armageddon should be slightly below average intelligence. Slightly *below.* That he's illiterate and lacking in imagination. That he should be dead broke because he can't get or hold a job. That he's a loner, unable to relate to anybody." Ambrose unrolled the report to find a marked passage. "And there's some more stuff in here that would puncture anybody's ego. For instance: 'Whining, self-pitying tendencies . . . one parent frequent-

67

ly alcoholic . . . unresolved sibling problems . . . sexually inadequate.' You and I know it doesn't fit. Armageddon knows it doesn't fit. But yet, it's what I'm telling the world on television. What I'm giving them as a true picture of Armageddon. As the facts—from an expert. The truth."

Standing up, Ambrose carefully put the report on his chair. "Assume for a second," said Ambrose, piercing the air in front of him with his long finger, "that you are Armageddon. Imagine you're sitting in front of a television set and hear that unbroken and insulting chain of characteristics come out a psychiatrist's mouth. You know—or at least have convinced yourself—that none of this is true. But there is a man on your screen—me— telling the world these lies about you. Furthermore, the same man says the authorities were willing enough to take you seriously, that they were originally impressed by the stuff you sent, but that he talked them out of it. Told them you would never go through with it. That you were incapable of carrying it out and that he, as a psychiatrist, has assured them of this." Ambrose smiled and threw his hands in the air with a shrug. "Your reaction would be very simple. Go find that man on television. Go find him and kill him."

Unhooking himself from his chair, Evan Evans now moved forward. "Only this will be harder to do than it seems. Even though we plan to publicize exactly where Dr. Ambrose can be found, he will be one of the most protected men in New York. We have plans to turn this entire floor into one gigantic trap for Armageddon. It's pretty simple."

Goddard passed his hand across tired eyes. It wasn't in the least bit simple for him. "I don't know. I'm not at all sure the government can condone using someone as bait for a trap. Dr. Ambrose, after all, is a civilian. I just don't know."

"The role as bait is a voluntary one," Ambrose pointed out. "And I have confidence in the protection Evans has worked out. Every confidence."

"It's still very risky." Goddard got to his feet and

scratched his head in discomfort. "You'll have to give me time to think about it. I just don't know."

Without warning, Ambrose felt his temper slide out of control. "Goddamn it, there's nothing to think about. It's a very simple idea. A good idea. And anything we can do is better than sitting here and letting him call all the shots. We're running out of time; can't anybody see that?"

Very sympathetically, Goddard nodded and then smiled. Ambrose began to apologize, but Goddard stopped him. "Look. We're all running on nerves. Forget it. Let me think a bit, and then I'll get back to you. I promise."

Although Ambrose tried to keep the conversation going and the subject open, it was clear Goddard didn't want to pursue it for the moment. He mentioned something urgent across town, but again reassured Ambrose he would get back to him with a decision. Quickly.

The moment he left, Ambrose lit up a Tijuana 12; he'd restrained himself during the meeting because he was trying to sell Goddard something and didn't want to do anything that might annoy him. Now, he turned to Evans in bewilderment. "I don't know where the hell we are. 'Time to think' is one of those all-purpose phrases that can mean anything."

"Code," grunted Evans sourly.

"Code?"

Evans laughed. "Code. Bureaucratese for 'I have to go ask somebody higher up—you're not going to pin a decision like that one on me.'"

Ambrose wasn't so sure it was that obvious. "That doesn't sound like Goddard. So far, he seems pretty much in charge of his own area. Maybe—just maybe—he is genuinely worried that it's too risky for me."

Evans snorted. "Risky my ass. Goddard isn't in the least worried about any risk to you. It's the publicity that bugs him. He's afraid *that's* risky."

With a diffident shrug, Ambrose collapsed into his chair and studied the smoke aimlessly rising from the Tijuana 12; it seemed as pointless as he felt.

"I have a prediction," announced Evans. "Our Mr. Goddard, for the time being, will do absolutely nothing."

Then, with an amiable sigh, Evans returned to his teeter chair against the wall, leaned back, and lit another of his tiny cigars.

But his predictions would turn out to be quite wrong, as would a lot else that had been said that day.

For Evan Evans had no way of knowing the contents of the envelope that Lars Colonius had placed in the mail a couple of days before, or the effect the contents would have when received.

Nor did Ambrose and the brain trust know that all their best guesses and psychological predictions about his ultimate target were completely off base.

It was to prove a costly set of errors.

Chapter Nine

At first, I suppose, the press isn't going to give me much of a break as a person. Particularly television. It's not so much what they say, but how they say it—those anchormen of theirs have a set of tricks they do with their faces, their mouths, their eyes, that lets the audience know when they really hate somebody. And no question, I'll be right on the top of their list.

Well, let them have their fun. The FCC guarantees a guy equal time, and my turn's coming. Then the world will know what I'm really like, not what Eric Sevareid's trick lips *say* I'm like.

—Extract from the
journal of Lars Colonius

Friday, June 19—Armageddon minus thirty-four.

TO COLONIUS, the actual timing of the news break almost seemed a sign from God. He had spent the last couple of days completing the details of his departure from Macon, already convinced his latest envelope to the Justice Department would produce fast results. The room at the Sweet Laurel was emptied of everything but the tape recorder, the journal, press clippings, his traveling clothes, and one suitcase. The small home developing kit, along with the fishing vest and the Brownie, would travel with Einstein in his tote bag. It was Colonius' plan to leave the same day the news broke, quietly and hopefully unnoticed by anyone. He would keep on sending rent checks to Mrs. Spiers, the Sweet Laurel's landlady; in her fogged condition, she would probably never even notice he was

71

gone, and keeping the money coming in would guarantee she didn't bother to find out.

One of the remaining details now caused Colonius to wrinkle his nose with displeasure; he couldn't get used to the odd smell of the store, a mixture of oiled leather fumes, hints of curing acids from somewhere in the back, and—just possibly—incense or herb vapors rising from a battered brass teapot over a small, open flame. He'd spent the last half hour here in this foul-smelling little shop off Wimbish Road, waiting for a final piece of his traveling equipment to be readied, and time didn't improve the almost Oriental stink of the place one bit. But in spite of it, the Algerian seemed to know what he was doing and coldly refused Colonius' repeated suggestions of speed. Colonius checked his watch and swore softly to himself again. He supposed the waiting was part of the ritual.

For when Billy-Joe had sold him the thirty-eight, he'd mentioned the Algerian's place and told him the man was a genius. Crazy as hell, but a superb craftsman. It was a place, he pointed out, where he could have a custom-fitted shoulder holster made for the thirty-eight—and no questions asked. Colonius hadn't wanted or needed a holster, but wrote down the man's name anyway—Yasir Arbadi was one of those Middle-Eastern names that just missed sounding poetic—and automatically filed it away. Now, suddenly, it became useful; earlier in the week he'd appeared at the store—but not to order a holster. And Billy-Joe was right. For although what he did ask to be made must have struck Arbadi as strange, no question was asked, nor was there even any indication of curiosity.

"There, mister," said the Algerian suddenly, slamming the first item of the order down hard on the counter for inspection and giving a satisfied grunt. "Just like you order, mister." Yasir Arbadi studied Colonius for a second, his fingers rubbing the highly polished leather lightly. "Is good, yes?"

Colonius examined it with a cold eye. It looked like a large canvas beach bag, perhaps two and a half or three feet high, trimmed at the bottom with a broad band of

72

black leather and decorated with a thinner strip of the same leather at the top, where two heavy black handles were attached. Nodding, Colonius studied it for a second, then reached down inside and began pulling something at the bottom. It wouldn't give.

The Algerian shook his head disgustedly. "No, mister. No. Is double cam lock at bottom you must disengage with finger. To prevent mistakes, a safety feature. Watch." Impatiently, Yasir Arbadi shook the loose, flowing sleeves of his gown free of his hands—he wore a simple cardigan over the elaborate caftan—and reached down inside the beach bag to demonstrate. There was a faint metallic click. He gave the bottom of the beach bag a hard pull and turned it inside out with one swift movement. Three-quarters of the beach bag's height disappeared in the process, folding itself neatly inside like pleats on an accordion, and what now stood on the counter was a black leather doctor's bag; only the two black leather handles still showed as reminders of the bag's earlier incarnation. Arbadi stared at it for a moment, patted it, and then smiled proudly at Colonius through his uneven, nicotine-stained teeth. "Double hand-stitched throughout," he volunteered. "Very durable." With a backward step, he aimlessly adjusted the dull, brown cardigan as it flapped open in front of him and waited for a reaction.

"Neat. Very neat." Colonius tried to think of something more positive to say, but was unable to; instead, he too patted the bag and offered a weak smile.

With a shrug, the Algerian fumbled with the buttons of his cardigan. "Your other work, mister. Ready also. But anybody could have done that." He slammed a medium-sized, hard-brown leather case on the counter with the expression of an expert whose talents have just been wasted. "Cheaper, too, than by Arbadi, I think, mister. Yes?"

Colonius ran his fingers across the fine, aged leather and nodded approval; he was probably being overcautious, but it had bothered him that the Wollensak, even with its opaque plastic cover in place, was so obviously a tape machine. He had no idea yet how much might be said in the papers about the tapes themselves, but he had decided it was wiser not to be seen carrying a recorder in and out of hotels and on and off airplanes. Inside the carrying case Yasir Arbadi had made for it, the machine now looked either like an overly large attaché case or a small overnight bag.

His heavy-lidded eyes almost closed in an appraising squint, the Algerian looked at him questioningly. "There is nothing else you need of me?" he asked. Colonius shook his head. Yasir wet the tip of a stubby pencil, consulted some strange writings on a small pad, and pronounced a figure. "Two hundred forty-five. It is expensive; this I know. But the workmanship is superior. And the inventiveness. Particularly with the doctor's bag." Straightening up—and in spite of the heat—he fastened the rest of the buttons on the cardigan. "Also," he added softly, "it is always expensive with a man who cannot remember any of his customers' faces, or if they are tall or short, or even if they are black or white." The Algerian cocked his small head to one side, produced a band of soiled teeth again in an attempt at an ingratiating smile, and leaned confidently back from the counter. Then, he turned away to adjust the flame beneath the copper kettle of pungent tea. Yasir Arbadi, Colonius told himself, was oddly at home for an Arab in Macon.

Sullenly, Colonius slowly counted out the money, transformed the doctor's satchel back into the beach bag, and left the dank mustiness of the store without a word.

Behind him, he could hear the shop's old-fashioned bell —arranged to announce the arrival or departure of customers—ring as the door swung to again, and felt relieved to be out of the place into the air of Macon once again. Arbadi's price was outrageous, even if it did include the name of a supplier in New York who would sell him *la plastique* without asking questions. That could provide a traceable link back to him that bothered Colonius; he wasn't at all convinced of the Algerian's inability to remember his customers' faces; any link was too important a point to be left to chance. It wouldn't be. Before he'd even gone to see Arbadi, Colonius had already made arrangements to foolproof the matter; and now that the Algerian had screwed him on the price, the arrangements almost caused Colonius to smile.

It was during the cab ride back to the Sweet Laurel that the message from God arrived. On the radio. Because of this, the message was partly obscured by static, blurred by music from an overlapping station, and sometimes almost lost in the whistling of an indifferent cab driver. But the import was clear.

An assassin, the announcer said, in a tone filled with urgency but obviously irritated by the lack of specifics, an assassin had gotten within inches of the Vice President; the occasion and place were as yet unnamed, details were sketchy and only partially confirmed, but the Secret Service had photographs (which might or might not be released) showing the assassin about to attack. At the last moment—and for reasons also unknown—he had withheld fire. The same man, continued the announcer, was reported to have also threatened a number of high figures in industry and the arts—the network news staff would try to get the names as soon as possible, but security precautions were understandably very tight. The alleged assassin's name was still unknown, the voice from the radio added, and the FBI would describe him only as "a male Caucasian, probably in his late twenties but with receding blond hair, habitually dressed in a broadly striped sports shirt, tight-fitting white trousers, and wraparound sunglasses." Through a sudden and violent burst of static, the announcer concluded by saying there were even rumors the same man had threatened the President himself, although, at this time, these reports were totally unconfirmed. Barely pausing for breath, the announcer started the whole recitation over again.

Lars Colonius pressed himself hard against the worn, imitation leather seat of the taxi and gave an anticipatory moan. He could feel the nerves tingle in his finger ends and the blood pump in his veins and the stirring that suddenly swelled beneath his clothes; he giggled to think of the effect this would have produced if he had been wearing the "tight-fitting white trousers" the FBI described. He wasn't, of course. The pants, along with the striped shirt and the wraparound sunglasses, were now only to be worn in front of Einstein's lens.

Abruptly, Colonius leaned forward and put his hands against the top of the front seat as if to hurry the cab homeward. His latest envelope to the Justice Department had produced the desired results; the first public part of the Armageddon plan was operational; it was now time to get his ass out of the Sweet Laurel and move on to the next stage.

At the Westbury, Ambrose's own plan was also operational, and the sparse progression of facts that so irked the announcer in Macon was part of it. Every new detail, every additional scrap of information and rumor, was carefully programmed by Ambrose and then fed to Washington by Goddard; from there, it was either reported directly to the media or leaked through the usual "reliable sources." The carefully orchestrated effect was that of an urgent news story boiling away under a lid clamped on by Washington.

Ambrose had been surprised when Goddard suddenly appeared at the Westbury, unannounced, three days earlier; it seemed too soon for an official answer to his proposal.

"I've got your approval for you," Goddard had said, slamming himself into a chair. "It wasn't hard; this turned up in the mail yesterday." Brusquely, Goddard slid an 8-by-10 glossy across the desk to him.

Ambrose studied it for a second and inhaled sharply; Armageddon, his arms folded and legs crossed, wearing his infuriating smartaleck kid smile, sat casually on the edge of the President's desk in the Oval Office. It was an incongruous, almost blasphemous combination, an effect heightened by the stark shadows the flashbulb cast across the flags, the paintings, and the walls of the historic room. Apparently, no one else was in the office, but the star-burst reflection of the bulb itself in one of the darkened windows behind the desk seemed to hover over the chair where the President should be sitting.

"It's a fake, of course," grunted Goddard after watch-

-ing Ambrose's face for a reaction. "But it raised all hell for a while."

"A *fake?*" Ambrose digested this and then tried to reorient himself. "Trick photography? A montage? Or what?"

"No, Armageddon was right there in the room. Just like you see him. It's the room that's a fake. In the LBJ Library in Austin. They've got this damned exact replica of the Oval Office on their top floor—the desk, the flags, the paintings, even the mementos—everything a precise copy. That's what gave it away so fast; the stuff gets changed around with each new President." Goddard snorted disgustedly as if his mind were still carrying on an argument with someone over the photograph. "Well, it didn't take long to spot it, but in the meantime, it had everybody climbing the Goddamned walls. And fake or no fake, most of them still are."

Ambrose struggled with it. "A fake," he repeated. "Armageddon's never used a fake before. And he must have known this one would be seen through quickly."

"He didn't even intend it wouldn't be." Goddard slapped a small reel of tape on the desk in front of Ambrose and stuck his hands in his pockets with a defeated look. "Brags about how easy it was to get into the museum at night. Cites parallels. Says he just wanted us to know he was still thinking about us—and promises next time it *won't* be a fake."

Glumly, Ambrose turned the white plastic reel over in his hands, shaking it occasionally as if the answer might fall out. "Anything else on it?"

"Laughing at us. The bastard's laughing at us. And oh, yeah—that countdown thing again. Armageddon minus thirty-six on this one."

With a sudden forward movement in his chair, Ambrose picked up the photograph again and studied it. The use of a fake picture might mean something, or it might mean only that Armageddon couldn't come by anything else; he wasn't sure that Armageddon was so much laughing at them as playing with them—and for a purpose. Once again, he had the uneasy feeling they were missing something terribly obvious and that they would pay

77

later for this inability to see. He looked at Goddard, who appeared as confident as ever and now seemed even relieved, apparently because they were free to take action. Even if the action were wrong. It was a quality about Goddard—and some other people he'd known—that bothered him, a seeking of refuge in the doing of things for the doing of things' sake rather than the careful analyzing of the basic problem.

"Anyway," said Goddard, annoying Ambrose further, "the picture did the trick of getting your plan approved. Now we can get moving and nail the creep."

To Ambrose, it was a particularly galling statement, further bruising his already strained sense of professional ethics by once again reducing him from analyst to supersleuth. If the stakes involved weren't so high, Ambrose probably would have rebelled; instead, he reached into his pocket, lit up a Tijuana 12, and inhaled prodigiously. He even gave a little cough just before exhaling to point up how satisfyingly deep that drag had been. Turning away with a flicker of displeasure, Goddard pretended not to notice. It was, as always, a petty victory and Ambrose knew it—but one he continued to find oddly satisfying.

Now, three days after getting word from Goddard on the plan's approval, the sixteenth floor of the Westbury was electric with preparations. Sparse details had been fed for midday release. By evening news time, the first major wave would hit the networks—along with the pictures from the All-Rite Shopping Center. In them, the background would be air-brushed out and neither date nor location mentioned, something insisted on by the Secret Service. For the early morning news tomorrow, a few more scraps of information and the first mention of Ambrose's name; it would appear as part of the growing impression—immediately denied—of drastic steps being considered by the authorities. By tomorrow night's news briefing, there would be two contradictory angles to the story, a pendulum of rumors swinging back and forth between a sense of great concern in government circles and heated denials of any real concern at all from the White House; Goddard's experts pointed out the quickest way to make a news story sound real was to deny it loudly and officially. The following day—under the guise of quashing the rumors of official concern once and for all—Ambrose's upcoming interview on television was to be featured in the stories. He would be pictured as an expert on criminal psychopathology, an analyst called in when the problem first arose, who had actively studied the psychological implications of the threats from all angles—and his findings as the reason the government no longer took the threats too seriously.

All of this careful buildup was to make sure that Armageddon was watching Ambrose's interview on television. Obviously, the facts from the program would be heavily carried in the next day's papers, but Ambrose felt that Armageddon should actually hear and see him on television, meet him face to face in the process of tearing him apart. The immediacy of television would make Ambrose come alive as the enemy, make it that much more compelling that Armageddon come try to kill him.

Restlessly, Ambrose strolled down the hall. He found himself stepping over the cables as carefully as a child avoids stepping on cracks in the pavement, and grimaced at the thought of what some of his fellow shrinks would make out of that. Inside the meeting room as he passed, he could hear the still-constant ringing of phones and murmur of voices coming from Evans' boilerroom operation. He didn't even pause to listen; God knows what misinformation Evans' network was now being fed.

Silently, Lars Colonius slipped the check for two weeks' advance rent under Mrs. Spiers' door. Along with it was a note saying he would be in and out of town the next few weeks, but that additional checks would come by mail if he wasn't back before the next was due; the room should be kept for him.

On the way to the Macon Hilton for the night, Colonius made only two stops. One was to drop a thick letter into the "Local" slot of the East Branch Post Office—doing this would guarantee its delivery the next morning—and quickly settle some unfinished business. The other stop—and a much longer one—was at the "Y," a faded red-brick building on Cherry Street.

There, by dropping a quarter in a slot every fifteen minutes, he bought the exclusive rights to an oversized dressing room. It was large enough for both him and Einstein to work in comfortably enough, although he found himself disturbed by the heavy antiseptic smell of the place, the almost-wet cement showing through the cheap rattan floor covering, and a general air of peeling paint and chipped mirrors. With a grunt, he dismissed the drawbacks and locked the door; Colonius had chosen the Y to change both his role and his appearance precisely because he knew a large turnover and a meager, uninvolved staff would guarantee little time to notice him arrive as one thing and leave as another.

"OK, Einstein. Not too damned short, now." Handing him a pair of scissors, Colonius carefully seated himself in front of a mirror almost brown with age and intently watched every move of Einstein's shears. All of it had been gone over with him in advance, but Colonius was still afraid Einstein would get carried away. Almost to his surprise, he discovered Einstein gave him a better than average crew cut.

A packet was taken out of the beach bag and poured into the yellowed sink; instantly, the water turned an intense, opaque black. Fifteen minutes later, before Einstein's awestricken eyes, Colonius was studying himself in the mirror, a crew-cut, black-haired, dark-eyed man. The dark, almost black eyes that replaced Colonius' hazel ones were provided by tinted contact lenses; he also had a pair of intensely blue lenses in case he later wanted to bleach his hair and look Nordic. The receding hairline mentioned by the FBI had vanished, almost unnoticeable as it disappeared into the crew cut; a touch of gray at his temples gave Colonius the air of a middle-aged man trying to keep up a youthful appearance with a Marine-style haircut. The effect was heightened by a pair of rectangular horn-rimmed glasses, a conservatively cut suit, and a narrow regimental tie. The clothes he wore in were easily fitted into the beach bag, now converted to doctor's satchel status. And when Colonius picked it up and added a dark homburg, it was difficult for even Einstein to believe he was the same man photographed grinning childishly at the near-great or perched impudently on the President's desk.

No new identity was needed for Einstein, since no one presumably knew he even existed, but, with some difficulty, Colonius helped him into a suit and tie for the first time in his life; he had to look respectable to play his role in Colonius' new life. Staring into the mirror, Einstein seemed disappointed, as if the suit should have changed him as much as Colonius had been changed. Gruffly, Colonius prodded him along until both he and Einstein could walk out of the Y and head for the Hilton to give their new identities a trial run before leaving for New York.

At the Hilton, it worked like a charm. There was some difficulty about the suite he'd called to reserve, but Colonius was insistent. "And, if possible, it should have color television. I specifically mentioned that on the phone. If at *all* possible," Colonius had told the desk clerk. The clerk looked bewildered and shook his head again. Colonius patiently explained once more that he—Dr. Kraus was the name he gave as he plunked the doctor's bag down on the counter in front of the clerk—and his patient, a deaf-mute, were on their way to New York so the boy could receive special surgery. Since his patient had been institutionalized for so long, Colonius added, he wanted to accustom him as quickly as possible to the changes in the outside world, a world so different from the one he knew when stricken. The desk clerk nodded sympathetically and rechecked his room diagram; finally, with a broad smile, he announced there was one suite with color TV available. It was reserved for another party, he said, but under the circumstances. . . .

Turning, Colonius solemnly flashed some sign language message to Einstein, who answered with the same. Einstein smiled; the desk clerk smiled; Lars Colonius smiled.

Colonius was still smiling half an hour later as he plopped himself down in front of the television set to watch the evening news and see how much the authorities were going to make public. Plenty. He stared at the picture of himself on the screen, trying to look at himself the way a total stranger would. He wished now he hadn't been wearing that damned smile. But maybe, he told himself, it was more frightening that way than if he'd looked menacing; there was such a contrast between what the announcer was saying about him and the smile on his face that it gave you an eerie feeling. And the fact that the picture of him was in black and white on an all-color program somehow elevated it to the status of a classic.

Lars Colonius had finally arrived.

Chapter Ten

Lately, the Armageddon project has been getting me back into gadgets. My father started me thinking that way when I was a kid—he was a mechanical draftsman—and he always had me tinkering with mechanical or electrical stuff. He was a pretty good draftsman, I guess, but then, all of a sudden, his eyes went bad, and he was out of work for good.

And if you ever saw someone be a bitch about it, it was my mother. Some women start taking in bachelor's laundry when the money gets tough; she took in the bachelors instead. I think that's why my father lit out finally; she never let him forget for a second who was making the money—or how.

> —*Extract from the*
> *journal of Lars Colonius*

Saturday, June 20—Armageddon minus thirty-three.

POSTMAN Perry O'Neil got to his deliveries on Wimbish Road early that morning; they were doing construction work on King Road, so he'd have to get to it after Wimbish Road instead of before. Starting down Wimbish, he was surprised to see the Algerian's door open. That guy, Yasir Arbadi, was so unfriendly he usually kept it shut all the time; maybe today it was open because the weather was so damned muggy.

Since the door was open, O'Neil couldn't slip the mail through the door slot like he usually did, but had to walk inside the store and hand it personally to Arbadi, who, in spite of his extra effort, stayed unfriendly as ever. When

O'Neil left the store, the Algerian was looking over the mail sourly—there wasn't much: two or three letters and a couple of large envelopes.

O'Neil didn't get more than a few doors down Wimbish Road when he was almost knocked off his feet by an explosion. Whatever it was was so close to him that he could see the plate-glass window on Arbadi's store first crack, then shatter all over the street. His first thought was that somebody on the King Road construction job had misgauged a blasting charge, but then he saw thin, gray smoke coming out of the hole where Arbadi's window used to be and ran back to the store.

Behind his counter, flat on his back, lay the Algerian, one jagged section of his eyeglasses sticking straight up from his left eyeball. That was about all you could make out of his face; the rest was just so much slippery red mush. O'Neil kneeled down and tried to get the Algerian to say something, but all he got was a couple of bubbling sounds and a sort of moan. Then, Arbadi suddenly tried to heave himself upward, swayed back and forth for a second, and fell back completely still.

By now, the musty little store was full of people, all of them talking at once, trying to find out what had happened, and telling each other how close they'd been when the blast went off. Half an hour after the police, two investigators from the Post Office Department showed up and began questioning O'Neil to see if he could remember anything unusual about the mail that morning. Yasir Arbadi had been killed by a letter bomb, they explained, and an unusual postmark or a foreign stamp or anything like that might be a big help. O'Neil could remember nothing; he was still too shaken by the piece of glass sticking out of the Algerian's eyeball, and the red mass that seemed to float underneath it.

The investigation into the killing didn't go on very long. The Macon police tried checking into Arbadi's list of customers, but discovered they were noted only by code numbers, as were the items they ordered; the matter was not pursued. The Post Office Department and the FBI had already produced an explanation that worked. For the letter bomb had not been filled with the usual combination of jagged metal scrap, but with several hundred small, six-pointed metal stars. Yasir Arbadi had been killed when these burst, virtually in his face. He was closer to the charge, they decided, than most victims, for he was near-sighted and had probably been leaning close down to the envelope when he opened it. Figuring out the rest was simple. And while the militant Jewish Defense League had never been active in these parts before, they could only assume that either the Algerian had been chosen at random by the JDL as a reprisal against any Arab anywhere, or because his completely untraceable background had Black September connections buried in it somewhere. This explanation seemed to satisfy everyone, even O'Neil, who could now understand why Yasir Arbadi had always stayed so unfriendly.

The next morning the Macon papers were full of the explosion, although Lars Colonius never got to see the articles. For by noontime, he and Einstein had checked out of the Hilton and were flying to New York, where they held reservations at the Regency as "Dr. Kraus & Patient." In fact, the only account of the event Colonius ever got was one he overheard on somebody's transistor radio at the airport, and about all the authorities were saying then was that an underworld figure, an Algerian named Yasir Arbadi, had been killed that morning in Macon, probably by agents of the Jewish Defense League.

"*Shalom*," whispered Colonius, and walked slowly down the ramp toward the plane to New York.

Sunday, June 21—Armageddon minus thirty-two.

The next morning at the Regency, Colonius finished his breakfast, lay back in bed, and began combing the newspapers again. The luxurious excitement of breakfast in bed at a place like the Regency was already deserting him, replaced by a gnawing fear that something wasn't working right, a sense he got from the newspapers of things happening he didn't understand. The story was getting all the play anyone could ask for; there was no denying that. But some of the omissions troubled him. For instance, there was still no mention of the other possible targets' identities—Henry Ford, Johnny Carson, and Leonard Bernstein remained anonymous. Odd. The text of his tape about the Vice President was printed faithfully, although the part about his not being a worthwhile target had been edited out. Politics, Colonius decided, and smiled grimly. The picture of him with his hand outstretched toward the Vice President dominated the front page, but the missing background—it had been deliberately blurred or totally removed in places—confounded him. A cutline under the photograph in the *Times* explained that portions of the picture had been altered for security reasons, but Colonius didn't buy that; there had to be some other reason. After another cup of coffee, Colonius decided the missing background actually worked in his favor, as fewer people in Macon would realize the event actually took place in their own town. The omission of the name Armageddon was easier to grasp. Revealing that almost necessarily led to explaining the countdown and the date of Armageddon itself; this would be an invitation to every crank in the country.

On his second, more careful reading, an item buried in the New York *Times* (and referred to obliquely in the *Daily News*) caught his eye and stopped him cold. A half-filled cup of coffee slid off the tray onto the floor as he sat upright, clutching the paper tightly. "It was reported that Dr. Carlton Ambrose, Chief of Staff of Connecticut's Living Clinic and an expert in the field of criminal psychopathology, has been called in to consult on the case with government authorities."

With a grunt, Colonius threw the paper on the floor in anger and swung his legs over the edge of the bed. A God-damned psychiatrist. Called in to consult. Consult on what? Some pious graybeard, cast in the image of Freud, who would ponder the text of the tapes and pronounce their author "disturbed." Damned right he was disturbed. But not the way Dr. Carlton whatever-his-name-was thought. He ran his fingers through his hair, paused, startled for a second, to examine his hands and see if any of the dye came off on them, and crossed to the window in a couple of long, impatient strides. Staring down from it at the teeming traffic of Park Avenue far below, Colonius calmed himself. There was a black knot of people waiting on the corner for the light to change so they could cross, and when it did, from twenty floors above, they looked like a swarm of ants marching in formation to the beat of some unseen drum. Anonymous ants. The difference between the ants and himself suddenly made Colonius feel better, and he strolled into the living room, where he could hear the television going full blast.

Einstein was lying in front of it, his overly large head cradled in his hands, watching *Captain Kangaroo*. He was giggling so hard at Mr. Greenjeans that he didn't even notice Colonius come into the room. Still giggling, and for no apparent reason, he abruptly leaned forward and switched to another channel. Silently, Colonius watched a few seconds of the animated cartoon that now appeared. Mostly, its action was made up of repeated scenes in which a very small, clever mouse kept beating a very dumb, big cat over the head with a stick of dynamite. It wasn't very funny but Colonius found himself smiling anyway.

This was the year of the mouse.

"No, no, doctor—you got to look at the one with the red light on." The director's voice from the control room had a hollow, booming sound when piped onto the studio floor, and its impatient tone rattled Ambrose even further. There were so damned many things to remember. Watch the cue cards the men were holding underneath the lens turret on each camera, but don't look like you're reading, please. The camera with the red light going is the camera taking the shot, so when you're not looking at Hank, look directly into the lens, please. It makes contact with the audience—sort of like looking them in the eye, understand, doctor? No, the cue cards for each camera-take are under *that* camera, and for Christ's sake don't keep nodding at the man with the cue cards—he knows when you need the next one.

They were taping Ambrose's interview—it would be shown tomorrow night—and Ambrose was hating every second of it. The oily feeling of pancake makeup on his face. The noise and confusion on the floor between takes. The sudden red gleam of the light on a camera, the angry eye of God warning him he was being watched. Hank Brady, the interviewer, had been clued in a little—not enough, Ambrose thought—to the interview's real purpose; he would try to ask the right questions, but Brady had so long been a hard-nosed investigative newsman that he almost instinctively led Ambrose into contradictions or tried to corner him into newsworthy overstatements.

Now, during a halt, while a stagehand did something mysterious with a long pole to adjust the lights more to the control room's liking, Brady leaned back in his chair and smiled encouragingly at Ambrose.

"Relax, doc. This stuff's always tough when you're not used to it. And we're taping in short sections, so if you blow one, forget it." Brady lit a cigarette and kept fanning the air in front of him so the smoke wouldn't show on the next take. Momentarily, Ambrose played with the idea of a Tijuana 12 but quickly dismissed it; a guy like Brady was too sharp not to identify the odor. "And don't worry about those cue cards," continued Brady. "They're a pain in the ass for anyone. And if you know your stuff the way you do, who the hell needs them?" Reaching down, Brady picked up a shallow tin-can cover, half-filled with water, from where it was hidden beside his chair; it served as his ashtray and Ambrose was fascinated to see how skillfully Brady maneuvered his ashes into it without spilling a drop of the water.

Suddenly, Brady leaned forward and Ambrose could feel the man was going to start trying to pump him. "Look," said Brady softly, "I know something big is up behind this interview, and I'm playing along just like I was asked. But, you know, if you could give me a hint of what the hell the scoop is. . . ."

Ambrose shook his head. "The interview is pretty much just what it looks like. A discussion, a portrait, of the psychopathology of the man behind these threats." It didn't sound convincing, even to Ambrose.

Brady sighed. "Sure." The director's voice crackled at them from the control room, Brady dropped his cigarette into the water-filled can lid, and smiled wearily at Ambrose. "Sure. Well, we're about to go again. Sit loose, doc."

Numbed, Ambrose listened to the electronic beeps and

watched the small board with the electric numbers count down the seconds before taping started; then he turned in his chair to find the camera with the angry eye of God on top.

Tuesday, June 23—Armageddon minus thirty.

"Goddamn it, Carlton," said Goddard heatedly, "I didn't know you were going to get into stuff like this." Goddard and Ambrose were watching the taped interview on a set rolled into their Westbury conference room for the occasion. From the beginning of the program, Ambrose found watching himself on the air—the mannerisms, the voice, the hesitant pauses and self-corrections—extremely painful; now, as he watched the always-smiling Brady neatly push him into a corner, he found he was squirming.

"What you're saying, Doctor Ambrose," the figure of Mike Brady on the television screen announced, "is that your profile shows a man like this self-styled assassin is something more than just an oddball. In his personal life, I mean." Ambrose watched himself nod and begin to answer, but then be interrupted by Brady. One of the tougher parts of dealing with Brady on the air was that the questions he was going into now hadn't even been touched on during the rehearsal runthrough. This kept Ambrose completely off-balance and he found himself saying things that Brady promptly made sound like something else. But the smile never disappeared from Brady's face, giving the impression that Ambrose was already agreeing with the interviewer's interpretation.

"For instance," Brady continued, "somewhere in that profile you said—you sort of skipped over it lightly, but I made a note of it—you said that this man you're describing is always—well, almost always, anyway—sexually inadequate. 'Can't relate to women,' I think that's the phrase you used." Brady made a show of referring to his notes and spoke again just as Ambrose was about to qualify the remark. "In other words, on top of everything else, this psychopath that's been scaring the country half to death is probably also some sort of deviate. Is that one of the angles you're using to try to track him down, doctor?"

Seeing himself on the tape, Ambrose could remember the anger he'd felt at this loaded, multiple question. At the time, he thought he'd been able to mask it; looking at himself now, it was clear he hadn't. "First of all," the Ambrose on the screen answered gruffly, "I'm not tracking anybody down. That's somebody else's job. I was only called in by the authorities to explore the psychological implications of the thing. And I never said the man was a deviate. Quite the opposite. I said he was sexually inadequate because he was probably unable to relate to anybody. Male or female. It's a usual facet of the syndrome." There was a pause on the screen while Ambrose took a swallow of water and struggled to collect himself; Brady nodded and gave an especially condescending smile that indicated he didn't believe a word Ambrose was saying. "But most importantly, Mike," the uncomfortable on-camera Ambrose added, trying to stay looking pleasant, "there's absolutely no reason for anyone to be scared 'half to death' or even nervous. As I pointed out earlier, we're dealing with a sick person. One who should be put away for his own good. Nothing more. The chances of his following up on his threats to kill someone are just about nil."

Brady closed in. "But somebody in Washington must be nervous or scared, doctor, or they wouldn't have a whole team of you consulting with them, would they? Somebody must be taking the threats seriously."

The attempt to brush this question off didn't work at all. Ambrose couldn't help but wonder if Armageddon, watching wherever he was, could see, as he could now, how badly the attempt foundered.

"Well, Mike," Ambrose saw himself answer, fencing for time and coming off very ponderously, "in a situation like this, in times like these, there's always bound to be a certain amount of hysteria, unfounded or not."

For the first time, the smile disappeared from Brady's face. "If I may say so, your statements just don't jibe with each other, doctor. On the one hand, you characterize the authorities as hysterical. All right. But at the same time, you claim"—Brady glanced down at his notes to find a sentence—"that there is no reason for anyone to be afraid of this man, that—"

"Hysteria, as a word, was just a figure of speech. What I meant—"

Goddard exploded, walking away from the set in disgust. "Jesus Christ. That tears it. 'Hysteria.' The government hysterical."

With a sigh, Ambrose stared into space, trying to ignore the sight and sound of himself, floundering away on the screen. "I was trying to do just the opposite—minimize any fears—but that guy Brady kept turning everything around. He didn't ask the same questions as he did at the rehearsal. And instead of being a lot of short takes, it was one long one. There wasn't any chance to stop him, to make him change what he was doing. Everything I said got twisted around." Ambrose was startled to hear how like a petulant child he was sounding.

Goddard glumly studied his shoes. "I warned you that's Brady's stock-in-trade; the bastard always does it. And you walked right into his trap."

The angry frustration in Ambrose spilled over. "Then why the hell did you pick Brady's show to put me on?"

"The show gets a lousy rating. And we were trying to keep the audience small." Goddard swore at himself. "Maybe it was a lousy idea."

Ambrose grunted and went back to watching himself on the screen, hating it, but unable not to look. It was torture. He only hoped Armageddon was tuned in and getting as mad at him as he was getting at Goddard.

Lars Colonius was very much tuned in and getting even madder than Ambrose could hope. He sat bolt upright in front of his television set, one hand curling and uncurling in anger, his eyes fixed hard on Ambrose's face. To Colonius, the program was a disaster. From the first mention of Ambrose's name in the *Times,* he'd had some misgivings about how he might fare at the hand of a psychiatrist, but he'd dismissed them in the excitement of looking forward to what they would say about him; this half-hour devoted to explaining him was a bonus—an unexpected one—for the Armageddon plan. Oh, the psychia-

trist might make up stuff about an unhappy childhood
or crap like that, but that's what they got paid for. And
there might even be a tinge of tragedy in the air as the
doctor explained how so brilliant but fragile a personality
could be transformed into an instrument of fear.

But it wasn't coming through that way at all. The God-
damned doctor was kissing him off. Phrases like "below-
average intelligence" and "born loser" hurtled out of his
television set and rocked Colonius. The jibe about sexual
inadequacy—and Brady's translation of it into deviation
—jolted Colonius with half-remembered taunts from childhood. And the insistent assumption, hanging over the entire interview like a challenge, that Colonius would never
carry out his threats, first staggered him, then brought
him to a near frenzy. For if people began to believe *that,*
the plan was foredoomed to failure.

Almost knocking over his chair, Colonius stood up and
began storming around the room. Einstein cowered in a
corner; he'd never seen Colonius like this. Roughly, Colonius grabbed him by the shirt and began shaking him.
"Do you hear what those bastards are saying?" Colonius
hissed at him. "Do you see what they're trying to make
people believe about me? Do you *see?*"

Einstein did his pathetic best to see, to understand, but
it was all beyond him. "Mr. Colonius," he whined miser-
ably and shook his head, "Mr. Colonius. . . ."

Colonius and he stood there for a second, staring hard
at each other, until Einstein finally could tear his eyes
away. Then, abruptly, the fury drained out of Colonius
and he released him with a diffident shove. No, Einstein
didn't see. Einstein would never see. Colonius turned and
let his eyes travel back to the television screen; the psychiatrist was gone from the picture and the camera was
moving in on the interviewer for the program's closing
remarks. Dispiritedly, Colonius walked back toward the
set.

Einstein shook himself like a wet animal and tried to
find something he could say that would help. "It was a
real good picture of you, Mr. Colonius, right up there
on the screen and everything."

"Oh, shut up." It was such an unusual way to speak to

Einstein that Colonius was about to say something to soften it, but the words from the television set demanded silence; Colonius help up his hand to make sure Einstein didn't start apologizing.

"And so, high above the city," Brady was saying, "in a small set of rooms at the sedate Westbury Hotel, Dr. Carlton Ambrose and his associates work to unravel the mystery of an unnamed psychopath. A psychopath who has threatened, along with others, the life of the President himself. Of course, if the doctor is right, the man is mostly only a danger to himself; Dr. Ambrose assures us that the chances of his carrying out any of his threats are, quote unquote, 'virtually nil.' " A new, longer shot showed Brady sitting in his chair, so back-lit he seemed almost in sil-houette, swinging himself back and forth as he clasped and unclasped his hands in front of him. But Colonius had had all he could take of Brady. Sullenly, he switched off the set, then moved over to click off the Wollensak as well. For a moment, he stood there, staring at the blank and darkened screen. Slowly, with what was almost a look of resignation, he leaned over to the desk, got a pad, and wrote down Ambrose's full name. Below this, he added the name of the Westbury, leaving a large blank space for the address. The hotel was an unfamiliar one to him, but it would, he supposed, be in the book. Tight-lipped, a man facing an unpleasant duty, Lars Colonius took the thirty-eight from the drawer, checked the chamber, and slipped it into his pocket. The address of the Westbury was found and memorized. Einstein was told to stay put.

Picking up his black doctor's bag, Colonius waved to Einstein, walked to the door of the living room, and disap-peared down the hall.

The elevator seemed to take forever to arrive.

Chapter Eleven

It's crazy how psychiatrists always try to bring everything back to sex. This Ambrose guy, for instance, obviously thinks I'm some sort of queer or something. Bull. At Taft Vocational, there was this creep, Herbie Blocker, who'd do anybody for a quarter. Just about my whole damned class, one time or another, paid Herbie that quarter. Except me. Oh, I thought about it. Once, I even had a dream about it. But if you just think hard about something else for a while, sick ideas like that go away. That's how wrong that doctor is about me.

I wonder what ever happened to Herbie. Two bits he wound up being a shrink.

—*Extract from the journal of Lars Colonius*

EVAN EVANS watched Goddard stalk out of the meeting room and head for the phone in his office, then walked in to join Ambrose. The doctor was leaning back in his chair, balancing it unsteadily on its two back legs, staring moodily at the black television screen. "Well, *he* didn't look too happy either," smiled Evans, gesturing with his head after the departed Goddard.

Pulling his eyes away from the set, Ambrose shrugged wearily. "He isn't. I don't think my show's going to get renewed." The chair's front legs hit the carpet with a muffled thud as Ambrose reached into his pocket, withdrew a foil packet, and lit up a Tijuana 12.

"I thought it was pretty good myself," noted Evans. "Except that bastard Brady pushed you around a bit. But, then, he's done it to Senators and members of the Cabinet and movie stars, so what the hell. And if Armageddon was tuned in, it ought to stir him up the way you wanted it to."

"He was tuned in, all right. I'm sure of that. But Goddard's afraid a lot of other people may have gotten stirred up, too. In Washington. He's down the hall making calls now to try to quiet things down."

Evans smiled and changed the subject, glancing at his watch. "About dinner. I can offer you a magnificent choice of two places: up here, room service, or the main hotel dining room. The Polo Bar is pleasanter, but I am afraid it's out—too much window area on the street for effective security."

"Anyplace but here."

Evan Evans started toward the door. "It'll take me a minute to make arrangements. I have to alert a lot of people where we're going."

Ambrose nodded and took a particularly deep drag.

At the door, Evans paused and turned back to him, sniffing with a sour expression and staring straight at the cigarette. "It's not the illegality of those things that bugs me; it's the stink."

The doctor smiled. "Arrest me." And after Evans had left, Ambrose leaned back in the chair again and studied the smoke slowly curling up toward the ceiling, trying to form some recognizable shape out of the thin, ominous swirls. A sort of cannabis Rorschach, he decided, and smiled at the idea. But no matter how he turned the ink blots around, no matter how hard he stared, he couldn't make Armageddon's face materialize.

Although it was only a ten-block walk from the Regency to the Westbury—it startled Colonius to realize how close together he and Dr. Ambrose had established their headquarters—the air and the exercise gave him time to cool off considerably. The revolver in his pocket was stupid; if he walked into the hotel and shot the doctor then and there, chances were he would get caught and that would be the end of the Armageddon plan. Gunfire in a hotel sounds loud; there would be other guests and maids and bellboys to contend with; he would also be at the

95

mercy of the hotel elevator for his escape. And for all he knew, Ambrose might have a guard watching him, although he doubted that the security was very tight, for they allowed the name of the hotel to go out over the air.

Still, the damage Ambrose and the program had done had to be handled somehow. The Armageddon plan, in its last phase particularly, was intricately constructed on a matrix of fear, of people believing he would do what he was threatening to do; without that fear and that belief, the plan would collapse.

Lars Colonius paused in front of a store window directly to the right of the Westbury's main entrance, swinging his doctor's bag to and fro slightly and pretending to study the overpriced antiques in the window display. What he needed, he told himself, was some plan to eliminate Ambrose and a plan that would accomplish this publicly, something that would destroy or discredit the doctor at the same time it reinforced the fear generated by the newspaper and television stories. But it would have to be a scheme that could be carried out long-distance—like the letter bomb to Yasir Arbadi—without endangering himself or the overall plan. The first step to this was to find out exactly where Dr. Ambrose was located in the hotel.

Looking between a Louis Quinze commode and a giant Chinese urn (circa 1700, if the card in front of it were to be believed), Colonius could see the antique store had another window, this one inside the lobby of the hotel itself. It seemed a reasonable place for a visitor to be browsing, and would give him a good spot from which to study the layout of the rest of the lobby. The doorman saluted and spun the brass revolving door for him; Colonius walked casually inside, then pretended something in the inner window of the store had caught his eye.

The lobby was not overly impressive. Across the marble floors lay a series of narrow rubber runways, apparently in expectation of sudden showers. To the left of the main entrance was a beauty shop, matching the antique store in size and position, but with no inner lobby window. Where the hall widened, the rubber walkways divided in direction, one going to the three elevators to the right rear

96

of the lobby itself, one going past the beauty shop to the doorway of the main dining room, and a wider one aimed resolutely at the thick glass doors of the Polo Bar. Through them, Colonius could see the late drinkers left over from the afternoon and the early diners of the evening settling down to the business of the day.

The front desk was set almost opposite the elevator doors; it was not very large, not large enough, in fact, to handle the four people crammed into the area behind it; the cashier's window seemed similarly crowded, a stoutish woman and a man in a gray suit struggling in a space barely big enough for one of them. Except for two ladies and a small child with accompanying nanny, clustered tightly together in front of the elevators, the lobby seemed mostly peopled with men. On a velvet settee near the door of the beauty shop sat two youngish men, one of them reading a newspaper; there was a grouping of two chairs and a small sofa to the left of the elevators, occupied at the moment by two more youngish men, one staring listlessly into space, the other, the one on the sofa, flipping idly through a paperback; down the rubber walkway that led to the dining room was an oversized oak and red-velvet chair, quite uncomfortable looking, in which yet another man was sitting, waiting, apparently, for someone from upstairs to join him for dinner.

Colonius could not immediately explain it, but something about the lobby automatically made him feel nervous; it bothered him, as if something were out of place. It was like one of those children's puzzle-pictures where they ask you to identify the one object in the picture that doesn't belong there. Colonius couldn't put his finger on it, but the vague feeling made him sharpen his senses.

It all became clear a few seconds later. The elevator door suddenly opened and Colonius could see, standing in the rear, the face of Carlton Ambrose. His hand tightened on the revolver and he could feel the surge of excitement swell through him; it would be so easy now to settle the score with the doctor—but too damned dangerous. The two men in front of Ambrose on the elevator stepped out and then paused, moving to one side to get around the child and the nanny and the two women waiting to get

97

on. Ambrose started forward, walking beside a short, al-most-round man with a tiny cigar stuck in his mouth. The latter looked around the lobby for a second and became suddenly angry. Striding forward, he held an unheard but heated conversation with one of the men in the grouping of chairs and sofa by the elevator. The man put down his paperback and, along with the man on the sofa oppo-site him, stood up, looking helpless in face of whatever the short, almost-round man was saying. During this, Am-brose stood waiting, looking embarrassed at his compan-ion's speech; he let his eyes wander around the lobby to avoid getting entangled in the dispute. In a strange replay of the scene with the Vice President at the All-Rite Shop-ping Center, Ambrose's eyes locked briefly with Colo-nius'. They stared at each other for a second, but Am-brose didn't appear to recognize Colonius from the pic-tures and the eyes moved on.

It was as Colonius turned his own eyes away, letting them wander across the lobby again, that the solution to the puzzle-picture—the object that didn't belong there—suddenly snapped into focus. It was the man on the velvet settee's newspaper. The paper was not today's; Colonius could remember reading it at breakfast yesterday. The pic-ture's focus grew painfully sharp. The man on the settee —probably, most of the men in the lobby—were plants. Add the overstaffed front desk and a hall porter who'd been sweeping the same spot on the marble floor for easily ten minutes now, and it spelled trap. They had wanted him to come here. That explained why the hotel's name was dropped into the broadcast. They had wanted him to come here looking for Ambrose so they could nail him. Very neat.

As casually as he could, Colonius slowly turned him-self around to study the contents of the antique store's window again. So far, his new identity as a doctor, his dark hair and black eyes were working, but he didn't care to test it any further than he already just had with Am-brose. Staring at the damned Chinese urn, he found him-self almost laughing. The trap was such an amateur setup. Obvious as hell. If he hadn't been so damned mad at Am-brose, he probably would have seen it the moment he walked in. Possibly, the present irritation of the almost-round man with the little cigar was on the same point; he appeared first to be startled, then angered to see all the plants scattered blatantly around the lobby. Colonius wondered if he'd noticed the newspaper yet.

With only a slight turn of his head, Lars Colonius could see him exploding all over the men staked out nearest him; then, Ambrose and the fat man disappeared into the main dining room, the man still waving his hands and irritatedly explaining something to the doctor.

Back on the street now, Lars Colonius walked back toward the Regency at a leisurely pace. Every now and then he would pause to gaze into one of the brightly lit shops on Madison Avenue. Most of them appeared to be in the antique business, with a couple of exceptions. It was one of these—a sports shop—that gave Colonius his inspiration for dealing with the Ambrose problem. His eyes flickered across the whimsically arranged display of everything from tennis rackets to skin-diving gear. Two mannequins in snorkling suits were hung from the window top in some fashion and appeared to be kissing underwater through a waving sea of underwater grasses made of paper. A school of cardboard fish were ogling them like Peeping Toms with gills. Like the tumblers on a combination, the pieces of the idea fell swiftly into place. It would undo the damage possibly done to the Armageddon plan by Ambrose's broadcast; it would reestablish the climate of fear he needed for the last stages of it to succeed; and, if in the process, it took a measure of personal revenge on Ambrose, even destroyed him, well, why the hell not?

Hands in pockets, Colonius began sauntering down Madison again. It was remarkable what a little exercise could do for a man's mind.

Wednesday, June 24—Armageddon minus twenty-nine.

The discussion was rapidly disintegrating into a bitter argument and both of the men were showing signs of wear. Evan Evans' miniature cigar had gone out from lack of being puffed, and was now being used as an accusative pointer, an extension of the Texan's angry right hand as he leaned across Goddard's desk and jabbed it into his face; only Evans' voice remained icily cool.

At first, Goddard struggled to stay looking calm and in charge, but the pose wore thin quickly. His lips were pressed tight together and now and then he spun his chair completely around to face the window, leaving Evans to stare at his back.

"All I want to know is one simple thing," said Evans in his frigid voice. "Either I'm in charge of security—things like the stakeout—or somebody else is. There isn't room for two people running it. That's all I want to know."

Goddard's chair stopped its swinging and turned around so he could face Evans. "You're running it. You know that."

"Then what were all those men doing down in the lobby last night? *I* didn't put them there. Enough FBI men to give the Mafia heartburn. It wasn't a trap—it was a convention." The unlit cigar gave an exasperated wave oddly in contrast with the completely controlled sound of Evans' voice.

With a small sigh, Goddard brought himself to the sticky part. "Well, from the moment that broadcast of Ambrose's finished last night, people started climbing all over me. Washington wasn't at all happy about how it went. The newsmen landed all over them, of course; that didn't help. Then they got to worrying if the plan *did* work and Armageddon showed up, he'd slip by us somehow. They had somebody—from the CIA, I wouldn't be surprised—checking out the lobby. He reported back he didn't see any evidence it was being covered at all."

In spite of his sour mood, Evans found himself laughing. "That's the idea. You're not *supposed* to see anybody. There was one man behind the desk, another in the cashier's window, and one inside the Polo Bar. Along with the elevator starter. Plenty."

Goddard offered a conciliatory smile. "I'm sorry about the rest of them. It was my fault, I guess. I should have said no, but after that broadcast. . . ."

Finally, Evans sat down. He could afford to be magnanimous now. "I got rid of them all pretty fast, so no harm done." He paused for effect and surveyed the unlit end of his cigar. "I mean, I don't *think* there was any harm done."

The bait was taken. Goddard turned toward Evans with a look of sudden concern. "Do you think he was around last night? That we—those men—could have scared him off?"

Evans was beginning to thoroughly enjoy himself at Goddard's discomfort, and pretended to study the tip of his unlit cigar and fumble for his matches. "It depends where he was at air time. New York, or someplace else. If it was New York—provided he got as mad at the program as you'd expect him to—the logical time to act in pure anger was last night. If he wasn't in New York, well, hell. You'd have to figure time for him to get here. As for scaring him off, nobody knows. It really would have been hard for him to get here that fast."

Goddard nodded, seeming relieved. He watched fascinated as Evans finally lit the little cigar, slowly revolving it in the flame to make sure it was burning evenly.

Over the glow of the match, Goddard's apparent relief so annoyed Evans that he couldn't restrain himself. "Unless, of course, Armageddon is staying at the Westbury himself."

There was a satisfying crash as Goddard knocked something over on his desk in surprise, then got control of himself as he realized he was being put on. He pretended to notice nothing and watched as Evans returned to the ritual of lighting his cigar, revolving it slowly and with great care. Goddard had seen connoisseurs give rare Havanas this sort of treatment, but it verged on the ridiculous with Evans' domestic miniatures.

Both Evans and Ambrose, Goddard decided, had definitely curious smoking habits.

Chapter Twelve

The police blew it—the handling of the thing—but it was a damned cagey idea and I bet this Ambrose guy was the man behind it. Because now that I've cooled off and stopped acting stupid, I have to admit he must be a pretty bright bastard and I guess the game just about boils down to him against me.

It's a funny thing, but I think if I could sit down and talk to him, man to man, he'd know why I have to go through with the Armageddon business. And I honestly think he'd understand me. Christ, maybe he'd even like me. But, hell, on television he had to say all that crappy stuff about me and that makes him my enemy and I have to fix his wagon for it or the whole plan will go up in smoke.

But it's too bad bright guys like him and me have to waste time knocking each other's brains out.

> —*Extract from the*
> *journal of Lars Colonius*

Sunday, June 28—Armageddon minus twenty-five.

THE SHOPPING list for "fixing Ambrose's wagon" took Colonius to a strange mixture of places. Some were in the heart of New York's most respectable and expensive shopping district, some were in areas where the store windows only got washed when the places changed hands or kids threw bricks through them. Almost all the items could probably have been picked up in one, or at most, two places, but Colonius wanted to cover his trail by spreading the purchases around.

From Abercrombie & Fitch—a store that fascinated him—came a pair of waist-high fishing boots, made of heavy rubber with double-thick soles, and of a size large enough to fit just about any foot. Offhandedly, he brushed aside the clerk's automatic inquiries about tackle, lures, and flies.

At Hammacher Schlemmers, he bought a complete skin-diving suit. There was a brief argument with the salesman, who kept insisting that so small a size would never fit him, but Colonius explained this away by saying it was a present for his wife.

The sports department of Bloomingdales provided two snorkeling masks, one large, one small, and a thick book on the ecology of the sea. Colonius had utterly no interest in the subject, but it appealed to his sense of the ridiculous to play the game out to its fullest limits.

By taxi, he then plunged out of the high-rent district down into the commercial district on the Lower East Side. Using the Yellow Pages, he quickly turned up the type of discount supply outlets he needed for the rest of his shopping list. At one electrical store—it was huge and harshly lit and smelled of people who worked with their hands—he picked up a pair of two-phase stepup transformers; they would deliver high-output but were designed to operate on ordinary house current. At a second store, farther down the same street, he bought a third, identical transformer and two large reels of heavily insulated copper wire. A neighborhood do-it-yourself store was able to provide two pairs of linesman's gloves, stainless steel wire-cutting shears, and a variety of relays, switches, resistors, and plates.

Finding a medical supply store required going back to the Yellow Pages again; there was one four blocks from where he was now, but this new order infuriated the cabbie (to handle the packages, Colonius moved from store to store and had the taxi wait; every time he got in or out, the driver swore angrily about people from out of town and how little money he was making on the trip). In its window, the store had a macabre display of gleaming wheelchairs, chromium crutches, and Medieval-vintage leather and steel-back braces, but it also had the item

103

Colonius needed: a giant tube of electroencephalographic gelatin.

This, Colonius figured, now completed his needs for his move against Ambrose. But in the cab on the way back to the Regency, Colonius spotted a small radio store, went in, and added a small, battery-powered record player to the pile on the taxi's back seat. Leaving, a collection of old LP's caught his eye, and he bought one of them, too; Dr. Ambrose might not be around to appreciate it, but a touch of irony seemed fitting for the finale.

Back at the Regency, he found Einstein still sprawled in front of the television set watching cartoons. He'd discovered that by switching back and forth among all the channels, including the two cable-TV ones provided by the hotel, he could damned near spend the whole day feasting on preschoolers' programming. To Einstein, it was the discovery of a whole new world; to Colonius, it was a pain in the ass, the shrill, clamoring voices of cartoon characters cutting hard into every train of thought he set up. Colonius' first instinct was to tell him to turn the thing off so he could do some work at the living-room desk, but he decided it was as good a way as any to keep Einstein off his back and took his paperwork into his bedroom to finish at the smaller desk there. Behind him as he was closing the door, he could hear Einstein giggling happily.

With a shrug, he sat down at the desk and took care of another preparation still needed for Armageddon Day. Pulling his checkbook out of the bureau drawer, he set his jaw and wrote out the check to The Institute for the Blind, Inc.—a $5,000 contribution. As he signed it, he felt three separate emotions, all incompatible, run through him at the same time: a sense of power that he could write so large a check at all, a sense of pain that it was necessary to write so large a check to a charity, and then, a sense of the ridiculous, since the check really had nothing whatsoever to do with being charitable. Carefully, he drafted a letter on a yellow pad that would go with the check; later, he would take this to be typed by a public stenographer somewhere. Considering the size of the gift, he felt sure the institute would get back to him quickly with the small favor the letter asked for.

Glumly, he recorded the figure in his checkbook. There was still plenty there, he told himself again, but it was a damned big check and the hole it made in the total shook him badly.

After a second or two of staring at the shattered balance, Colonius stood up, stretched himself, and went over to the pile of packages he'd brought home. On top were a couple of underground magazines he'd picked up on his tour of the Lower East Side. He thumbed through them intently, looking for a location that would be right for his neutralization of Ambrose. The Regency was out. So was any respectable hotel in the city. His original notion had been to find something in Greenwich Village, where there would also be a ready supply of the kind of performers he needed, players who'd do anything for a buck and wouldn't find the parts they were asked to play too offensive.

Neither magazine had any suggestions that sounded right in the city. The *Village Voice* wasn't very helpful about anyplace anywhere; it was too full of political invective. But the copy of *Screw* had an article on Fire Island that fascinated Colonius. Parts of it, apparently, were very much wide open ("MacDougal Alley with sand in the smack" was their description of Ocean Grove). It sounded full of the sort of people Colonius needed, and, as a bonus, it struck him that in a small but nearby resort like this, he could milk the thing for all the publicity it was worth. In fact, instead of just neutralizing Ambrose's TV appearance, a little luck with the newspapers might turn this Fire Island maneuver into an actual plus for the Armageddon plan. Colonius began to feel good about things.

For the copy of *Screw* not only provided him with a location, it gave a complete listing and description of hotels as well. Whistling, Colonius stepped over Einstein in the living room—he was now watching the Galloping Gourmet careen his way through a fondue with the same fascination he gave Bugs Bunny—and went downstairs to place a call from one of the phone booths in the Regency's lobby; he didn't want any record of the number he dialed on their books.

The lady at the Blue Goose Hotel sounded startled. "A *reservation?*" There was a long pause, an intake of breath while she considered, then: "Honey, are you sure you understand about this place?"

"I read about your hotel in *Screw*." The credentials had been presented. "And, yes, I want to make a reservation. It's important."

"Well, doll," the lady's voice said after another long pause, "what I mean is, honey, usually people don't make reservations here. They just sort of show up, you know?"

"I want to make a reservation. For two people."

The pause again, followed by a sigh of resignation. "Man and woman, two men, or what, doll?"

"Two men," Colonius provided a pause of his own. "But separate rooms." He added it much too quickly for the words to sound right and the lady laughed.

"Well, all right, honey. Two rooms. Adjoining, OK? Starting Tuesday." She took the name he gave her and talked about the ferry schedule from Bay Shore on Long Island and how bad traffic was on the Cross Island and suddenly tacked on a parting shot in an almost severe voice. "But, honey, no leather-jacket stuff if it's going to be noisy, understand? And nothing—even if it's a pet turtle—nothing under sixteen, OK?" Then she giggled.

As he hung up, Colonius smiled. *Screw* was accurate; the lady understood. He smiled again as he stepped out of the phone booth and headed for the elevators; somehow he doubted that Dr. Ambrose read *Screw* or even kept a copy of it on his waiting-room table.

Chapter Thirteen

Lately, I've started to worry that I could get so involved finishing off Ambrose the plans for Armageddon Day might suffer. I don't think so. Actually, because of that damned broadcast, one thing now pretty well depends on the other. I've got to prove I mean business or the plan just won't work. And by time I get through with the Fire Island job and Ambrose, the whole crazy country's going to know what I say, I mean.

The reason I keep coming back to this point—running it around in my head all the time—is that I'm beginning to look forward to the Fire Island deal so much it scares me. I don't know why. And I just want to be certain I'm doing it for the good of the plan and not for the kicks.

—*Extract from the*
journal of Lars Colonius

Tuesday, June 30—Armageddon minus twenty-three.

FORTY MINUTES by train from New York, and an additional fifteen by ferry, Fire Island lies off the southern shore of Long Island like a footnote to an appendix. It is almost sixty miles long, roughly half a mile wide, and virtually impossible to explain. Considering its small size, the island's several different communities are remarkably isolated from one another, although this is not by accident. At one end is Point O'Woods, very wealthy, very social, very WASP—and with a very high steel-mesh anchor fence to keep people out. Cherry Grove and The Pines are made up almost exclusively of artists, interior decorators, and hair stylists—and don't need a fence to keep people out. Saltaire and Seaview are bastions of New York liberalism, insulated from the rest of the island by a moving wall of baby carriages, kids' bicycles and upper-middle smugness.

Squatting in the middle of all this is Ocean Grove. Unlike the communities around it, Ocean Grove tolerates—even encourages—transients, and is therefore the wildest in life-style. It boasts the island's only midway, an unpromising alley of small stores, saloons, bars for swinging singles, bars for gay boys, bars for prostitutes, for male hustlers, and for barefoot teen-agers who just like to watch. Besides small, easily rented beach houses, there's a clutch of rickety boardinghouses and dubious hotels. Pot is sold on the sidewalks, smack is for sale in the bars, and bodies are peddled just about everywhere. It was the perfect setup for settling his problem with Ambrose.

Up a side street from the plank-boarded midway is the Blue Goose. Lars Colonius, who arrived on a midafternoon ferry, had installed himself and Einstein in their adjoining rooms; these were depressing, with sagging wallboards, uneven, bare-plank floors that creaked when you walked, and scraps of thin, woven matting in lieu of rugs. Against the wall of each room stood a single, iron bedstead from which most of the paint had long ago been chipped and worn. Colonius surveyed them and shrugged; Einstein was still excited from the ferry trip over and didn't appear to notice.

Carefully, the equipment was set up and checked out. Nothing blew. To make sure, Colonius slipped downstairs and replaced the fuses with pennies; the Blue Goose might burn down from the overload, but at least the equipment wouldn't konk out on him. Pulling a comic book from his suitcase, Colonius presented it to Einstein with a flourish, ordering him to stay in his own room and talk to no one until he knocked on the thin wall for him to come in with his camera. Colonius thumped on the wall to show him what it would sound like. Einstein was already restless and complained about there being no television set, but Colonius began pointing out things in the comic book to him and pretty soon Einstein seemed to be settling

108

down happily enough. Outside, Colonius sat down on the rickety wooden steps of the Blue Goose and began his own wait—the darkness would come early, he figured, because of a forbiddingly gloomy sky that hung over the island that night. Finally, he decided it was dark enough, dusted the sand off his trousers, and set off toward the midway.

Tucked away on another side street off the midway was The Arrangement, another name provided him by the *Voice*. It was a typical male hustlers' bar, long and narrow, with the buyers lining either side of its front end. This way, they could inspect everyone who came in. On display at the other end was the merchandise; the room widened here slightly and the boys stood or walked around the resulting open space so they could be easily studied by the buyers' gauntlet up front. Occasionally, the hustlers would exchange a word or two with one another, but no conversation was allowed to start; it might discourage a buyer.

After one look, Colonius found himself worried by this layout. Many of the hustlers obviously knew each other and all of them would see him leave with his purchase. To make himself hard to remember, he had, soon after arriving, outfitted himself in the native costume of the island: sports shirt, dungarees, and sneakers—with a swordfishing hat covering as much of his hair as possible. But it bothered him that someone with a particularly good memory might be able to describe him at all: "He had a dark crew cut under that hat, I think—I mean, his hair was dark but he had bright blue eyes." Some way around the problem of the layout had to be found; both a cooperative male and female were needed for his operation, and they were the one set of props he hadn't been able to bring from the mainland with him. A minute later, Colonius decided to go find the girl first—there was a pross bar farther down the same street—put his untouched drink on the counter, and walked out the front door. Maybe the girl would have a suggestion.

Outside, he took a deep breath and studied the overcast sky, trying to decide if rain was going to be added to his problems. Then, he turned sharply to his right and started to walk. He almost tripped over the outstretched legs of Vernon Tuckerman, Jr., who was leaning casually against the outside of The Arrangement.

Tuckerman was an eighteen-year-old refugee from Granger, North Carolina, with wide, innocent eyes that were an insult to your intelligence. He was new to the North, even newer to the Island, but an old hand at his profession; if you stayed outside, you not only got first crack at the marks, you didn't have to plank down a buck for watered beer. In silence, Colonius and Tuckerman studied one another.

Until that moment, Lars Colonius hadn't faced up to how you went about buying a person. The boy was obviously a hustler, but putting the proposition into words threw Colonius badly and he ended up painfully blunt. "Do you want to go with me?"

Tuckerman eyed him with curiosity; usually there was at least a pretense of small talk. He stretched elaborately to cover his own confusion. "I guess. As long as you understand I'm not into it for kicks."

"Of course."

"And that hanging out on Fire Island is very expensive. *Very* expensive."

"Of course." There was an uncomfortable pause, then: "One hundred?"

Tuckerman blinked, but managed to hang on to his pose of nonchalance. A hundred was four times the going rate. "OK," he drawled.

"It's not me," Colonius said in a voice that suddenly seemed to be talking too fast. "It's with a girl." He tried to read some reaction in Tuckerman's face, but could detect only a slight flutter. "I mean, you *can* go with a girl, can't you?" It was a question that had troubled Colonius ever since he had worked out the details of the Fire Island thing.

And it was a question to which Tuckerman didn't know the answer himself, so he hid from it by playing it extra-cool. "For a hundred, mister, I could go with Smokey the Bear."

Lars Colonius laughed because he knew he was supposed to laugh, and then quickly started Tuckerman and

110

himself off in the direction of the pross joint. No one on the street, he was pleased to note, was paying any attention to him or had even noticed his transaction with Tuckerman. It was going to work.

Getting the girl was a cinch.

The dive, also from *Screw,* was whimsically named the Princess Grace; Colonius left Tuckerman outside, fifty dollars stuck in his pocket to guarantee his hanging around. Inside, the Princess Grace looked very much like The Arrangement, except here the buyers and sellers were all mixed together instead of being staked out at opposite ends of the room. The girls were younger and not as hard-looking as Colonius expected—many of them, according to the *Voice,* worked in places like this only to support a habit—but they were thoroughly businesslike in handling themselves.

Colonius' way of picking one was simple: He propositioned the first girl inside the door. She was about his own age, he guessed, with long blond hair that fell loosely to her shoulders; you could not call her pretty, but neither could you say she was ugly. The clearest impression you got from her was a feeling of total, grinding boredom. Asked to go, all she said was, "Why not?" Told it was not for himself but for a friend ("He's a little crazy—only likes to watch"), she just shrugged. It was only when Colonius mentioned a hundred dollars—he figued she should get the same as Tuckerman—that she finally reacted with a troubled look. "What's the catch?" she demanded, her eyes narrowing.

"You have to wear a sort of costume."

"Two hundred," she said flatly.

Colonius nodded and they slipped out the door, the girl a couple of feet behind him. The girls at the Princess Grace were used to just about anything.

Or thought they were.

On the way back to the Blue Goose, having to step off the path often and into the soft sand as they went, Colonius began preparing them for the roles they would play. Since they would consider them peculiar, he thought it

111

was best to do this a little at a time, rather than throwing the whole thing at the boy and the girl in one piece. He knew they had no moral scruples—the glint in both of their eyes when the amounts of money were mentioned had not escaped him—but he didn't want them to get scared and chicken out on him.

"This friend of mine, the man who's paying for all of this," Colonius began, reaching down to pull a stone loose from his sandals, "he has, well, some pretty funny ideas. Sick, I suppose you could call them. But there's nothing to worry about—you'll never even see him." Colonius watched them out of the corner of his eye and could see the beginning of worry grow in the boy's eyes; the girl remained phlegmatic. "You'll never see him," he added, "because my friend will be watching from behind a two-way mirror in the next room; he always insists it be done that way." Colonius thought of the yellowed and cracked mirror from over the dresser which he'd rigged to bolster this piece of fiction, and smiled brightly. He was also amused to notice the worried look vanish from Tuckerman's eyes.

"You will, of course, see the guy taking the pictures. He'll be in the room with us."

This statement made the girl stop dead in her tracks and shake her head vigorously. Angrily, she stared at Colonius. "No pictures. That's asking for trouble. You didn't mention anything about pictures before or I wouldn't be out here wasting my time."

Colonius laughed. "There's no trouble with the police to worry about. The costume," he reminded her with a reassuring smile, "your face, your whole body will be covered up with it. Nobody could recognize you in a million years."

"No pictures," the girl repeated. "No pictures and that's final." Tuckerman, standing alongside her now, nodded in agreement.

Colonius pretended to sigh and began reaching into his pocket. For three hundred dollars the pair agreed to the pictures, and the three of them started on toward the Blue Goose again. Promising the couple a lot of money—as long as the amount stayed sounding believable—didn't

112

bother Colonius at all. They wouldn't be around to collect it.

Once inside, Colonius carefully laid out the costumes on the bed. The girl laughed when she saw the rubber skin-diving suit with the hole cut in its front, but climbed into it without argument. "This friend of yours must be *real* sick," she giggled, "but what the hell. It's his money." She darted over to the mirror and waved into it cheerfully, then mouthed a silent "hello" to the friend supposedly on the other side.

Tuckerman wasn't as amused. His costume would consist only of the Abercrombie fishing boots. That and the snorkeling masks and linesman's gloves Colonius said they both were to wear. Standing there, virtually naked, trying to get his feet used to the boots, Tuckerman felt both silly and increasingly nervous. He wanted very much to find some excuse and back out, but couldn't bring himself to; three hundred dollars would keep him away from Granger, North Carolina, for quite a while.

"Watch the mike wires," said Colonius suddenly. "Don't get your feet tangled in them." Both the girl and Tuckerman looked at the wires with mistrust. While they were undressing and getting into their rigs, Colonius had told them that his friend, watching through the mirror from the next room, would also be listening to their electrically amplified heartbeats; tiny microphones in the costumes carried the sound through the externally attached wires and into his room, Colonius explained; this was his friend's big kick. Awkwardly, they shook their feet free of the wires, still looking at them uneasily, particularly the girl. Her need for a fix was beginning to make her irritable.

"Oh, hell. Let the creep get an earache," she snorted finally, and then, walking carefully around the wires, plopped herself on the bed. Colonius half-pushed Tuckerman toward her, smiling a little as the hustler sat down on the edge of the bed uncomfortably. With a quick movement, Colonius walked over to the wall, told them to adjust their snorkling masks, and then rapped on the wall for Einstein to come in with his equipment. Colo-

113

nius had peeked in on him earlier and told him it would only be a few minutes now.

The door opened hesitantly and Einstein shuffled in with the Brownie and the flashbulbs, but stopped, confused, the moment he got fully inside. Colonius had done his best to prepare him for the skin-diving suit on the girl and the lack of anything but fishing boots on the boy and that wasn't what was bothering him. It was what the man and the woman were doing. Einstein had seen pictures of it drawn on the walls of men's rooms, and this was a little like that, he supposed, but he'd never really seen *it* before. Now, suddenly, the girl had slid back the snorkle mask with a disgusted "Damn!" and her mouth was working directly on the boy's thing; he'd seen drawings of that, too, but it mystified and frightened him anyway.

The girl wasn't in the least bit mystified. This fag-hustler—she supposed they'd gotten him at The Arrangement—was having trouble getting it up with a woman, so she had to get him going or she'd never get out of there. The whole scene bothered her: the male hustler, the creep who'd picked both of them up, the crazy man behind the two-way mirror, now this goggle-eyed kid with his damned camera. She probably should have held out for more money. But what the hell, all she wanted to do now was get it over with and cut out on this bunch of weirdos. She couldn't put off the fix much longer.

"The pictures, dammit, the pictures," Colonius whispered angrily to Einstein. Back in familiar territory, Colonius figured, Einstein would shake himself out of it and stop being so frightened. And, slowly, Einstein started to respond; the viewfinder went to his eye and the flash-bulb began to blink. But there was a terribly uneasy look to Einstein's face suggesting that while he might feel a little better now, this new game Mr. Colonius was playing disturbed him in some far deeper way than he could understand.

Patiently—he was also a little amused—Colonius waited until Tuckerman was finally up to starting and then told him, for Christ's sake, to get going. Tuckerman gingerly inserted himself through the hole in the diving suit and felt himself enter her. Automatically, he began moving and allowed himself an inner sigh of relief. The scary part was no longer a worry; he could perform.

Backing up slowly, Colonius let his fingers slide onto the switch that would start the tape machine, then inched them over to the one beside it that controlled the three transformers. These were wired in parallel, 20 amperes, 115 volts each, to give a cumulative charge of 60 amps. at 115—one hell of a wallop. The positive lead ran through the wire to a small copper plate buried inside Tuckerman's boot, very far up, just beneath the left buttock; the negative lead was attached to a gauze-padded, copper-mesh disk in the girl's rubber diving suit, set just below the small of the back so she would be in tight contact with it. Both the plate and the gauze-padded disk were well saturated with electroencephalographic gel to be sure of a full power flow.

Colonius took a deep breath and threw the switch. The current surged through the wires, the negative and positive charges seeking union like particles in an atom. There was only one uninsulated point of contact where they could join, and that was where Tuckerman's prick stuck through the diving suit into the girl. When the surge of power reached them, their pelvises were jammed together as if slammed tight by some awesome giant's hands. Uncontrollably, the girl's back arched far off the bed in an upward thrust, lifting Tuckerman with it; his body seemed to straighten at first, then arched too, but in the opposite direction, as if the two of them were struggling to escape from some giant spike that had nailed them together. His hands in the linesman's gloves shoved frantically against the mattress as he tried to heave himself away from the girl and the pain and the spasms that were running through him, but the hold of the giant spike was too strong and his arms beat helplessly and began to go rigid.

Colonius threw the switch to "off" and the two bodies seemed to collapse into each other. He waited for a couple of seconds, still calm enough to remind Einstein to keep going with the damned pictures, but Einstein was so terrified Colonius had to speak twice before he was even heard. Then, Colonius closed the switch again. This time, Tuckerman's head snapped backward so sharply that it made an ugly crackling sound, but it was a sound almost lost in the tight strangled moans from the girl and a child-like whimpering that was coming, Colonius suddenly realized, from Einstein. Again, the lights dimmed and flickered dangerously from the drain of the transformers, but Colonius kept the charge going until the room's air was bitter with the acrid smell of electricity; he could see a small curl of smoke begin to rise from the fused pelvises and smell the sticky-sweet incense of burning hair. Finally, he decided it was enough.

The switch was thrown open and the transformers turned off. The bodies stopped thrashing and collapsed. A half-choked "Ohmygosh!" came from Einstein, a phrase so inadequate it sounded almost funny. The lights, tentatively and uncertainly at first, returned to full strength. Colonius was surprised to discover he was breathing heavily; slowly, he became aware of a damp-ness, suddenly cold and uncomfortable, inside his shorts and he swore at himself angrily. Einstein, the camera still half-raised, stared blankly at the bed, his mouth hanging limp and open. With a cough to reassure himself, Colonius strode across to the bed and placed two fingers on Tucker-man's neck to make sure the job was complete; there was no pulse. As he withdrew his hand, Tuckerman's head re-acted to the movement and slipped suddenly sideways, his eyes bulging at Colonius through the glass in the snor-keling mask. Oddly, Colonius could see the girl's eyes were closed, like she was just resting. He reached down and tried to roll back the linesman's glove on her left hand so he could check her pulse, too, but the hands had frozen into a clenched position and pulling down the glove wasn't easy. There was no indication of pulse with her, either. Colonius straightened up; it was done.

Abruptly, from behind him, the sound of Einstein's whimpering changed. Turning, Colonius could see he was shaking his head and desperately trying to say something, but couldn't, because he was starting to cry. Colonius spoke to him sharply, hoping to calm him with the reassuring sound of familiar commands. "Get moving, now; we've got a lot to do."

But the strangeness of it was too great to be so easily washed from Einstein's mind. His shoulders began to shake convulsively and the crying grew louder and more uneven. He was losing his control completely, not because he understood what had happened, but because he didn't. In two steps, Colonius moved in front of him and slapped him hard across the face. It was something he had never done before, but it worked.

Einstein shook his head, as if trying to jar loose the scene from his head, and let an uncomprehending hand slowly rise to touch where he'd been slapped. His eyes blinked at Colonius and his hand moved back from his cheek, turned over, and ran itself under his nose. "I'm sorry," he whispered, "I'm sorry." He fumbled in his pocket for the handkerchief he never remembered to carry and used the back of his hand again.

Quickly, they stripped the skin-diving suit from the girl and the fishing boots from Tuckerman. Colonius folded them neatly and stuffed them into a laundry bag. On top of this went the three transformers, the snorkeling masks, the linesman's gloves, and the rolled-up wire. The note to Dr. Ambrose had been written before they left the Regency and was carefully propped up against the mirror. Colonius checked his watch; they were ahead of schedule. But arranging the bodies for discovery by the police— it was an elaborate setup, as Colonius wanted to be sure of milking the publicity value to the limit—took longer than he'd thought. When he checked his watch again, it was almost twelve thirty, about half an hour behind. Colonius shrugged and had Einstein shoulder the laundry bag of equipment, while he picked up their personal luggage. Going out the door, he set the trip wires and closed it carefully behind him.

At the marina, he located the small speedboat he'd spotted earlier in the day; it had a neglected look about it and he was able to jump the ignition wires easily without anyone on the almost deserted docks asking questions. Halfway across Great South Bay to Long Island, the laundry bag was heaved over the side; the transformers were very heavy and it plunged to the bottom almost instantly.

Lars Colonius felt good. The brooding sky of earlier evening had given way to a clear, deep blue, and the stars—you could always see them better out on the water like this—seemed to be flashing a personal victory salute to him. By this time tomorrow, the whole world would know he meant business and Ambrose would look like an ass.

And now he could get back to preparing for Armageddon Day, which, he suddenly realized, was only twenty-two days away. Then, the stars would really have something to applaud about.

Chapter Fourteen

I wonder what that kid from The Arrangement thought when the current first slammed into him. It's really almost comic: His first—and only—piece of nookie, and look what happens to him. I suppose, somewhere in the back of his head, he was always afraid of women, and that's what made him like he was. He was a real case; that crazy whore had to work like hell just to get him going.

Jesus, and Ambrose had the nerve to call *me* sexually inadequate!

—*Extract from the journal of Lars Colonius*

Wednesday, June 1—Armageddon minus twenty-two.

"I DON'T know what to make of it." Ambrose handed the picture back to Goddard and shook his head. It was a shot of Armageddon standing a couple of feet away from Mick Jagger; Jagger was waving, although from the angle you couldn't tell whether it was at Armageddon or at someone else in the small crowd beside him. A fast check with booking agents showed it was taken following a recording session in L.A. some weeks before. "Except," continued Ambrose, "that it's more of the same old game he's playing." He paused for a moment to think. "I don't know why, though. By now, he must figure we get the message. Or figure that we're awfully stupid."

Goddard looked embarrassed. "He does—figure we're stupid. And in my case, he may just be right." With a

119

resigned sigh, Goddard walked slowly over to the tape machine and switched it on.

"This is the voice of Armageddon," the familiar, changing tones crackled out of the small speaker. "And you were pretty dumb with that trap you set at the Westbury. Stupid. The next time you want to catch somebody, I suggest you don't have a small army of guys sitting around a cramped hotel lobby. It shows. Also, you might at least give them the right day's newspapers to read —theirs were a day behind. Anyway, I'm not so stupid as to blow the Armageddon plan just to get even with Ambrose. I have my own way for getting equal time, and you'll be finding out about that pretty soon now. In the meantime, if I were you, I'd spend my time worrying about Armageddon Day—only twenty-six days until air time, men."

There was the usual click and the sound of the narrow ribbon of tape beating against the tape deck until Goddard reached over and stopped the machine. Ambrose looked at him incredulously. "Did they *really* have the wrong day's newspapers?"

Goddard shrugged. "I don't know. There's no newspaper stand in the lobby, you know, and maybe one of them just picked up what he could find. Hell, apparently he'd spotted them anyway. Too damned many of them. Which is my fault. I don't know what to tell Evans."

"Well," said Ambrose, trying to ignore Goddard's fit of self-castigation, "maybe Armageddon will come back and take another look—this time with something planned. Obviously, the fact that he showed up at all means the interview bugged him plenty. So it served a purpose."

"Maybe." Goddard and Ambrose looked at one another. Goddard didn't believe what Ambrose had just said any more than Ambrose did, but they were both willing to let the fiction stand to make Goddard feel better.

Inside himself, Ambrose was struggling with something that didn't make him feel good at all. It was a strange sensation he'd had once before—that Armageddon could somehow see into his mind and guess what their next move would be before Ambrose had even decided it himself. (If he could have read Colonius' journal, he would have been interested to see it described by him as "like playing chess with somebody in the dark.") It was an eerie feeling that Ambrose sometimes got with his patients at the clinic—a feeling that they were finding out as much about him as he was about them.

The thought bothered him and to dismiss it he changed the subject. "This new tape. It's an odd one, somehow. There's no relationship—not even a mention, in fact—between it and the picture of Mick Jagger. I don't know what that means. And the phraseology's different; 'equal time' is a funny way to put getting even with somebody. And 'air time' a strange set of words to describe Armageddon Day. It's show-business language, more or less. Maybe Dr. Sochi can find other hints of it in the earlier tapes."

While talking, Ambrose had moved slowly across to the "probability board" on Goddard's wall. This was an intricately laid-out panel, covered with blocked-off squares of acetate marked up with china-marking pencil. It looked like a giant checkerboard, possible targets lettered in and cross-related to comments from the tapes, dates of receipt, and probable dates of sending, then vectored by locations, dates, and times of possible opportunity. No one in the room knew it, but it looked remarkably like the one Colonius had used in his original search for a proper target.

His hands behind his back, Ambrose turned away from the chart, talking as much to himself as to Goddard. "There have been several show-business, art-world, television people before, of course: Namath, Bernstein, Johnny Carson. And now Jagger. But up until now I've been assuming it was just because they were highly visible personalities—names with impact to them." He turned back to the chart and suddenly thrust a finger toward one of the squares. "Look here, though. On the Bernstein tape, Armageddon says he could have been a concert pianist. Don't worry about whether it's true or not; it's the idea behind it that counts." A small trace of excitement was creeping into Ambrose's voice as he jumped his finger to another square on the chart. "And on the Carson tape

—remember?—he rambles on about how tough it is to get into show business. Now, Mick Jagger. And those phrases like 'air time'."

Ambrose had turned away again from the probability board and was standing with his back to it, his eyes half-raised to the ceiling, playing with an idea that was growing in his mind, twisting, turning, reshaping it like a dissatisfied sculptor with a hunk of clay. "Maybe, when all's said and done, Armageddon was an actor or something, a frustrated actor, maybe that's what we haven't been looking at. And maybe the target isn't a person at all, but a *thing*. A concert, a program, an event. Something where Armageddon can act out his fantasies. Demand and get his equal time. Maybe, maybe. . . ." Ambrose was sounding unusually excited, the smooth mask of unflappable cool strangely absent; now, as he listened to his own voice and realized how little solid fact lay behind his reasoning, the enthusiasm collapsed abruptly. "Oh, hell, dammit, I don't know."

Goddard's enthusiasm didn't need collapsing; this line of thought didn't mesh with his preconceptions, and his reaction was sour. "He also sent tapes and pictures about the Vice President and then the President. That makes his target a legitimate concern of the Justice Department. On the other hand, if all Armageddon plans to do is blow up some damned actor, well, I don't mean to sound unconcerned, but then it's a job for the police."

Already half sunk into a chair, Ambrose let himself down the rest of the way loudly and heavily, staring at Goddard with disbelief. He realized the man was still angry with himself over blowing the stakeout in the lobby and could be expected to overreact and lash out at anything handy, but the peculiarly bloodless form the overreaction took mystified Ambrose. He struggled briefly with a growing petulance in himself and ended by succumbing to it. "Maybe," he suggested softly, "you should let *me* tell Evan Evans that Armageddon saw through the trap in the lobby. There's no point getting him any madder than he'll be anyway."

Goddard grunted. He had nothing to say.

The Ocean Grove section of Fire Island is administratively part of the town of Bay Shore, Long Island. In return for the right of collecting taxes, the town provides Ocean Grove with essential services, as well as backup firefighting equipment, personnel, and police protection. In Ocean Grove itself, there were, in addition, two constables. These were native islanders whose jobs consisted mostly of seeing that no one broke into the resort's homes in either winter or summer; anything more important was handled out of Bay Shore.

And what happened that morning rapidly became too important for Bay Shore itself to handle. At approximately nine thirty A.M., an anonymous voice called the Bay Shore police to inform them of a drug overdose victim in Ocean Grove. He could be found, the caller said, on the floor of room two zero two of the Blue Goose, which he described as a small hotel on Dune Street. Just before hanging up, the voice added it was even possible the victim was still alive. Bay Shore Deputy Chief De-Fazio had twice tried to reach the constable in Ocean Grove by phone, but was told by the man's wife the constable was down at the other end of the island on some errand or another. There was no answer at all from the phone at the Blue Goose. Grumbling, DeFazio had climbed into the town's emergency powerboat with another officer, Patrolman Daniel Hicks, and—along with two hastily summoned interns from Misericordia Hospital —headed for Ocean Grove, the rear of the powerboat stocked with oxygen tanks, respirators, a stomach pump, and other general emergency equipment. The trip took about fifteen minutes.

Now, DeFazio stood face to face with the proprietress of the Blue Goose, a fat lady dressed only in a wrinkled flannel bathrobe. She was visibly annoyed to have been wakened so early and so rudely.

"Why the hell don't you answer your phone, lady?" asked DeFazio belligerently. "This is an emergency."

The fat lady looked at DeFazio with indifference and wrapped the bathrobe tighter around herself. "This *what* is an emergency?"

"You got an o.d. in room two zero two."

123

"I don't take junkies here. Or acid heads."

"There was a phone call. You got an o.d. in two zero two."

The fat lady bristled; this kind of trouble could get expensive. "I run a clean place and I don't wan' no trouble. You're crazy, honey."

DeFazio started through the front door. "I gotta look anyway. Like I said, it's an emergency."

There were a couple of seconds when it was unclear whether the fat lady would try to block the entrance with her body—you could almost see a demand for a search warrant forming on her lips—but suddenly she turned around and led DeFazio toward the stairs. "What the hell," she mumbled resignedly. "But it's a big pain in the ass you guys come busting in here like this."

Outside the door of two zero two, the fat lady paused, fished into the pocket of her bathrobe, and pulled out a jumbled fistful of keys. Carefully, she selected the right one and firmly stuck it into the lock. From inside came the sound of a record dropping and the starting of a snatch of music. The fat lady turned on DeFazio triumphantly. "See, honey? Some poor bastard's just playing a record or something. But you guys—"

"Open it."

With a shrug, the fat lady turned the knob, pushed open the door, and stood there, stepping back silently to let DeFazio see past her. She didn't stay silent very long. There was a popping sound as a wire somewhere across the room broke with a loud snap and a sort of *whooshing* sound through the air and the sudden white blur of something swinging across the room almost directly at her; the expression of triumph on the fat lady's face turned first into one of surprise, then into one of terror, as the arcing white blur knocked her backward, away from the door and almost across the hall; her voice found itself and she began to scream, a scream that had no beginning or end nor top nor bottom, but ripped open the whole spectrum of sound, bouncing off the walls of the narrow hall and seemed to gain in volume as it went. Mouth open and sagging, DeFazio stared bugeyed past her into the bedroom and struggled to say something but could manage only a half-swallowed groan before he had to do some ducking himself as the white blur swung back across the room at them again.

Hanging from a pipe on the ceiling, naked and upside down, were the bodies of Vernon Tuckerman, Jr., and the girl from the Princess Grace. Their near hands were joined together by a lacing of wire, so that they looked like the inverted image on a photographer's ground glass of a young couple strolling through some park. Until now, a trip wire attached to the doorknob had held them in position far up against the top of the room's rear wall, but the turning of the knob had snapped the trip wire and released them to swing back and forth in graceful, sweeping arcs, almost in time with the LP on the record player, set to playing when the key went into the lock and closed a circuit. The LP was a vintage recording of Gertrude Lawrence singing "Hello Young Lovers, Wherever You Are . . ." and her thin, uncertain voice sounded almost pleading as it cut through the dim sunlight that here and there pierced the black opacity of the drawn window shades.

Later, when asked by reporters to describe his first reactions to the scene, DeFazio would dwell at some length on the curious blue cast to the bodies and on his own estimate of how long they had been dead. At the time, what actually struck him was how ridiculous naked people look when hung upside down; breasts and testicles drooping in the wrong direction are so crazy-looking that your first reaction is to giggle, but it was an inappropriate reaction and DeFazio quickly dismissed it.

Turning now, he grabbed the fat lady and shook her until she stopped screaming. This made DeFazio feel a little better. Not only was the screaming a nerve-shattering sound, but doors were opening, left and right, down the long hall as the still half-asleep tenants cautiously stuck out their heads to find out what the hell was going on. Patrolman Hicks, left behind downstairs with the two interns by request of the fat lady, had been brought bounding upstairs by the screaming and, after being allowed a fast look into the room, was now sent to telephone Bay Shore for reinforcements. Everything they had available,

125

DeFazio said. Then, Hicks should take up position at the front door of the Blue Goose and keep everybody out; DeFazio himself would stay inside the room with the evidence—glancing up at it hanging from the pipe on the ceiling, he found the thought disturbing but necessary—as well as launch a preliminary search for clues. It would be a futile search, he knew, one that should really await the arrival of detectives from Bay Shore, but it would be better than just standing around staring at the bodies.

The only out-of-place item he ran across—it was propped up on the bureau and apparently forgotten in the killer's flight—was a bulky, carefully stamped and addressed envelope. It was unsealed and when DeFazio shook it a small reel of home-recording tape fell out, followed by a neatly typed letter. This, he told both the detectives that finally arrived from Bay Shore and a growing crew of newspaper reporters that came with them, was addressed to one Dr. Carlton Ambrose, MD, at the Hotel Westbury in New York City. The contents, he assured the reporters, would undoubtedly be released as soon as the letter and the envelope had been gone over for fingerprints. He did not mention the tape.

The reaction at the Westbury to the news was first disbelief, then shock, then fury. For while Ambrose's name had meant little to DeFazio, it was quickly connected to Ambrose's broadcast and the Armageddon plan by the first city reporters who arrived to cover the story. And the UPI and AP, along with the network news teams, soon had chartered every available small boat in Bay Shore and were pouring into Ocean Grove.

Had Deputy Chief Inspector DeFazio called the Westbury first, the Justice Department might have been able to turn on enough pressure to keep Ambrose's name out of it. But as it was, by the time Goddard even heard of the killing, Ambrose's name was pouring out of every telex machine from one end of the country to the other.

With this sort of clamor, the best Goddard could do was to keep the actual contents of the letter itself from becoming public; however, an enterprising reporter from the New York *Post* easily flattered DeFazio into giving him the gist of it, and this too was soon a matter of public record. The killer's letter, DeFazio allowed, was signed by someone who called himself Armageddon; the writer accused Dr. Ambrose of lying about him on some television program or other, and the murder in Ocean Grove was by way of proving how wrong the doctor was in not taking his threats seriously. According to DeFazio, the letter also accused the doctor of lying about his IQ, his personality, and his sex life—there was something specific mentioned here, DeFazio thought, but he couldn't remember what it was—and finished with a statement that the double murders were the first installment of something so vast the world would finally give the writer the equal time it had, up until now, denied him. No, DeFazio insisted, he was quite positive about the phrase "equal time"; it was used twice in the letter and he was sure about it. Yes, there was also a reel of tape inside the envelope, DeFazio admitted; he hadn't mentioned it earlier because he didn't think it was important. Sorry, he had no idea of what was on the tape; it had already been sent to Bay Shore, and from there to New York. The newspapers, radio, and television began having a field day with catch phrases like "the equal-time murders," the sensationalism of the killer's "Armageddon" signature, and the link between Ambrose's television interview, the photograph of the Vice President, and the rumors about the Oval Office.

Numbly, the waves of news swept through the sixteenth floor of the Westbury. Evan Evans said little, but ground out one of his cigars angrily and coldly noted that there was a good chance Armageddon might have been behind bars by now if the stakeout in the lobby hadn't been the victim of overdirection. Goddard was so harassed—Washington had called three times by then, and kept coming back on the line every few minutes—that he didn't even bother to answer him. The FBI was already on its way to Ocean Grove; the Secret Service was redoubling its guard around government figures; members of a Senate subcommittee were talking about an investigation.

In the midst of all this, Ambrose sat, his lanky feet

propped on a chair across from him, a Tijuana 12 hanging lit but untasted from his hand, and pondered the sudden and repeated use of Armageddon's new phrase, "equal time." More than ever, he was convinced that the ultimate target would not be a government person. But he had abandoned his earlier notion that Armageddon might be a former actor or performer in search of revenge—without, however, abandoning the idea that the target might be a person or thing somehow associated with show business. The words in the Mick Jagger tape kept bothering him, and he wondered what relation there would be to the words on the Ocean Grove tape when the helicopter from Fire Island arrived with it. The words. Somewhere in the words was the key.

Standing up and straightening himself out slowly, Ambrose quietly left the room and headed down the hall toward Dr. Sochi.

By three thirty that afternoon, the manhunt for Armageddon was reaching into every corner of Greater New York. But Colonius was no longer there. His phone call to the Bay Shore police that morning came from a phone booth at Kennedy, and by the time Deputy Chief DeFazio had climbed aboard the emergency boat to Ocean Grove, the early-morning flight to L.A. had already taken off. The first playing of "Hello, Young Lovers" didn't take place until Colonius was well over Pennsylvania, and by the time the New York *Post*'s reporter had squeezed the contents of the letter out of DeFazio, Lars Colonius was about over North Dakota. The intensive manhunt for him in New York began almost precisely at the same time he climbed off the plane in California, dressed once again in his dark suit and carrying his doctor's bag.

A little later, he and Einstein were unpacking in a bungalow at the Beverly Hills Hotel, registered as doctor and patient as they had been at the Regency, but with a new set of names. These touches, Colonius told himself, were probably being overly cautious, even as skipping out of New York for a while was, but he felt himself drawing too close to the payoff of the Armageddon plan to take any chances of any kind. The intensity of the manhunt, the flavor of the press coverage, and the fast tieup between the killings and Ambrose's television interview delighted him; the tone of public fear necessary to pull off Armageddon Day was evident in every new news item.

At the moment, his only problem was Einstein. Although he had not expected Einstein to understand what really went on at the Blue Goose, Colonius was unprepared for the dramatic change it would make. The scene had left visible scars on him. Frequently now, Colonius would find Einstein staring at him vacantly, not with either fear or disgust, but in what appeared to be unhappy confusion. When Colonius would try to draw him out on the subject, bringing it up himself in an offhand way so he could dismiss it lightly to show how little it mattered, Einstein would seem to shrink inside himself, sometimes twisting his hands nervously and staring at them as if they held the answer to some great secret. He no longer spent hours watching television, although several times Colonius found him sitting in front of the set just staring intently at the blank screen. He still obeyed any command Colonius gave him, but no longer with any trace of eagerness; it was a sullen performance and the closest to rebellion Colonius had ever seen him. Time, he told himself, would quickly erase it.

This was to be a classic misjudgment.

But one that passed easily from his mind. Although Colonius spent a good deal of time around the pool of the hotel, enjoying being pampered by the staff, he still had plenty of work to do. The journal needing expanding and completing, his case against the world had to be distilled and made sharper, his thoughts and actions crystallized and readied for Armageddon Day. The home movies sent him by his mother were still to be spliced together and a script written; commentary was needed for the pictures from his school classbooks. Carefully and sometimes painfully, all of this was set down on yellow legal-sized pads while Einstein lay on the terrace beside him, sulking in the sun.

It was not until the middle of the following week that Colonius felt ready to return to New York and put the machinery of Armageddon Day in operation.

A small but lavish office in a converted townhouse just off Fifth, manned by two secretaries and a changing directorate of socially prominent volunteers, is all there is to the headquarters of the Institute for the Blind. The matrons who run the institute see their function as twofold: the dissemination of facts to help prevent blindness, where possible, and the raising of money through charitable contributions to help the afflicted. In the past, the ladies had mostly concerned themselves with the latter, while the publicity was handled for them by a public relations firm, John Connover Associates. This particular year, Connover had talked them into a program which combined both functions. The institute, he said, could stage a nationwide telethon which would raise money and, at the same time, publicize their blindness-prevention campaign. With the contacts he had personally—and because of the compellingly worthwhile objectives of the telethon—Connover assured them he could deliver enough big names to make the program worth watching; he had already sounded out one of the networks and gotten what he described as "a good reaction."

Mrs. Alwyn Vreeland, the institute's vice chairman and one of its leading figures over the years, sat in the office that morning and watched with suspicion as the morning mail arrived. She had harbored—and to some extent, still did—reservations about having the institute associated with anything that smacked of show business, but had been badly outvoted by the rest of the board; Connover was far too effective a salesman to be beaten on his home turf. Originally, her response to this defeat had been to sit the telethon out at her place in East Hampton—a far pleasanter spot than the city this time of year. But slowly, as more and more big stars agreed to appear, as the telethon's prepublicity hit the columns, and as she saw the rest of the board climb on the telethon bandwagon, she began to worry that her initial opposition to the scheme might let other members of the board get ahead of her, and reluctantly started driving into town twice a week to help with preparations. Connover had told her that several big donations at the beginning of the telethon would be needed to start the ball rolling, and Mrs. Vreeland had been writing and calling everyone she could think of to try and line them up. So far, the largest she'd been able to swing was a three-thousand-dollar gift from a business dependent of her husband's; Eleanor deKay, who was also in the institute's office that hot, summer day, was already far ahead of her, and Mrs. Vreeland suspected she was probably gunning for her spot as vice chairman.

"Well, I'll be damned," exclaimed Eleanor deKay, letting a check flutter out of a letter one of the secretaries had just handed her. "Five thousand dollars. From somebody I never heard of. And without even being asked."

Under her breath, Mrs. Vreeland swore a not very ladylike swear. Eleanor deKay was definitely out to get her and even the secretaries were helping her. Why else would they have steered the check to Eleanor instead of her?

But Mrs. Vreeland merely smiled an enormously pleased smile; only by the sudden and nervous flutter of her left hand to the triple strand of pearls at her neck could anyone have known she was anything but ecstatic. "Five thousand dollars. How nice." There was a pause while she regrouped and searched for some way to turn things to her advantage. "What's the name?" she asked offhandedly. "Perhaps it's someone I talked to."

"A Doctor Walter Kraus. From the coast. But he just says he read about us in the paper somewhere." Wordlessly, Eleanor deKay handed the letter to her.

Institute for the Blind,
12 East 83rd Street,
New York City, New York 10028

Dear Sirs:
I read recently of your upcoming telethon on behalf of the blind. To my mind, there are few worthier causes, and I enclose a check as my contribution.

I prefer to make my gift in this manner rather than on the telethon itself, as I have discovered such events in-

131

variably bring the donor's name to public attention, something which I personally always avoid.

I trust you will respect this request for anonymity.

The only thing I would ask, beyond a receipt for income tax purposes, is a pair of tickets for the telethon itself. I shall be in your city on that date, and will have in my care a young patient, a deaf and dumb boy, who has frequently expressed interest in seeing a live television broadcast. He would be accompanied to the program by his own interpreter, someone who can explain what is going on, so there would be no need for any special provisions to be made in his behalf. In fact, I would definitely rather none were, as I try to encourage my patients not to become used to any sort of special attention.

If tickets are available, I would appreciate a pair greatly. If not, please do not concern yourself; I am sure I can make arrangements for him to see some other show.

My sincerest best wishes for a successful telethon, and I hope you are able to raise a goodly sum for the commendable cause of blindness prevention and treatment.

Yours Sincerely,

/s/ Walter Kraus, MD,
c/o Hotel Regency
Park Avenue,
New York City, New York.

(*Please mark envelope "Hold for Arrival"*)

Mrs. Vreeland sighed; it would be impossible to claim this odd California doctor as her own, and suggesting his check might bounce would be too obvious. She smiled at Eleanor deKay again. "No, I don't know him either. But he's certainly generous." Then she glanced at her watch, smiled determinedly at her rival, and got ready to leave for lunch at the Colony Club. There, she would gather her friends and tell them what that awful Eleanor deKay was trying to do to her.

Eleanor deKay, who could have given an extremely accurate account of precisely what was going on in Mrs. Vreeland's mind, smiled back gracefully and got ready to leave for luncheon herself. Still smiling, she handed the note and check—along with instructions about sending the tickets to Dr. Kraus immediately—to the secretary, who nodded and smiled back at her.

Everyone, it seemed, was smiling. But if Lars Colonius could have heard himself described as generous, he would have been smiling the biggest smile of all.

Chapter Fifteen

Trying to put my rage against the world into words isn't easy. Yet, what I say on Armageddon Day—the philosophy I express—is just as important as the explosives, the timers, and the batteries in Einstein's fishing vest.

I only wish words were as easy to wire together.
—*Extract from the*
journal of Lars Colonius

Thursday, July 9—Armageddon minus fourteen.

WITH A sudden lurch, the helicopter slipped sideways, veered away from Fire Island, and headed back toward New York. It was an unsettling motion and Ambrose looked at Evan Evans seated beside him to see if he were alarmed; the doctor had ridden in all sorts of airplanes, but travel by chopper was new and a little frightening. He was answered by a reassuring smile that didn't really reassure him and forced himself back to thinking about the interviews at Ocean Grove. Hard police questioning of the fat lady had produced no usable description of Armageddon—she was, from long experience, unhappy with direct questions—and Ambrose was there to try his own hand to shake loose information from her indirectly. Not too much was produced, but it was better than nothing.

"Well, it was pretty damned dark in the lobby, honey. It's always dark in here, sort of, but that day was a real murky one—I can't remember if there was a storm coming or what—so I didn't get much of a look at him." The fat lady paused and then shook her head firmly. "And damned if I can tell you one sure fact about the color of his hair. He had this hat on—a swordfishing hat, I think —so you couldn't see much of it anyway. For all I know, honey, it could have been green." She stared at Ambrose for a second, then added: "I had a customer staying here like that once. Green hair. So help me. Caused one hell of a stir down on the beach."

Ambrose nodded sympathetically and looked around the dim little lobby, then: "It *is* pretty dark. It must be tough on your eyes, working in here. I'm surprised your guests can even see enough to register."

The fat lady pursed her lips and suddenly brightened. "Hey, I can tell you one thing, though. His eyes. Blue. Damnedest bright blue eyes I ever saw. Didn't think of that before, but Goddamn, they were blue. Like—like dime-store sapphires."

With a self-congratulatory smile, Ambrose looked at Evan Evans. Of course, the color of his eyes was, in itself, not significant. But what it did indicate was that Armageddon hadn't dyed his hair, something both of them had wondered about. For Armageddon was too cagey to go dye his hair dark brown or black if he had the sort of eyes the fat lady was describing; the effect would be too startling. It was the first of many wrong conclusions they would reach in the next few days.

Nothing much more was gained from the fat lady. Adroit use of thought-association got nowhere with her in trying to pin down her only other recollection—that the man had some sort of accent. No, it wasn't foreign. Well, no, she didn't think it was Southern, but it could be.

Evan Evans cut in. "Well, I have a Texas accent. Southwestern, I guess you'd call it. Would you say it was like mine?"

The fat lady pondered. "Sort of. Only mushier, honey."

Quietly, Evans and Ambrose abandoned attempts at getting more information about Armageddon from the fat lady. Nor was she able to help them at all on Armageddon's accomplice. She'd never seen him.

The rest of their visit to the Island was fruitless. The girl from the Princess Grace was identified quickly enough by her peers there, but no one had seen her leave that

135

night or whom she was with. First she was there, then she wasn't.

The helicopter banked and Ambrose stared out the window at the waters of Great South Bay below them. It was as bright and sparkling a blue as Armageddon's dime-store sapphire eyes.

Friday, July 10—Armageddon minus thirteen.

Identifying Vernon Tuckerman, Jr. took a little longer (the clothes of both victims were in the same bag with the transformers and other equipment at the bottom of Great South Bay). A couple of people at The Arrangement knew him slightly, but didn't think he'd been in at all the night of the killing. His fingerprints disclosed only that he'd never been arrested or in the service.

It was not until a blowup of his face ran in the *Daily News* that the information finally surfaced. An anonymous call to the *News* not only provided his real name, but established his home address as Granger, South Carolina. It was the wrong state by one, but close enough so that his real home could be found. Eventually, a mystified family came to New York and claimed the body. The city's police are occasionally brutal in such cases, and spared them few of the details in their effort to uncover any friends of his the family might know of in the North. They could remember none.

Putting these scraps of information together, Evan Evans began to build a curious hypothesis: It was possible Armageddon was a Southerner. The first tape and picture came from the All-Rite Shopping Center in Macon; it could be an accident of geography, or it could mean that Armageddon had chosen someplace close to home for his first effort. Vernon Tuckerman had arrived in New York from North Carolina only three months ago; the victim of Armageddon's "electric orgasm" might represent a random choice, or might have been an acquaintance of Armageddon's from the past. Then, there was the matter of the "mushy" accent described by the fat lady. People from Texas like to think their accent is distinctively their own, yet, if you sharpen an accent from the Deep South, add a slight elegance of rhetoric while subtracting the bombast of expression, and then pipe the result through a well-dried set of adenoids, they are really pretty close. Evan Evans reluctantly faced this; the lady from the Blue Goose, inhabiting a world no larger than her hotel on the Island and a similar setup in the West Forties, could be forgiven her confusion. And it added another small element to his rapidly expanding premise.

Evans mentioned it to no one; it was too speculative for the moment. But he did direct his officers in the task force to pay special attention to the South in their manhunt. New flyers of Armageddon were sent to the police departments there, for Evans knew only too well how quickly the old ones get buried beneath new material. With all of the publicity recently given Armageddon, it would seem incredible that such a step was necessary, but Evan Evans also knew that policemen have a parochial way of looking at life and frequently tend to separate what they see in newspapers and on television from what they see firmly tacked on the station-house wall.

Thus—and for all the wrong reasons—the first steps that would ultimately bring the authorities crashing into Armageddon's New York hotel suite were taken.

But taken too late.

"It doesn't tell us anything about Armageddon, but it gives us some interesting, if curious, insights into his accomplice." Dr. Sochi said this almost apologetically, and then stood facing them, strips of recording tape draped around his neck like a Mexican bandit's cartridge belts. Ambrose had come to the semanticist's workroom to see if he could check out the sudden rush of show-business words on the Mick Jagger tape, but never got to pursue it. For he discovered that Sochi had just about finished analyzing the tape of the killing Armageddon had left behind at the Blue Goose, and everything else was put aside. Beside him stood Evan Evans, who had arrived on his own, wanting to test his Southern thesis with Sochi. Like Ambrose, he now tabled it for later.

"The accomplice," Ambrose repeated absently, and shook his head in confusion. Up until now, because of all of the other things he was caught up in, he had no time to even hear the tape and Sochi was talking completely over his head.

"At least, I believe we can assume it's his accomplice. You can hear the shutter of his camera working and what is probably Armageddon whispering instructions to him in the background. Unfortunately, these are just about drowned out by the moans and struggling sounds of the victims; I can't catch an intelligible word of his, only the fact that there are whisperings. With the accomplice, however, it is a different matter. I've had my findings corroborated by the sound engineers, comparative voice-track matchings, and a child psychologist. Not everything fits, of course, but we are generally in agreement."

"A *child* psychologist?" asked Ambrose, now totally confused.

"For the crying," explained Sochi. He studied Ambrose's face for a second, trying to be sure whether the doctor had heard the tape or not, and decided it was possible he hadn't. "Perhaps we should listen to the whole thing again before going into it in detail."

They listened. Even completely separated from its events, it was a shattering experience, and Dr. Sochi's narrow eyes closed to avoid showing any expression. The tape began with the sound of normal sexual breathing, suddenly interrupted by the struggling and thrashings as the first wave of current hit Tuckerman and the girl. Their strangled moans as they tried to escape the current were at times almost overwhelmed by the groaning of the bedsprings and even of the bed itself. Softly at first, you could hear a bewildered whimpering begin that grew louder as it went, building up to a series of sobs and then a sudden but totally inappropriate "Ohmygosh!" that was more of a wail of fear than an interjection. Intermittently, there were the whisperings in the background, vague, unclear, unintelligible, followed by shorter sobs showing some effort at self-control. Finally, the sound of the camera clicking started again. The tape ran out and the three of them stood staring at the machine in silence.

"I think I know what you're getting at," said Ambrose softly, "although it doesn't quite fit."

138

Dr. Sochi smiled faintly. "I know, I know. But Dr. Fermi—he's the child psychologist I called in—has an explanation for that."

There was a grunt from beside Ambrose as Evan Evans spoke up impatiently. "Well, *I* don't know what you're getting at, Dr. Sochi. Except that that's the damnedest tape I ever heard."

Turning, Sochi faced Evans. "Armageddon's accomplice is young, very young. A boy, really. Dr. Fermi and I agree that he is probably somewhere between thirteen and fifteen, which could explain the timbre of his voice. It is too deep for a child's, you see."

"I don't know what makes you think it's a child to begin with."

"The crying pattern. It is not that of an adult. More of fear and bewilderment at what he is seeing than anything else. An adult cries because of pain, or bereavement, or a situation that he understands but cannot tolerate. A child, on the other hand, cries more from bewilderment; he does not understand pain or death or the reasons behind the intolerable situation. And his crying pattern expresses his fear of the unknown as much as anything else. It is a much less inhibited sort of pattern than an adult would demonstrate."

With a vague nod of agreement, Ambrose shoved his hands in his pockets and began pacing the room. But Sochi's small area was too cramped for this, almost every available foot of it filled with equipment of one sort or another, and Ambrose gave up. "That voice, though," he said thoughtfully. "Even for thirteen to fifteen, it's awfully deep."

Sochi sighed. "Of course, some boys mature physically quite early. Even given that, it strikes one as strange." After a pause, Dr. Sochi added a thought he obviously didn't agree with. "Dr. Fermi did suggest you might get the same pattern from certain kinds of defective adults. Someone mentally retarded, for instance. But then, of course, he would be of no use as an accomplice."

Both Evans and Sochi nodded in agreement. "He couldn't even work the camera," Evans pointed out. Ambrose was not so sure, but decided it was no time to argue the point.

"If he'd only said a little more," sighed Sochi. "His 'Ohmygosh' doesn't really tell us anything. Except that it's completely out of scale with the situation."

Evans had almost forgotten the accomplice had spoken at all. Now, he brightened. "Could you tell, Dr. Sochi, if by any chance he was a Southerner?"

He received an odd look from Ambrose and an exasperated one from Sochi. "You can't tell much from three words spoken under that kind of stress," Sochi noted. But as he ran Evans' question over in his mind, it obviously began to grow on him. "But there is a trace of something regional to it. I suppose it could be Southern. At least, it's possible."

For Evan Evans, another chink had fallen into place. Slipping one of his tiny cigars into his mouth, he hurried down the hall to the workroom to tell the officers to add something new to their description: that Armageddon might be accompanied by a young Southern boy.

For the moment at least, the one truly significant fact —that the accomplice could be a mentally retarded adult —was ignored. Except by Ambrose. Slowly, he developed a picture of Armageddon and a retarded adult in what was an almost slave-master relationship. Armageddon with someone advanced enough to do simple errands and run the camera, but someone not developed enough to challenge—or even understand—what Armageddon was doing. An unquestioning worshipper at his feet. And suddenly, it became a picture that fitted Armageddon compellingly well.

Sunday, July 12—Armageddon minus eleven.

Lars Colonius would have smiled at some of these developments if he'd known about them. And if he'd had the time. But he was as deeply concerned with getting ready for Armageddon Day as the authorities were. From Goddard on up, the government still clung to a thin ray of hope that the date would pass with nothing having happened; their private world of the important and powerful was more than amply protected, and there was to be a meeting with Ambrose later in the week to check out his point of view on the areas they might have missed. Already, elaborate security precautions were planned for any possible government targets within the entire time frame on either side of Armageddon Day. Ambrose kept trying to broaden Goddard's point of view on targets to include other than political or governmental figures, but so far was not having any great success.

Although Colonius still faced a good deal of work getting ready, his problems were more concrete. He knew the precise time, date, and place of the target and was armed with something the government *didn't* have: absolute certainty that he would go through with it. Colonius sat now, carefully crossing items off a master checklist. Instead of the Regency, when he and Einstein went back to New York, it was to the Americana. There were several reasons for this. The Regency was by no means small, but it was run with the intimacy and personal attention of a small hotel; the desk managed to keep a discreet eye on the comings and goings of its tenants, something which was all right for the earlier stages of the plan, but a possibly dangerous inconvenience in its final phase. The Americana was huge and impersonal, filled with the ebb and flux of conventions arriving, meeting, and leaving. It was an easy place to lose yourself in. And importantly, the Americana, with its location on Seventh Avenue and the Fifties, was only a handful of blocks away from the site of Armageddon.

An item on the checklist caused Colonius to raise his head and study Einstein briefly. There was one thing on it which would not only be easy enough for Einstein to carry out, but would be safer for him than it would be for Colonius. But it was a fairly important one, and Colonius still wasn't sure if enough time had gone by since the trauma of Blue Goose to trust him entirely. Einstein had gone back to watching television cartoons, which probably was a good sign, but watched them with no trace of laughter, which probably wasn't. A suppressed giggle from him as he watched *Superdog* convinced Colonius that part of his remoteness was pure acting, and that the assignment might shake him out of his funk. It seemed to work. Einstein offered no comment, but merely nodded when told to go to the Hotel Regency and pick up mail waiting for them there; some of the sullenness seemed to disappear as he accepted the order.

Half an hour later, he was back with it. There wasn't much—but it was all that Lars Colonius expected: a pair of studio tickets to the Institute for the Blind's telethon. With them was a letter from a Mrs. deKay, thanking him profusely for the contribution and assuring him of anonymity. She quite understood, she said, how he would not want to be hounded by other charities. In the letter, she also said she was taking him at face value and not making any special provisions for his deaf and dumb patient; if, however, he changed his mind and wanted anything done to make the show more rewarding for the boy, Dr. Kraus had only to call her or her secretary and it would be handled promptly.

Colonius allowed himself a wan smile as he put the letter down. He had taken steps Mrs. deKay could never dream of to make the show more rewarding for himself. Walking back to his desk, he sat down and neatly crossed the item off the checklist and slipped it between the pages of the journal. The next major thing to get out of the way was the plastic explosive. He thumbed through the pages until a small slip of paper fell out. It was the name and address of the New York supplier passed on to him by Yasir Arbadi in Macon.

Colonius had already sent the Algerian his personal note of thanks for it.

Monday, July 13—Armageddon minus ten.

The head of the giant clamshell in the stern of the dredging barge hit the muddy water with a splash and disappeared. For a second, there was a crest of white foam; it was the solitary touch of white to the mud-clay surface of the Ocmulgee, and it only lasted briefly. Then the bubbling foam dissipated itself in the opaqueness of the river's surface and eddied away.

In the cab of the clamshell, Dell Witburn, a thick cigar stuffed into his pale, pasty face, worked the lever and pedals that controlled the scoop. Occasionally, he would lean out the opening of the cab to spit and see if he could clear the barge with it; so far this morning he hadn't made it. It was so hot that even his saliva was drying up. He swore and pushed the lever that dumped the clamshell into the stern of the barge, narrowly missing Titus with the load of sludge and mud just scooped from the bottom of the Ocmulgee. Titus' job was to rake, shovel, and hoe the sludge as flat as possible so it wouldn't make a pile too high for the sides of the barge; he was also supposed to shove any items not suitable for landfill off to one side, so the truck on Front Street, following their slow progress along the river, could pick it up and take it to the city dump. So far today, the Ocmulgee had yielded up one icebox, a variety of battered motors, wheels, and chains, and the badly rusted remains of a 1932 Buick.

As the new load of sludge hit right beside him, Titus jumped to one side as quickly as his hip-high boots would allow, swore, and looked angrily up at Dell Witburn in his cab. It was not on purpose, he supposed, but you never knew; a few years back, Witburn probably kept a white sheet neatly folded on the top shelf of his closet.

Witburn met the angry look by wrinkling his nose, not at Titus, but at the stink of the sludge. If it was bad up here in the cab, he hated to even think what it must be like down where Titus was. He waved good-naturedly to apologize for dropping the load so close—he'd seen the angry stare from Titus and figured that crazy black would find some damned way to take it personally—and started the cab slowly turning back around toward the bow to pick up another load from the river bottom.

But fool Titus was still yelling something at him, something so urgent the sound of it even cut through the roar of the clamshell's motor and the rasping clank of the gears. With a sigh, Witburn put the crane into neutral and leaned out of his cab to see what the hell was up with Titus now.

Titus was pointing to something his heavy rake had hit, backing away from it, still yelling something at him

143

Witburn couldn't understand. But the look on his face demanded attention. Swearing again, Witburn turned off the ignition, climbed slowly out of the cab, and started down toward Titus in the hold of the barge.

When Titus had first seen it, he thought it was another bottom chunk, the kind formed when enough sand mixed with silt to make a compact lump. Usually they weren't anywhere near as solid as they looked and he'd attacked it with his rake almost without thinking about it. But this one was different. When the rake bit into it, the tines cut into something and there was a ripping sound. The lump seemed to explode. Titus was hit in the face by a foul-smelling rush of gas so powerful it overwhelmed the stink of the mud-silt; the lump appeared to open up and split as the water ran off it, revealing edges of some sort of plastic covering; a partly decayed, wrinkled hand clawed at the air around Titus's feet as if trying to find something it could hang onto while pulling itself out of the mud-covered plastic sack.

"Jesus," Witburn whispered softly, and tried to spit over the side again. But his mouth was so dry now he barely cleared his own shoes. He nudged the sack with his boot and it split open wider to reveal more body stuffed inside. Wordlessly, he and Titus stared at each other, then quickly sloshed their way to the side of the barge and started waving frantically at the truck on the shore. It had a two-way radio in it, and somebody could call the police, and they could get their asses off this damned barge with its frightening sack full of human flesh.

Reemerging in Macon, Billy-Joe Armbruster was as lovable as ever.

Chapter Sixteen

You know, if they'd had to live in my time, Henry Ford and the Wright Brothers would still be running bicycle shops, Thomas Edison selling newspapers, and Marconi, I guess, working in a barbershop. Because the way things are these days, there's no room left for the brilliant odd-ball, the aggressive loner, or the self-taught genius. And those guys would've been just as unsuccessful and un-known as I am.

Every now and then you read an article saying this is because the world's grown so big and complicated. Balls. It's the system the Goddamned intellectuals have sold the world. They've got everybody so ready to trade indi-vidual risk for collective security, people don't see they're also trading personal potential for collective mediocrity. That, of course, is just the way the intellectual aristocra-cy wants things; it turns the world into an anthill society with them as Queen bug.

Well, the world's about to meet one guy that didn't fall for it. One guy with the brains and the guts to buck the system. Individual violence may not be the nicest way to prove my case, but it's the only way I could get anybody to listen.

This is an important point to make in the script for Armageddon Day. Otherwise, people could think I did it just to get attention. Or even worse, that it was the ran-dom act of a madman.

—Extract from the
journal of Lars Colonius

EVAN EVANS came into Ambrose's room early that morning, barely even stopping to knock. He had an exultant smile on his face and a torn-off sheet of telex paper in his hand; as far as he was concerned his Southern theory about Armageddon was now proven fact. "Read this," he said, shoving the telex at a still sleepy Ambrose. "It came in last night."

Groggily, Ambrose struggled to sit up in his bed and took the paper. It was from the FBI, but that's about as far as Ambrose got; Evans was already explaining it. This was one of Evans' more irritating habits when excited. Like many impatient people, he'd give you something to read and then tell you what was in it before you even got your eyes focused.

"The FBI's finally located the 'Binet' in 'Stanford-Binet.' Only it's not in Stanford-Binet," said Evan Evans happily, and lit up one of the tiny cigars. "It's in *Benay Venuta,* badly pronounced. From a radio broadcast—a nostalgia thing—talking about the thirties. The announcer who made it got a call from the station manager, who remembered the broadcast from about two months ago. The FBI's checked it out—compared voice prints—and it's the same recording Armageddon used."

Evan Evans, Ambrose thought, was looking very pleased with himself, leaning against the bureau and puffing contentedly. A whiff of the cigar smoke reached Ambrose and he felt a little shaken by the idea of a cigar so early in the morning. He put his feet over the edge of the bed and tried to generate some of Evans' enthusiasm in himself. "Do they know which town?"

"Well, it was a regional radio broadcast. You know the kind of thing—they make a recording of it and send it to several stations on a regional network. But, Goddamn it, Carlton"—Evans paused and looked straight at Ambrose for effect—"it was a *Southern* regional network."

When Ambrose still looked confused, Evan Evans had to explain his Southern theory—the All-Rite Shopping Center in Macon, Vernon Tuckerman's coming from North Carolina, the "mushy" accent described by the fat

146

lady at the Blue Goose, Dr. Sochi's new analysis of the Fire Island tapes indicating at least a possibility that the "ohmygosh" had a Southern inflection—and now, the tracking of a word on the original tape to a Southern regional radio network. It was pretty conclusive.

But as Evans continued, explaining how the police network had special instructions to concentrate on Southern areas, Ambrose began to wonder if it was as useful as it was conclusive. He used the time calling room service gave him to find a gentle way of exploring this. "I'm not terribly sure where it gets us at this point though, Evan. I mean, Armageddon may come from the South all right, may be a Southerner along with his accomplice, but he certainly isn't there now. He's been strangely quiet, but the last we knew for sure he was in Ocean Grove."

Evans appeared unfazed. "Agreed. But if we can get a line on his hometown—or where he was operating from when he started all this—we can probably get a line on where he is now. My bet is that he's in New York. Or Washington. But there are all sorts of ways to get an exact location if we pin down his home base. People who knew him. People who saw him. People who know what he looks like now. Underworld types who may have supplied him—or may still be. Somebody somewhere has an address or telephone number that will tell us exactly where he's hanging out right now. In this kind of work, one thing leads to another. A mass of little details and unrelated facts, each one somehow aiming you toward the next. It's that simple."

Ambrose laughed as he slipped into a light bathrobe. "And that's as polite a way of telling me to stick to the business I know about as anything I've heard all week."

Evans shrugged and puffed furiously on his tiny cigar, which seemed in danger of running out of oxygen from all his talking. "OK, but I'm a hunch player. Every good cop I've ever known *is;* it's the one thing TV gets right about us." He gave up the puffing, forced to relight. "And my hunch tells me that we're nearer to closing in on Armageddon than anytime since Goddard blew the lobby stakeout."

By now, Ambrose desperately wanted to brush his

teeth, wash his face, and go to the bathroom before breakfast arrived. But Evan Evans, in his excitement, showed
no sign of leaving. "I hope so," Ambrose said, and leaned
against the bathroom door to help get the point across.
"But I wish to hell we had a better idea of what the
target was. On that, I've got my own hunches. But not
built on facts or details or anything much else. Pure instinct. And as open to being wrong."

Evans finally took the hint and started for the bedroom door. With one hand on the doorjamb, he turned
and paused. "If we can nail him first, we don't have to
worry what his target is."

Despite his effort to encourage Evans' enthusiasm by
looking cheered by his news, Ambrose found his voice
growing grimmer as he thought of the elusive target again.
"There's so damned little time, Evan. Nine days. That's
all we've got."

It was Evans' turn to sound encouraging. "Don't worry.
It's plenty."

Going out through the door, Evan Evans wished he
felt as confident as he sounded.

In Macon, some more of the little details and unrelated facts that Evans had mentioned were coming together. But once together, there they stayed. The Macon
police had no reason to connect the discovery of Billy-
Joe's body with what they'd seen on television, read in
the papers, or seen in the new set of flyers on Armageddon currently tacked to their bulletin boards. Fingerprints
and dental records established Billy-Joe Armbruster as
pretty much what he was: a petty criminal with underworld connections, but so minor as to be very much on
the outer periphery of even the kind of organized crime
Macon supported. They had no address for him, and
none was forthcoming.

The body was naked, so there were no pockets to
search for notes or letters, and no billfold to suggest his
current connections or activities; the only clue they had
was the plastic clothing bag used to suffocate him, and
there was only one small fragment of a store name re-

maining on it by now. Not very much hope was held out for tracking this down.

Even after his name and the story of his being fished out of the Ocmulgee River by the dredging crew was printed, there was no one in town willing to admit they even knew him.

This included Mrs. Spiers, landlady of the Sweet Laurel. Her first reaction on seeing his name in the paper was a shriek of pure anger. Billy-Joe had disappeared without paying his bill, but this was not a new experience to her; since he'd left all his belongings in his room, she assumed he would return one day, pick up his things, and pay her then. Quite a few people had done this in the past. But Billy-Joe had gone and gotten himself killed somehow, his head inside one plastic bag, his whole body stuffed into another, and both dumped into the Ocmulgee. To Mrs. Spiers, this was unpardonable.

In her initial fury, she considered calling the police and telling them. It wasn't mentioned in the papers, but maybe he was carrying money when he sank. A variety of reasons made her decide not to. Mrs. Spiers harbored a deep mistrust of the police, one heightened by the fact her license had long ago expired. Too, calling would bring police crawling all over the Sweet Laurel, and some of her other tenants might get nervous and disappear on her. But mostly it was the thought that they would surely impound Billy-Joe's collections of guns—she'd seen it only once during her weekly "lick and a promise" treatment of the room, but it appeared extensive—and the guns represented hard cash on the market.

This thought, along with her morning pint of bourbon, sustained her until noon. At twelve-thirty she investigated Billy-Joe's room and found the collection both extensive and intact. By one o'clock she had made a couple of telephone calls and arrangements for their sale were already underway.

By two thirty, there was no sign at the Sweet Laurel that Billy-Joe Armbruster had ever existed.

"You're going to have to practice moving around more naturally." Lars Colonius made this observation while sitting backwards on a desk chair, his legs straddling the seat and his arms folded and resting atop the chair back. "You know, *loose*. Right now, you're as stiff as a robot."

Einstein giggled. Now that they were back to playing games, the last trace of sullenness seemed to be disappearing. He rocked back and forth the way he'd seen robots do on television and giggled again. "I am the servant of Ur," he mimicked in a deep, toneless voice. But the expression of displeasure on Colonius' face brought him up sharply and he stopped clowning. "It ain't easy, Mr. Colonius. With all this stuff. It just ain't easy."

They were practicing with the fishing vest and other equipment for Armageddon Day. Every loop and pocket of the vest was stuffed with tightly rolled newspaper to represent the bulky plastic he would be carrying. These didn't provide room enough for a sufficient charge, so Colonius had stapled additional pocketlike holders on the inside of the vest as well. For the moment, to accustom Einstein to the real weight, lead sinkers were pinned to the bottom of the vest; knocking together as he walked, they made a dull, ominous sound that rattled even Colonius.

In each trouser pocket was an energy cell, wired independently from one another so that the accidental breaking of one circuit wouldn't cut out the other. In each hip pocket of the pants, Colonius had put a thin electrical timer which could be set to close the circuit at a preset moment; these were also independently wired as fail-safe devices. And as further insurance, Einstein's jacket pockets would each have a manual switch with a safety cover.

The effects of what he was carrying—as well as the reason for his carrying them—were not told to Einstein. In fact, all the wiring was carefully hidden inside rubber tubing covered with bright red cording so that Einstein would have nothing to remind him of the Blue Goose. The timers —before being wrapped in adhesive tape so that only their setting dials were visible—were explained away as "a sort of alarm clock—you'll use it to interrupt the show, you see." They would interrupt the show all right —but not before the threat of them had made Lars Colonius, if only briefly, the most highly visible person in the country.

As it often did, the thought of how close this was swept through Colonius's mind without warning and made him feel suddenly and intensely contented. Very easily, it could have extended itself into a daydream, and Colonius had to fight himself to push it out of his brain.

He cleared his throat loudly. "Loose, stay *loose*," he commanded Einstein. "Now, try sitting down. Nice and easy . . . watch it . . . don't tighten up . . . *that's* it." Einstein was sitting in the desk chair, upright and stiff as stone, looking straight ahead of him with a petrified expression on his face. Colonius sighed and patiently started him over again. As with the camera and the deaf and dumb imitations, once he had fully accepted it as a game, Einstein would do just fine. It was only the thudding of the lead sinkers that was making him self-conscious.

With a reassuring smile, Colonius unhooked the sinkers from the vest and decided to let him practice without them for a while. He'd have to think of something else that didn't make so much noise. For Armageddon Day itself, of course, the plastic would provide its own weight.

Einstein turned toward Colonius, his face eager but anxious. "Am I doing it right, Mr. Colonius? Am I doing it right?"

"Fine, fine. It's getting there. You'll be the hit of the show." And Colonius laughed, because he hadn't counted on the double meaning. And because long before they got to Einstein's role, he would have stolen the show for himself. And without even leaving his suite at the hotel.

The daydream threatened to intrude again as Lars Colonius began to figure how many million people would be watching. Twenty? Thirty? With numbers that big, it didn't really matter.

His figuring stopped abruptly. Einstein, taking Colonius's laugh as a sign of approval, was doing his robot thing again. "The servant of Ur will steal the show, the servant of Ur will steal the show," he boomed in a thundering singsong, and walked stifflegged across the room.

This time Colonius's laugh was genuine; Einstein *was* fully back in business. But it was time to silence the servant of Ur for a while and give himself time to catch up on his own work. With a gesture, Colonius waved Einstein back into the desk chair and told him to practice sitting down and standing up without looking so self-conscious about it, and then turned to finishing up the script. It would take a lot of words to cover that much film. A lot of words.

Chapter Seventeen

Once this thing breaks, people are going to go looking for all kinds of reasons why I picked the Institute for the Blind telethon. Because he's a shrink, Dr. Ambrose with probably say it was to get back at my old man; he walked out on us, you know, when his eyes went bad and he couldn't work anymore. But that's a crazy idea. The New York *Times* editorial—they always do one on anything that shakes them up, so I think I'll rate at least one—will probably find symbolism in a guy standing up to a society blind to its own indifference. But that's even crazier.

The one and only reason I picked the Institute for the Blind show was that it was live. With just about everything, even the news, on tape, finding a live show these days isn't easy. But this is really a kind of hijack—the ultimate hijack, with millions and millions of people watching—so it had to be on the air live or it just wouldn't work.

Maybe I shouldn't go putting this fact down on paper. Maybe I should let people think I really had some deeper reason for picking it. That *Times* kind of symbolism begins to grow on you after a while.

> —*Extract from the*
> *journal of Lars Colonius*

Wednesday, July 15—Armageddon minus eight.

"I THINK this whole operation ought to be moved to Washington. There's a few days left so we still have time for it. That's where we've set up the command post for Armageddon Day, and it's crazy to have your part of it still operating out of New York." Goddard, pacing the room, stopped to turn and see what sort of reaction he would get from Ambrose and Evans. He got about what he expected.

"No." Ambrose said this flatly, in a tone indicating it was a statement of intent, not opinion. "It's better here." Evans nodded agreement through a puff of cigar smoke.

With an expression designed to look as if he were giving Ambrose's reply serious consideration, Goddard stood in the center of the room, staring at the ceiling, his hands jammed into the back pockets of his trousers. He suddenly brought his eyes down to the two men, giving his head a small shake of bewilderment. "I'm not sure I agree. Communications, for one thing. Much tougher. I think we should all be together in one place. And Washington's the obvious one. Kern Eckhardt is outside for the briefing and I was hoping I could tell him that—"

"No."

"To begin with," explained Evan Evans, trying to soften the edge of Ambrose's tone a little, "we have the police network all over the country geared to reaching us here. In New York. Right now, some of the things they're coming up with show a lot of promise. Changing signals on where we are would slow everything down."

Goddard faltered. Dealing with Eckhardt—he represented the National Security Council in the Armageddon crisis—obviously worried him; possibly moving the operation to Washington was Eckhardt's suggestion, and Goddard was used to taking suggestions from people like him as orders. In any case, the degree of resistance he was getting to the move clearly surprised him.

A Tijuana 12 was produced to indicate that Ambrose's rebellion was not to be easily put down. "Moving it would also affect Armageddon himself," noted Ambrose. "He knows where we are—here. There's just a chance he might try to talk to me on the phone. Well, we blew the lobby stakeout by having too much officialdom hanging around; if Armageddon had to get himself transferred by a series of operators all the way to Washington, we could do the same thing all over again."

Ambrose received a grateful look from Goddard for putting the fate of the stakeout in such gentle terms, but it was rapidly replaced by one of skepticism as Goddard considered the rest of what the doctor had said. "You don't really expect Armageddon to just pick up a phone and call you, do you?"

"It's possible." Ambrose rocked back and forth in his chair studying the thin curl of smoke from the cigarette. "To relaunch a time-honored platitude, hate is very close to love. A man like Armageddon probably doesn't allow himself to display much of either, yet he allowed himself to show hate when he came looking for me with a gun. And he might now allow himself to display the reverse—disguised as something else, of course—and try to make at least verbal contact with me. A sort of love/hate, father/son thing. I want to be where it's easy for him to reach me. And that's here, not in Washington."

A look of wariness crossed Goddard's face. Ambrose didn't usually go in for this sort of psychological speculation, which was one of the reasons Goddard could put up with him at all. But it gave him a face-saving device for giving in to Ambrose's virtually flat refusal to shift operations to Washington. "Well, if there's any chance of that, of course. . . ." Goddard let the sentence trail off and shrugged to show he wouldn't press the move any further. "Eck's outside. I suppose we ought to get him in here and have him brief us." There was a pause while Goddard considered saying something further and finally decided he would. "I'd appreciate it if you didn't mention that love/hate thing or the possibility that Armageddon might call you; Eckhardt's very bright but I don't think he'd understand it."

With a laugh, Ambrose looked at Goddard. "What you mean is, *you* don't understand it, isn't it?"

The remark appeared to go unnoticed by Goddard, although his next request to Ambrose was posed in sharper tones than he usually used. "I'd also appreciate it, Carlton, if you'd put that damned reefer out before Eckhardt comes in. I have no idea whether he can recognize the smell or not—I would doubt it, somehow—but I don't want to take any chances on embarrassing the Justice Department." With a flourish, Goddard opened a side door to the office and began fanning the room to help chase the smoke out.

Feeling like a truculent child, Ambrose took another long puff and made an elaborate display of grinding out the remains of the Tijuana 12 in the ashtray. Goddard stared at it a second as if it might poison him to touch it, then picked up the ashtray and dumped it down the toilet in the bathroom, flushing it several times more than necessary. Ambrose and Evan Evans exchanged a smile; it was remarkable to realize that even in a situation as serious as the Armageddon crisis, Goddard's primary reaction to Eckhardt was mostly simple, bureaucratic reflex.

"Eck" was ushered in and introduced. He was almost a caricature of a White House adviser, with a slim, black and chrome attaché case apparently growing out of his left sleeve. His briefing was succinct, clipped, and allowed very little room for minority reports.

The prevailing view in D.C. was the same as Goddard's: Armageddon's target would be a governmental figure, function, or object. For the two days on either side of the date announced by the tapes as Armageddon Day, the President would stay at Camp David. This, Eckhardt pointed out, was already kept so closed to the press corps that additional security measures and forces could be put in place without drawing attention. While there, the President would see virtually no one; he went into isolation often enough so that it should arouse little suspicion.

The Vice President would also disappear for the same time period. He would spend the time at the underground National Security Headquarters, the alternate command post built during the days of nuclear saber rattling. Without any comment, Eckhardt pointed out that this arrangement, besides protecting the Vice President—he had, after all, been the subject of the original threat—would provide for an orderly succession in the event something unexpected should happen at Camp David. Calmly, Eckhardt paused in his briefing, silently decided his last statement overstepped the bounds, and immediately and loudly reassured the room that the possibility of anything happening at Camp David was, of course, very small indeed.

156

Reaching into his pocket, Eckhardt lit a cigarette, then discovered he had no place to put the match; Goddard had left the ashtray in the bathroom. Evan Evans, his face a mask, provided him one from a side table.

The Cabinet, the Supreme Court, and the White House staff, continued Eckhardt, would be given particularly heavy protection. The leaders of the Congress were more of a problem, since any increase in the security on them would be immediately noticed by their peers and tend to pinpoint Armageddon Day. This raised a point on which the President had only given them a decision that morning. On July 22, the day before Armageddon Day, a joint session of Congress had long been scheduled. The Congress was to be addressed by The Honorable Mr. Selden, Prime Minister of New Zealand, who was already miffed that his private audience with the President would now be an informal one at Camp David instead of a full-blown formal affair at the White House. Since a joint session would involve all members of both houses, the Supreme Court, the Cabinet, and the *corps diplomatique,* the security forces desperately wanted it canceled; the session would almost be an invitation to Armageddon. But the State Department felt that Prime Minister Selden might take this as a further slight, since he was already aware that his Socialist government was not popular in Washington. When the question was put to the President, he was adamant. The joint session would be held. Canceling it would be an admission that the United States government could no longer protect its officials from its citizens.

A look of pride appeared below Eckhardt's trim crew cut as he finished quoting the President. "He was firm, very firm."

"I hope," said Evan Evans, "that he was equally firm about the joint session having ample security, preentry checks, searches, and so forth."

Goddard looked outraged. "You can't very well frisk Supreme Court justices and ambassadors."

But Eckhardt stayed icily calm. "There will be no one admitted to the visitors' galleries. Press coverage will be by pool reporters, and television by pooled camera facilities. It's going to cause a fuss, but it's the best we can do."

157

An entirely different area he wanted to explore was waiting poised on Ambrose's lips, but Eckhardt was determined to plow ahead. He ignored the expression on Ambrose's face that indicated the doctor was about to speak, consulted the schedule of major events he was working from, and went on to the next matter. On the other side of Armageddon Day, he noted, there was a large function scheduled for the United Nations in New York—a reception for the members of the new government of Zambia. The Secretary General had been spoken to, and, although the details of the problem could not be fully explained to him, he had agreed to postpone the meeting until later in the month. A total breakdown in the air-conditioning system would be used to account for the delay.

Putting the list of events to one side, Eck extracted another sheet from his attaché case and outlined precautions being taken around government buildings. The White House was to be closed—for "repairs." The Lincoln Monument would be roped off for "cleaning and refurbishing of the stonework"; the Statue of Liberty would be banned to visitors because of a "threatened demonstration by militant American Indians." These subterfuges would protect the buildings from being damaged in case Armageddon's target was a symbolic object rather than a person. But the Washington Monument, Eckhardt conceded, was giving them double fits; a skilled marksman could both use its symbolism *and* kill any number of people simply by barricading himself in its top and using a long-range rifle with a sniper scope. From there, he could pick off strolling passersby almost anywhere in the Capitol complex. It was to be closed and sealed for the entire time period on either side of Armageddon Day; the Capitol engineer would issue a statement that there was a possibility of sinkage in part of the monument's foundation, rendering it temporarily unsafe to visitors. This last item caused Eckhardt to offer his only smile of the briefing. "The engineer—he couldn't be told the real reason he was being asked to issue the order, of course—got incredibly upset. He thought it made the monument sound like the Tower of Pisa."

No one laughed. But the pause gave Ambrose a chance

158

to ask his question. "What if Armageddon doesn't have a government 'thing' or figure in mind? What if it's some entirely different kind of event or person?"

Turning, Eckhardt looked confused. With an annoyed wave of his hand, Goddard sought to dismiss the question. "Dr. Ambrose has a personal theory that Armageddon might go after an entertainment event or figure rather than a government one. He thinks Armageddon himself may be a former actor." Goddard laughed too loudly. "If that's all he is—an actor—I'm not too worried."

"So was John Wilkes Booth," snapped Ambrose. He felt himself reaching for his cigarettes, but struggled with his hand and brought it under control; there was no point in getting Goddard any angrier than he already was.

The hostility between them was reaching Eckhardt. And Ambrose's riposte had gotten to him, too, although he didn't quite know how to handle it. "Well," he said, looking back and forth between them, "it's built on a different assumption than ours, but I'm not sure we shouldn't be prepared to handle it."

Abruptly, Ambrose leaned forward. "That list of events you have. Is it only government functions, or is it everything?"

"Everything of any importance, doctor." Eckhardt scanned the list, then handed it to Ambrose with a helpless gesture.

Ambrose quickly ran down it. Since the five-day period fell in the middle of summer, there wasn't a great deal on it: The gala openings of two movies, one in New York, one in Chicago; a jazz festival on the Hudson River; a special chess tournament with Bobby Fischer in Denver; and a rock concert in L.A. The list also noted that the Tanglewood Music Festival and the Jacob's Pillow Ballet would be in session during the period, and listed the dates and cities of the various baseball games. At first, Ambrose concentrated mostly on the Tanglewood Festival; the tape of Bernstein and Armageddon's claim to have been a concert pianist made it intriguing, but it didn't quite feel right. Not enough important names involved.

"Bobby Fischer, Bobby Fischer," mumbled Ambrose, as Eckhardt and Goddard studied him; Evan Evans had settled his vast roundness into a chair and was doing his teeter-totter act against the far wall. "Bobby Fischer has the kind of big name Armageddon would be attracted by," Ambrose said slowly. "But the audience at a chess tournament is necessarily small. So *it* doesn't fit either."

His eyes came to rest again on the rock concert in L.A. Mick Jagger and the Armageddon tape hadn't made sense at all. Or maybe it had. Maybe Armageddon was trying to tell them something. The rock group on Eckhardt's list of dates was the Jefferson Airplane, and it was set in the Hollywood Bowl. That would be a big audience, how many he wasn't sure, but big enough.

"This Jefferson Airplane thing in L.A. How many people see a show like that?" he asked. It was an idle question in a way; Ambrose was buying time to let the idea better form in his head, while keeping the subject open with Eckhardt and Goddard.

For a second, Eckhardt looked lost, but tugged at an earlobe and struggled with an answer. "It depends whether it's being televised or not. If so, it's probably on tape here and blacked out there. I can find out, of course. In the Bowl itself, possibly sixty or seventy thousand."

"The television part," said Ambrose thoughtfully, "probably doesn't matter too much. But that event should definitely be given full security. Sixty or seventy thousand people is enough for anybody."

In retrospect, it seems curious that Dr. Carlton Ambrose should come so close to the heart of the plan, and then miss the most critical ingredient. But he, as had everyone from the very beginning, continued to underestimate the size of Armageddon's dream.

Thursday, July 16—Armageddon minus seven.

At first, the Macon police thought they might have got lucky. For while the plastic clothing bag they'd found knotted around Billy-Joe's head had only fragments of a store name left on it, they discovered a printer's code number, fully intact, farther up on one side of the bag. With this number, and the few letters of the store name they *did* have, they were able to trace the clothing bag back

to the men's store on Hawthorne Street. The police hoped
that someone at the store might remember Billy-Joe's
face or his name. Or that, if nothing else, the store could
provide an address list of its customers and who'd bought
what. That, even assuming Billy-Joe was using a phony
name, they might get a line on where he lived, and from
that, who his friends were, whom he'd been seeing, and
possibly some clue to who killed him.

But their luck ran out on them quickly. No one in the
store could identify Billy-Joe's picture or remember ever
having heard the name. The store manager said they sold
well over two hundred garments a year that came in plastic bags like that, and that virtually all of their sales were
for cash. No addresses were kept for cash sales, he explained. The best he was able to do was to supply a small
mailing list of their regulars, and the police glumly had
tracked all of these down without discovering anyone who
had ever seen or heard of Billy-Joe.

They had no way of knowing that nobody in the men's
store would remember Billy-Joe Armbruster's face for a
very good reason: He'd never even been inside the place.
Or that their plastic clothing bag had originally come
with a suit bought for Einstein by a man named Lars
Colonius. Or that there was any connection at all between
the Armageddon plan and the body found half-buried in
the silt of the Ocmulgee.

So when Evan Evans' private police network called
them (because of a growing suspicion that the location of
the All-Rite Shopping Center was no accident, Ambrose
had suggested a special check with Macon authorities),
they had little to report. No, nothing unusual going on.
Well, their murder rate was up a little—it usually ran
about eleven or twelve a year—but with the exception of
the usual winos, these were mostly crime-connected killings. Well, there'd been one odd one, but it had been
solved: an Arab knocked off by the JDL. Yes, the new
flyers had been received and posted. And they hoped it
was cooler in New York this time of year than it was in
Macon.

Evan Evans read the report on the contact with Macon

161

and frowned. After a second, he asked Deputy Chief Le-Clerc of New Orleans to call Macon back in a couple of days and check again.

His hunch was itching.

Chapter Eighteen

There are some people I hope very much are tuned in Armageddon Day. Dr. Ambrose, I know will be, because by then he'll be part of it. My father, of course. My mother—well, I'll have a few things to say about her, so it's a pity she's dead and can't hear them. Then, there's the principal of Taft Vocational and the bastard who turned down my audition at WDBT. The President? —I suppose it depends where he is.

Too bad I can't preempt a football game.

> —*Extract from the*
> *journal of Lars Colonius*

Friday, July 17—Armageddon minus six.

"AND I want the additional two sets to be color, too," Colonius said, his voice rising slightly.

The man at the desk looked at Colonius, rubbed the back of his neck thoughtfully, and went off to consult with somebody. Colonius had upset the Americana's desk clerk by demanding two additional television sets be installed in the living room of his suite. It wasn't a matter of money—Colonius had offered to pay whatever the charge would be—but the desk clerk had never gotten a request for three sets in one living room before. And this was especially odd because there already were sets in each of the two bedrooms of this particular suite.

Colonius spent the time drumming his fingers on the desk, looking irritated. The desk clerk returned to say that it was all right; the hotel's engineer thought the room's cable antenna would carry the extra load without problem. He and Colonius exchanged small nods and the clerk promised the sets would be in place by afternoon.

There was a considerable press of people at the desk, but Colonius thought he could still see a small shadow of doubt on the man's face. He decided to give the clerk an explanation; it was better not to leave anybody feeling too curious about him. "Good. I know it's an unusual order. But I'm doing a paper on the psychology of television commercials, and sometimes I have to be able to watch more than one channel at a time to catch them all."

The desk clerk smiled broadly to show that he understood, and that besides that, he hadn't really been curious anyway. It was not very convincing.

After another exchange of smiles, Colonius turned and fought his way toward the elevator through the milling people in the Americana's lobby. He wasn't sure where the inspiration for the television commercials came from; it had just appeared. But in a way, he supposed the Armageddon plan *was* a sort of commercial—for himself. And without any question whatsoever, the longest, most expensive, and most impactful commercial since the invention of the cathode tube.

Upstairs, Lars Colonius went quickly to his desk and checked the item off his master list. There was very little left to be done. The time needed to get from the Americana to Thirty Rockefeller Plaza had been stopwatched and recorded. The scripts, films, pictures, and sound tapes were ready. A few days earlier, he had considered buying a home video-tape camera and putting himself on tape addressing the audience directly, but the mechanics of it became impractical. Studios use a different size professional tape and probably wouldn't be able to broadcast it, the man at the store had told him, and Colonius himself had reservations about Einstein's ability to master the machine. A Brownie was one thing; even the simplest videotape recorder was something else. Grudgingly, he could also admit he might not come off too well on tape, and finally decided it was better to remain a disembodied voice. There was something more frightening about that anyway.

With a sigh, Lars Colonius pushed back the desk chair and looked at the list again, wishing there was more left on it to do. Or less time to do it in.

Fifteen minutes later, out of sheer boredom, he lay down and was sound asleep on his bed.

Saturday, July 18—Armageddon minus five.

The tenor of things at the Westbury was precisely the opposite. All of a sudden, there seemed an enormous amount to be done and very little time left to do it. The security of governmental figures, both national and international, as well as the protection of national monuments such as the White House and Mount Rushmore, was now completely in the hands of the National Security Council. Through Goddard, the council would be kept informed of any developments that would affect its arrangements; similarly, through Eckhardt, Goddard and Ambrose would be kept up to date. Reluctantly, Goddard had decided he should be in New York for the critical time period. His own instinct was to be in Washington—he was still firmly convinced the target was there—but Eckhardt convinced him that it was more important for him to stay with Ambrose and try to head off Armageddon or find what the target was. Goddard grumbled, but obeyed.

Evan Evans at first considered flying to L.A. to be on hand during the concert by the Jefferson Airplane at Hollywood Bowl, but decided against it; he wanted to stay near the police network in case the Southern theory paid off. Recently, one more piece of evidence had been added to support it; the regional Southern radio network that had broadcast "Binet" covered Macon. But this in itself proved little, and for the moment, Evans decided merely to continue pressure against the whole Southern region.

He ran into unexpected difficulty with Ambrose on this point. "Look," said Ambrose suddenly, "I want you to zero in on Macon. Call the police there—go there yourself if you have to—and tell them you think it's Armageddon's home base. Tell them to pull out all the stops."

It was unusual for Ambrose to give him a direct order, and Evan Evans found himself mystified. "Macon? You're

165

that sure? Just because the first picture was taken there?"

"Not just because it was the first picture," snapped Ambrose. "Because it was the one *different* picture." Evan Evans stared at Ambrose. The doctor usually worked by indirection; he was now close to dogmatic. "Think about it," Ambrose continued, tracing an imaginary diagram in the air with one finger. "A man as insecure as Armageddon has to have a home base. It may be a hole in the wall, but it's a place where he can feel safe. Now, tie that fact to the picture. It was the only one not arranged for in advance. Taken by a newspaper. By accident. Which means the idea for the rest of the pictures probably started right then. And if the idea for the pictures only started then, it follows that Armageddon didn't go very far out of his way to be at the shopping center that morning. The best explanation for this is that his home base, the place he could feel safe, was in Macon."

For a moment, Evan Evans said nothing. He felt Ambrose was building a very large pyramid on a very small base of facts, but as long as it didn't interfere with the intensification of the Southern effort, it couldn't hurt anything. "Well," he answered, trying not to sound irritated at Ambrose's playing detective, "it's certainly worth a try." He heaved himself to his feet and started toward the door.

"There's one more thing." Like a good television DA, Ambrose's statement caught Evans just as he thought he was home free. Wearily, Evans turned to listen to him. "For Macon particularly, I want the stuff about his accomplice to include that he may not be an adolescent boy, but a mentally retarded adult."

Evan Evans was stunned; it was a point he considered settled days ago. "But, Carlton, you and I and Sochi agreed way back that it was a kid. That it had to be. Remember?"

"You and Sochi and the absent Dr. Fermi agreed; *I* didn't. The more I've thought about it, the more right a mentally defective adult fits my picture of Armageddon. A slave/master kind of thing."

"We went all over it, Carlton. He wouldn't be able to run the camera right."

"They're not always that helpless. It could be someone

166

just bright enough to do what Armageddon wanted, but not bright enough to figure out what his boss was up to. There are quite a few like that."

Evan Evans found his temper slipping out of control as he was backed into a corner. "The voice. Dr. Fermi said the voice—"

"Didn't quite add up," finished Ambrose for him. "And something Dr. Fermi didn't point out: A fifteen-year-old would have a hell of a lot more to say than 'Ohmygosh' if he saw two people being electrocuted *flagrante delicto*."

Inside, Evans was seething; ordinarily, he would have argued the point bitterly. But Ambrose's mood, his whole tenor, left little room, and with a shrug, Evans gave in. "You're the boss."

"I'm sorry." It made Ambrose uncomfortable to be reminded he was in charge of the task force, but he was sufficiently sure in his belief about the accomplice to resort to outright pulling of rank when it became necessary.

"It's going to raise a hell of a lot of confusion," Evans said, giving resistance one final little fling. But the expression on Ambrose's face didn't change, and, shaking his head, Evan Evans went out through the door.

Reluctantly, he had LeClerc call Macon and change the police flyer there to reflect the possibility Armageddon might be accompanied by a mentally retarded adult rather than by an adolescent Southerner, as originally noted.

If the Macon police could have acted on this last piece of information quickly and fully, a great step forward would have been taken. But they had their hands full with a local crisis, and, in spite of the pressure from New York, were not able to respond immediately. A young black activist, Blaine Carey of Chicago, had barricaded himself on the roof of the Ocmulgee Bank, smack in the center of downtown Macon, and was lobbing hand grenades and fire bombs—as well as taking an occasional well-aimed sniper shot—at anybody who got near the building. As with the Mark Essex affair in New Orleans, the first assumption was that there was more than one man on the roof. Virtually all of the Macon force, along with state police and special teams from Atlanta, were committed first to surrounding, then storming the rooftop. It was nowhere near as lethal an operation as the one in New Orleans (except for Blaine Carey), but it tied the police up in knots for days.

As a result of this, what police were left over—those in the field—were still operating on the old information, combing the flophouses, motels, and stores with a flyer describing Armageddon as a man with a Southern accent and his accomplice as a young Southern boy. The information was being revised, but owing to the confusion over the bank shooting, it was taking far longer than it should.

Still, when the break in Macon finally came, it was entirely due to Ambrose's stubbornness. And was entirely too late.

Sunday, July 19—Armageddon minus four.

The telephone call to climb on the first shuttle and fly to Washington immediately left Ambrose with little choice. It also left Goddard furious. When he asked Ambrose if he knew what it was about, the doctor could honestly answer he didn't. When he asked Ambrose who he was to see, Ambrose had to resort to evasion; Eckhardt had specifically instructed him to mention neither his, nor anyone else's name. It was the kind of evasion predestined to failure. Less than thirty seconds after he'd told Goddard he would be in Washington for the rest of the day, Goddard was already on the phone with Eck demanding to know why. Whatever Eckhardt told Goddard worked; Goddard raised an eyebrow, hung up the phone, and waved Ambrose toward the door. "My car's downstairs," Goddard grunted. "Take it and get your ass out to LaGuardia." From his expression, it was obvious that Goddard wasn't happy about it, but it was also clear whatever it was left him in no position to argue.

Coming through the entrance gate at Washington airport, a man from Eckhardt's office identified himself and then led him to Eckhardt, who sat waiting in the back of a black government limousine. During the trip into town, Eckhardt carefully steered away from any discussions on what Ambrose was doing there and kept them on light, noncontroversial topics. With some strain, they managed to devote almost the entire trip to the fate of the football Redskins next fall, although it was a subject Ambrose knew little about and one which he suspected interested Eckhardt very little either.

Sometime after they got into Washington proper, Eckhardt reached over and pulled down shades over all the windows of the limousine. "Your face—well, after that television interview it's a little too well known to newsmen to chance it," he explained. "And they've almost always got someone covering the gates."

They entered the White House grounds through a small door off the side drive. Half an hour later, they were ushered into the Oval Office. The President was sitting behind the vast desk and nodded at Ambrose as he entered, but did not rise. Ambrose was surprised that he appeared so much shorter than in his pictures, but part of this, Ambrose admitted, might be due to the size of the desk. Still—and Ambrose could not tell whether it came from the man or stemmed from the sense of awe and history that the room exuded—there was a feeling of power and urgency that seemed to flow from behind the desk directly toward Ambrose. Standing there awkwardly, Ambrose watched him as he made a small marginal note on the top page of a pile of papers, and thought of the picture of Lars Colonius perched impudently on the edge of the same desk in the LBJ Museum. He shuddered; it was pure Kafka.

There were two other men in the office besides the President, but they were neither introduced nor acknowledged. One of them—he looked vaguely familiar, Ambrose thought—indicated a chair with a tilt of his head and a small smile, but Ambrose stayed standing. The other man studied Ambrose without expression.

"Has Doctor Ambrose seen it yet?" asked the President. He was still writing something on one of the papers, and seemed to address the question to the room.

"No, sir." Eckhardt reached into his pocket and handed Ambrose a letter with a picture attached to its top. The letter was from Armageddon, and to make sure it got straight through, he'd clipped to it a copy of the photograph Ambrose had just been thinking about; news of its existence had not been released anywhere and it guaranteed its sender immediate attention. For Armageddon, it was an unusually short message—the first received in writing—but typically brash:

Dear Prez: Jul 19
The time is Armageddon minus three.
Please hold yourself available at around ten-thirty P.M. of the obvious day. A telephone call from you at that time could save a few lives. Some of them may even have voted for you. You will receive further instructions later.

—Armageddon

When he lowered the letter, Ambrose discovered the President for the first time had raised his head and was looking at him. "Why did he send that?" asked the President, still staring directly at him.

It was an easy question, but Ambrose found his voice had a sudden flat ponderousness to it. "He's a paranoid-schizophrenic, Mr. President." Ambrose was shocked to hear himself lapse into jargon, something he had scrupulously avoided since the day Goddard first brought him into the picture. "What I mean is, the man is torn between delusions of grandeur on one side, and feelings of total inadequacy on the other. To get a response from you would satisfy one and dispel the other." Ambrose thought a second, then added: "Temporarily, at least."

The President continued to look directly at him, his eyes expressionless and unmoving. "Should I? *If* it ever comes to it, doctor, should I respond?"

"We don't know yet what you might be asked to respond to. He mentions saving a few lives, so it is, in a sense, a ransom note. It may be for the lives of an airplane full of people. Or for a handful of performers on a stage. Or it could be for one person, one important person —possibly from government—that he somehow manages to get at gunpoint."

Ambrose saw a flicker of displeasure cross the President's face; he had not answered the question directly. The stare bore into him. "And my response?" the President insisted.

170

"You would have to weigh the lives involved against the possibility that responding at all would give encouragement to other psychopaths to re-create the situation. However, Mr. President, you should know that, in my opinion at least, anything this man Armageddon threatened, he is both capable and willing to carry out. As a doctor, then— and with other lives involved—I would have to recommend responding as he asks."

"That's the easy way out." The direct question had received its direct answer, and the answer was found wanting; the eyes now left Ambrose and moved thoughtfully on to the other men in the room, one after the other. "I don't see how I can be in the position of giving 'encouragement to other psychopaths to re-create the same situation.' It's the skyjacking thing all over again. When our policy was not ro resist, we merely stimulated imitation by others; air travel became a national disgrace. When our policy got tough, it stopped."

The other men in the room—with the exception of Eckhardt—nodded. Eckhardt gazed out a window, apparently to avoid having to commit himself. Ambrose had a feeling the President was trying out an explanation that could be used later publicly—there was a blatant flaw in the logic he'd expressed—and rose to the challenge. "I'm sure you've been told before, Mr. President, that one of the motivations of the skyjacker is to commit suicide— with someone else pulling the trigger. Resistance *aboard* an aircraft only made the act more appealing to him. The getting tough didn't work until it was done on the ground *before* boarding—the X-ray devices, the luggage and body searches, the quarantine areas established in airports. It was a policy of prevention, not resistance."

The President's eyes returned to Ambrose; a small flicker of a smile crossed his face and he shrugged affably. The President was as aware of the logical flaw as Ambrose was; the explanation had been given its trial run and proved not to be serviceable. He put both hands behind his head, leaned back in his chair with his eyes closed, and sighed. "That brings us back to square one—my response. If I don't give in, lives are perhaps lost and half the country blames it on my being too hardnosed. And they could be right. If I do give in, those particular lives are saved, but a week—a month—six months later, someone else is encouraged to try the same thing. Perhaps with even more lives at stake than the first time. Now, the other half of the country is heard from—it wouldn't have happened if I'd been tough enough the first time around. And *they* could be just as right." Opening his eyes, the President brought down his hands and swung the chair back toward the desk. "It's not an easy decision. And unfortunately, unlike skyjacking, there is no preventive response —unless you can think of one, doctor."

"Catch him. Or figure out his target, get there first, and stop him."

For the first time, the President stood up. Ambrose assumed it was a signal to Eckhardt that the interview was finished. So did Eckhardt. But as they moved toward the door, the President's voice stopped them.

"You don't think there's any chance he's just bluffing?" asked the President.

There was a wistfulness to this question that affected Ambrose; it was an appeal to spare him from having to make the decision. But Ambrose could only shake his head sadly. "I am afraid not, Mr. President. From what we know of the man, we have every reason to believe there's very little bluff involved. He has all the cards."

The President was back in his chair again. He returned to his papers to make the dismissal final, nodding slowly as he worked. The decision would have to be made, but not today, not now; a student of poker, he knew there were still too many variables.

All the way back to New York, Ambrose struggled to remember if a good poker player tries to beat a man with all the cards by running his own bluff. It would probably shape how the President played his hand.

But a quick comparison of the date on the letter to the President and the original countdown would have shown that Armageddon was already second-carding them all.

Lars Colonius slapped the journal shut for the last time. He had nothing more to enter in it. The case was either made clear, or it wasn't. Tomorrow, carefully wrapped and sealed, he would take it down to the Americana's front desk and have it locked in the safe. If something went wrong with the plan and he were killed before he had a chance to air his thesis, it was all there for posterity to read. If the plan went smoothly, there would be no need for the journal, and it could sit in the vault forever——or until the hotel took whatever legal steps are necessary to open an unclaimed item.

Half-heartedly, Colonius went over his plans for escape. This phase of the plan still needed refinement and work, but he was having trouble staying interested in it. Sometimes he wondered if he really expected to escape—— or if he really wanted to. He didn't want to be killed, that he was sure of. But the question of what he would do with himself after getting away was of so little interest to him that it was frightening. The idea of sinking back into obscurity, of once again being just another tiny black speck in an anthill society, was suddenly impossible. A grinding existence as a faceless automaton——and one always destined, apparently, to fail. Maybe, he thought, Dr. Ambrose was right in describing him as a born loser. For if he got away with the plan and then escaped free, it would be a fantastic accomplishment. But while his name, his voice, his thoughts, would be famous, he himself would have to stay in hiding. So to win would be to lose. He toyed with those words and by mistake they came out backward: To lose would be to win. The thought of death made Colonius shudder and he dismissed it.

From behind him came the sound of Einstein putting something down on top of the television set. Colonius turned. It was the package of films, tapes, and scripts that would be stashed in their hiding place tomorrow, waiting for H-hour. Everything else was ready. Colonius stood up.

"You know what we're going to do tonight, Albert?"

Einstein was so surprised to be called by his real name

that it took him a second or two to realize that Mr. Colonius was talking to him.

"We're going to have champagne, Albert. The biggest damned bottle of champagne this hotel can turn up."

"Whoeeeeee!" Einstein clapped his hands and hit his knees in excitement.

As an act, it was pretty convincing. Einstein didn't have the faintest idea of what champagne was.

Chapter Nineteen

Tuesday, July 21—Armageddon minus two.

THE FIVE-DAY maximum security time frame began at eight A.M., two days before Armageddon Day. Half an hour before that, the President helicoptered to Camp David, where he would stay until July 26. If the newspaper wag who dubbed it "Festung David" in the early days of the President's term could have seen it this morning, his sally wouldn't have seemed very funny: A mosquito couldn't get into the place unless invited.

At about the same time, the Vice President descended into a command post, deep under the ground, on the other side of the Potomac in Virginia. The National Security Council had, when it built the installation, equipped it with all the comforts of home, but the Vice President viewed these arrangements dimly; in spite of its spaciousness, the place was completely windowless and the idea of spending five days in the glare of artificial light was bringing on a touch of claustrophobia. Silently, he cursed the All-Rite Shopping Center and Georgia's Governor Jimmy Eggans; this was illogical, he knew, but Macon was where the whole Armageddon rhubarb began and he held the town, the state, and the governor personally responsible.

Would-be visitors to the Washington Monument, the Lincoln Memorial, and the White House grumbled on discovering they were all closed for one reason or another; one tourist reported this angrily to the Washington *Post*, but the paper assumed him to be a crank and never checked the story out. A similar report was received by the New York *Times* from a Brownie troop leader annoyed there had been no public mention of the "Indian uprising" at the Statue of Liberty (the closings were not announced in papers anywhere to avoid drawing attention to them). But the *Times,* afraid it was a criticism of their reporting rather than of the authorities, likewise ignored the report.

At the Capitol Building, FBI and Secret Service men were giving the House chamber a thorough search in preparation for Prime Minister Selden's address to the joint session the next day. They had reluctantly agreed not to frisk anyone, but had managed to install X-ray scanners at the entrances to the chamber (similar to those used at airports, only larger). These would, at least, alert them if someone was carrying a weapon, provided it was big enough to show up on their screens; Eckhardt only hoped none of the Senators wore steel back braces or metal-soled elevator shoes he didn't know about.

Out on the coast, a similar search would be made of Hollywood Bowl before the Jefferson Airplane appeared, but there was no way to monitor the entrances there for weapons. The most Eckhardt could get was a promise there would be an agent at every gate armed with the photographs of Armageddon.

Ambrose himself spent most of his time in his room, staring at the wall, trying to discover any possibly overlooked angles. He'd been over every tape, every photograph, every transcript, to see if there were any psychological clues to the target he might have missed. The probability board had been checked and rechecked. Sochi was still working to make sense out of the sudden input of show-business language, but so far could find no new evidence that might help. Armageddon's target remained as elusive as Armageddon himself.

In the "boiler room" of the private police network, Evan Evans was squeezing out the last ounce of effort in behalf of the Southern theory. On Ambrose's orders, Macon had been called twice more, but still had nothing relevant to report. Quite correctly, Evans suspected they were too preoccupied with the aftermath of the Ocmulgee Bank sniper to give them much attention; New York might be yelling at them, but the governor's mansion in Atlanta was yelling just as loudly and was a whole lot easier to hear.

176

Goddard seemed to be spending most of the time on the telephone to Washington.

At the Westbury, FBI and Secret Service men met endlessly. Telexes chattered back and forth, spewing out endless rolls of futile paper. Couriers crowded the elevators to the sixteenth floor.

The authorities were braced and ready. But, unlike Lars Colonius, not ready enough.

And no one was drinking champagne.

Wednesday, July 22—Armageddon minus one.

The call from the Macon police came in at four forty-five P.M. Evan Evans was down in the Westbury's Polo Bar, sipping a *Punt é Mes* and soda with Deputy Inspector LeClerc of New Orleans, "massaging him a bit," as he later was to put it, into making one final effort on the Southern theory. They shot for the elevators.

The information they got over the phone was a definite breakthrough: Armageddon *and* his accomplice had definitely been placed as living in Macon. And over a period of time. There was no address as yet, but they were working on it now; furthermore, they had strong suspicions that Armageddon was connected to the death of a minor underworld figure named Billy-Joe Armbruster, and they would work their stoolie grapevine to see what they could find out about Armageddon from that quarter.

Evan Evans was so exuberant he almost inhaled his entire cigar in the excitement. "Jesus Christ, if you can get us an address for him up here, you'll be national heroes. Goddamn. How'd you do it?"

There was a long pause; it was a question that Macon would rather he hadn't asked. Slowly, they told Evans the story from the beginning—the discovery of Billy-Joe's body in the Ocmulgee, the plastic clothing bag with the fragmentary store name, and the inability of anyone from the store to identify Billy-Joe from his picture. It seemed, they said, like the usual dead end to the usual gang killing.

But the district attorney's office, they explained, was under heavy pressure because of the town's rising crime rate, and refused to be as sanguine; the office insisted the police go back and get sworn statements from everyone involved before it would allow the case to be slipped quietly onto the inactive list.

Among others from whom affidavits were needed was James Corchran, manager and owner of a men's store. Waiting in the police station for a justice of the peace to show up and hear his oath, Corchran whiled away the time listlessly studying the bulletin boards. There he came across the flyer on Armageddon. It took him a few minutes to put it together in his head, but then he tentatively identified him from the picture as a man who had been shopping in his store. About two months ago, he thought. He wasn't sure at first—the man looked different from his picture —but he became surer when he read about the accomplice. It was the accomplice that made the incident stick in his mind at all, Corchran explained. The flyer, see, described him as possibly mentally retarded, and maybe that would explain the fight he and his wife had had over the pair after they left the store. His wife, Corchran said, insisted the giant of a kid was deaf and dumb, and that had been his own initial impression, too; he made noises, but no words, and did all his talking with those hand signals you see deaf and dumb people using. But when the kid was back in the changing room and thought no one could hear, he began speaking and Corchran overheard him; it was a crazy kind of talk, like a little child's, all excitement over the new suit. In spite of this, Corchran continued, his wife still insisted the youth was deaf and dumb and accused her husband of having made up overhearing him talk just to win his argument. The bitterness of the dispute was the only reason Corchran remembered the pair out of the thousands that came through his store every year; maybe, he suggested, the deaf and dumb thing was just an act to conceal the fact the youth was mentally retarded. Corchran couldn't wait, he said, until he saw his wife's expression when she heard he was right.

The police could. They got Corchran to deliver an astonishing number of details about the sale: The man bought two suits, one for himself and one for his deaf and dumb accomplice, and he must have been living in Macon at the time, because while the boy's suit fitted well, the man's did not. And the man, who seemed in no hurry about it, didn't return for a week to pick it up.

Evan Evans was staggered at the amount of information suddenly in their hands. Because of Ambrose's stubborn stand on the accomplice—as well as the truculence of the Bibb County district attorney—they now had established Macon as Armageddon's home base; through the underworld stoolie network—who would want to get the FBI and others off their backs as quickly as possible—they would probably shortly have an address for Armageddon. And an address in Macon should quickly lead to an address somewhere else. Incredibly, they not only had a description of the accomplice, but as soon as Corchran had gone back and checked his sales slips, would even know what clothes each was wearing.

There were at least thirty-six hours before Armageddon Day. As soon as the phone call from Macon was over, Goddard issued orders and FBI agents were called in from all over the South to help out in Macon. Special local TV news cut-in's were asked for by the Macon police to describe the accomplice. The underworld, badly shaken, was showing every sign of being almost pathetically eager to cooperate. It looked good.

Evans' enthusiasm even spread to Goddard. For the first time Goddard genuinely believed they had a chance of nabbing Armageddon before the fact—and it was no longer a matter of relying on questionable psychology, but on sound police practices.

Only Ambrose remained skeptical. It was too easy, almost. Corchran was right, and his wife was wrong; there was no question that the accomplice was not deaf and dumb. For Ambrose, the strangled "ohmygosh" on the Fire Island tapes was ample proof of this. But why, then, the deaf and dumb act? Was it done to confuse them, and had it been used elsewhere? Certainly, if so, it was a performance easily remembered and should perhaps be added to the police descriptions. But the doctor remained silent while he tried to figure out what this new element in Armageddon's game meant and if it could have any bearing on his ultimate target. Prudently, he had decided to keep all of these unanswered matters to himself for the moment.

There was too much enthusiasm on the sixteenth floor of the Westbury just now to raise somber questions like that.

If Evan Evans, Goddard, and Eckhardt could have seen what was going on in Armageddon's suite at five thirty that afternoon, their enthusiasm would have shriveled up and died.

Colonius had just put Einstein through a last rehearsal with the fishing vest—and this time the pockets and loops were not loaded with newspaper, but with plastic. Only the wires needed connecting and it would be operational.

"Very good, Einstein," said Colonius, and carefully hung the vest over the back of the chair. "You have about three hours until it's time to go, so you can watch television in your room or whatever you want."

Einstein looked wistfully at the three sets arranged in a shallow arc at one end of the living room, but Colonius shook his head, and Einstein, after grumbling a little, moped his way into his bedroom. Sometimes he didn't understand Mr. Colonius.

But Lars Colonius understood Einstein. He didn't want him in the room when he did the actual connecting of the wires from the batteries and timers to the charges. It was not because he was afraid Einstein would realize he was a walking bomb; the boy had accepted the story that all that would happen was a bell ringing to interrupt the show. As usual, he'd even made a game of it, sometimes racing around the room clanging like an alarm clock. But Colonius was nervous about anything that might remind Einstein of the "electric orgasm." The initial sullenness had long ago disappeared, but Colonius didn't know when something might come along and trigger it into action again. And letting him see the wires, he felt, might just be one of those things.

Pointlessly, he checked his wristwatch again. It would, according to earlier timings, take a maximum of fifteen minutes for Einstein to make his way to the old Belasco Theater on West Fifty-fourth street; the package of films and stuff was already stashed, waiting, at Thirty Rockefeller Plaza. There was nothing for either of them to do until it was time for Einstein to leave. To double-check, Colonius walked over to the desk and gave the checklist a final once-over. He could think of nothing, which was just as well; there was very little time left.

Because unlike the countdown they had both in Washington and at the Westbury, Colonius's calendar for today didn't read *"Armageddon minus one,"* it read *"Armageddon Day,"* and then was broken down into hourly components. From the beginning, he had been consistent about this deception. The only exception had been the letter to the President, when he had felt particularly arrogant and used the actual date. He assumed no one would notice the discrepancy. And no one had.

The more than thirty-six hours that Evans, Goddard, Ambrose, and Eckhardt thought they still had was actually less than three.

The activity in Macon, on the other hand, paid off more quickly than they had any right to expect. It was at six ten P.M. that "Fatback" Johnson, a smalltime bookie, appeared at Macon police headquarters. He was not there entirely of his own accord, police stations being a complete anathema to him. But in an earlier visit from a pair of higher-ups, men he laid off his bets with—and men who were aware that Fatback not only knew Billy-Joe Armbruster but occasionally used him to collect delinquent accounts—had bluntly suggested he volunteer all of his information about Billy-Joe forthwith.

At first, Fatback resisted, but the two gentlemen pointed out that the sudden descent of local police, state police, and federal agents into the Macon underworld was extremely bad for business, and that certain people even more important than themselves were very unhappy about it. A short unpainful call to the police would clear the air. Otherwise, they suggested, Fatback might go swimming in the Ocmulgee himself.

From Fatback, after a little sparring and fencing to make sure he wasn't incriminating himself, the police learned the name and address of the Sweet Laurel. Twenty

181

minutes later, a distressed Mrs. Spiers found herself letting the police not only into Billy-Joe's room, but into Lars Colonius's as well—the new description of the accomplice as a "blond, mentally retarded youth" was quickly connected. But there, once again, the search seemed to reach a dead end. The checks for room rent from Colonius, Mrs. Spiers told the police, came from different parts of the country at different times, although most of the more recent ones came from New York. The bank in Macon on which the checks were written had no other address for him. There was nothing found in the room to help the police, although there was plenty of evidence that it was Armageddon: excess film, stains from the home-developing kit, scraps of unused recording tape tucked away in a drawer, and a large supply of the heavy manila envelopes in which all the tapes and photographs had been sent to Washington. There were also plenty of fingerprints of both Lars Colonius and his accomplice, whose name Mrs. Spiers said was Albert. He had a last name, she supposed, but had never heard anyone use it.

All this information was telephoned immediately to New York, including the fact that they had, for the moment, reached an impasse. The bank was having its time locks breached so that an official could examine the microfilm record of other checks Lars Colonius had written, in hope the name of a New York hotel would be discovered, but this would take time. Meanwhile, the FBI was working on another angle: Somewhere close there must be a telephone Colonius used—and phone company records would show any long-distance calls made from it once it was found. But this too would take time.

Evan Evans and Goddard received the news calmly, although without taking any of the pressure off the people currently swarming across Macon. Evans, particularly, seemed confident. Passing Ambrose in the hall, the tiny cigar bobbing up and down in his mouth with excitement, he tugged on Ambrose's sleeve. "Goddamn it, Carlton. This time we're going to nail him. And *before* he gets to do anything."

Ambrose smiled and said nothing. He was through underestimating what Armageddon might have up his sleeve.

Chapter Twenty

THE FIRST telephone call came into the Westbury at nine zero two P.M. It said only that the caller was Armageddon and that he would call back in one minute. Dr. Ambrose should be prepared to talk to him immediately; the caller would only stay on the line a short period of time to avoid any attempts at tracing the call.

By the time the second call rang through, Ambrose was sitting in a room crammed with people, telephone amplifiers, and recording equipment; Goddard was walking nervously around the room, and Evan Evans leaned against one wall studying the tip of his cigar. When Ambrose's extension rang, an FBI man picked up another extension and dialed the waiting operator to start the tracing process and another FBI man started the tape recorder, which was hooked directly into the telephone line.

"Dr. Ambrose?" Coming out of the telephone amplifier, Armageddon's voice had a rattling, scratchy sound. Ambrose, for so long now used to hearing him as a patchwork of recorded voices spliced together, at first found it difficult to believe it was really Armageddon.

"Yes, this is Dr. Ambrose."

"Hi. This is Lars Colonius, although you probably only know me as Armageddon."

Evan Evans waved vigorously at Ambrose to make sure he didn't contradict this assumption; there was no point in letting Armageddon know they had been given his real name by Mrs. Spiers at the Sweet Laurel. Ambrose shook his head, annoyed at what he considered too many signals coming from the onlookers at the same time. "Of course. Hello, Mr. Colonius."

"Lars."

"Lars." Ambrose began taking notes. He found it curious that Armageddon wanted to be called by his first name; he had expected the opposite. "It's nice to talk to you, Lars. I thought you might call." Ambrose said this with a hint of desperation. There was something insane in the casual tenor of their conversation.

Possibly Lars Colonius felt this. Both his tone of voice and what he had to say changed abruptly. "I want you to listen very carefully. I'll only say it once, but, of course, you undoubtedly have a tape machine going and can double-check your memory." There was a pause, followed by a near-giggle, then: "I'm afraid I've been cheating, doctor."

There was another pause, of the kind familiar enough to Ambrose from sessions with patients to know what was expected of him. "I see, Lars," he said. "Cheating me how? . . . In what way?"

"About the timetable. The countdown I gave you. Armageddon Day isn't tomorrow; it's tonight. In fact, right now."

Ambrose struggled to stay calm as Evan Evans, moving quickly and agilely considering his size, raced out of the room to alert the police network. Goddard was only a few steps behind him, on his way to let Eckhardt know in Washington. Ambrose was waving his free hand, signaling them to be quieter as they rushed out of the door. "I understand, Lars," said Ambrose in a voice that fought to sound calm. "Although I don't understand why."

"A precaution, just a precaution." Colonius appeared to evaluate this for a second before adding defensively: "And I *did* put the right date on the President's letter. Two bits nobody noticed."

There was a querulous note to Colonius's voice now, and Ambrose decided to capitalize on it. If he could get Colonius involved enough, they might get the time they needed to trace the call's origin. "Oh, we noticed all right, Lars. It just seemed a little unfair after all those earlier tapes giving us another date."

There was another giggle from the other end of the phone, then Colonius's voice, which had gradually been growing more casual as he talked, suddenly changed back to a crisp, almost taunting tone. "You're trying to trick me, doctor. Into talking a lot so you can trace the call. It won't

184

work, of course. I've got one of those little black boxes phone freaks use, so the call is untraceable. All you'd probably find is that it's coming through Alaska or someplace. But I won't take the chance anyway." Colonius cleared his throat and over the amplifier they could hear him moving a piece of paper—a list, probably—to where he could read it more easily.

"Now, then. Instructions for the moment. *One:* Get a television set. Right there where you can watch it. *Two:* Have the bomb squad in downtown L.A. standing by— they might be busy. *Three:* Alert the networks the President may have a message of importance." The voice was speeding up as if Colonius were checking himself against a stopwatch to see how much longer he dared to stay on the phone. "I'll give you time for that and call back in precisely four minutes, doctor." A click and a buzz and he'd hung up.

The FBI man with the phone in his hand listened to a voice on the receiver, nodded, said something like "Thanks," and shrugged at Ambrose. There hadn't been time to trace the call.

The other FBI man reached down to stop the tape recorder. "Get a television set in here—fast," Ambrose ordered him. Goddard was already back inside the room and had heard the end of the conversation; Evan Evans followed a few seconds later.

With one hand on a phone Goddard stared at Ambrose. "What do you think?"

"He's a cool customer. Very cool," said Ambrose slowly, pulling at one earlobe as he tried to make an accurate assessment. "The only indication of any strain at all is the way his speech pattern alternates between the overly casual and the authoritarian. Whatever he's got cooked up, he means it."

Goddard, who had decided it was better to stay in the room rather than making further calls from outside, picked up a phone and asked to be connected with Eckhardt in Washington. Priority. Urgent.

The cigar in Evans' mouth stayed unlit as he raised his eyebrows in an unspoken question to Ambrose. "The bomb squad in L.A. I suppose I'd better call them. Your hunch about the Jefferson Airplane thing may be right."

Putting his hand over the mouthpiece as he waited for Eckhardt to come on the line, Goddard leaned forward impatiently. "It's not being televised. I checked it. In fact, I don't understand the demand for a television set in here at all. Or about calling the networks. Eck will faint."

"I'm sure our boy will make it all too clear to us when it suits him," noted Ambrose dryly. Goddard was beginning to annoy him again.

By now, Evans had decided that since Deputy Chief Gerhardt of Los Angeles was in the police network room, it was better if he handled alerting L.A. He grabbed the first passerby and sent him for Gerhardt, stepping back as two men with the television set rolled it into the room, hooked up the aerial to the cable box, and plugged it in. "Should we have them alert the Hollywood Bowl, too?" Evans asked.

Ambrose thought for a minute. "The FBI there, yes. The Bowl—well, we'd better wait until we see what Armageddon's up to. It could cause a full-fledged panic if they tried to empty the place."

Goddard was losing his temper. "Goddamn it," he yelled into the phone. "Where the hell is Eckhardt?"

A little self-consciously for once, Ambrose lit a Tijuana 12; it was not in his usual gesture of rebellion, but because he wanted and needed one. Suddenly, he slapped the top of the desk in front of him. "Somebody should have caught that changed date on the letter to the President. It was right there in black and white."

Covering the mouthpiece again, Goddard stared angrily at him. "*I* never saw the letter."

With a small sigh, Ambrose tried to think of a fitting answer. But his telephone rang again. Armageddon. Glancing at his watch, he checked the time. Two and a half minutes instead of four. Armageddon was cheating again.

"Hello? Is that you? This is Doctor Ambrose."

"Lars Colonius." The voice was back sounding cool and calm and unhurried. "Have you got the television set yet?"

186

"Yes I do, Lars. Right in front of me."

"Good." You could hear the crinkle of paper again. "Now, have somebody—I am sure you're not in the room by yourself, doctor—have somebody turn it to Channel 4."

"OK, Lars." Ambrose nodded at the nearest FBI man, who adjusted the channel selector. The picture flopped over once or twice, then steadied; the camera was showing a stage on which were set up long rows of tables. Behind the tables sat men and women—and some extraordinarily pretty girls—each one with a telephone in front of him. In the center of the stage was a raised platform flanked by two swiveling guest chairs. A large mock-up thermometer—its cardboard column of mercury currently registered zero—was at the rear of the stage. Behind this was a backdrop with giant cut-out initials spelling "I.F.B." The men and women behind the tables were all standing now, bowing slightly as the audience applauded them at the urging of some unseen voice.

"What the hell?" hissed Goddard at Ambrose.

Abruptly, his expression changed as Eckhardt finally came on the line and Goddard plunged into an urgent—but unheard—conversation with him. Evan Evans dived for a copy of the *Times* and scrambled his way through the second section looking for the television page.

"Channel 4 is on, Lars," said Ambrose calmly. "We're seeing it fine."

"OK. Now hear and understand this, all of you. What you're seeing on your screen is the telethon in behalf of the Institute for the Blind. It's a live broadcast. There is a bomb hidden in the studio, the Belasco Theater on West Fifty-fourth Street, but don't bother trying to figure out where; you'd never guess in a million years. It is a large bomb—about two kilograms of high-explosive plastic—and there is a large audience at the Belasco—maybe four hundred to five hundred people. The bomb is not controlled by a timing device, but is activated by a radio transmitter I have here with me." The paper rattled again; Armageddon was clearly reading directly from it. You could hear him clear his throat and when he resumed talking, his voice had the same speeded-up quality as it had toward the end of his last call, as if he'd just checked himself against a watch. "What I want you to do is keep cutting to shots of all the exits so I can be sure no one is leaving. The cameras are my eyes in the studio. If anyone appears to be—or if I even suspect anyone is trying—I shall fire the bomb immediately. I also want a package picked up at the reception desk of Thirty Rockefeller Plaza. It was left there to be picked up by a Mr. Armbruster—that's a phony name—and should be given to the television director at the Belasco as soon as you've briefed him. The package gives him instructions and material for what I want presented. My equal time, you see. Now these orders must be followed to the letter, or—well, I don't have to belabor the point. I shall call again in five minutes." The buzz of the phone after it was hung up seemed startlingly loud to the men in the room.

Shaking his head, the FBI man working the telephone trace turned to look at them. "No luck. It's almost impossible with a call coming in to a busy switchboard like a hotel's."

"Call all the rooms and tell people not to use their telephones, it's an emergency," snapped Goddard. His face showed that he'd come out on the losing end of an unpleasant talk with Eckhardt.

"There are over four hundred rooms," said the FBI man, helplessly, and shook his head. "All we've been able to establish so far is that it isn't coming from anywhere inside the hotel; we're getting the telephone company to spot any long distance calls coming to the number, but with direct dialing, that's no guarantee they'll catch it." The man's face clouded as an additional problem struck him. "And if he's really got the phone freak's 'black box' he mentioned, we'll never trace him."

Goddard shrugged wearily. He turned toward Evans. "Evan, would you handle the New York police? The theater should be cordoned off, but not—repeat NOT—entered. Also get their bomb squad on alert. I don't know why the hell he had us put the L.A. one on standby—either it was to throw us off, or this is just the beginning of something bigger."

As Evan Evans started out the door, Goddard began to tell someone at the FBI to go get the package from Thirty

188

Rock and bring it here. Ambrose was on the verge of protesting when his phone rang again. Ambrose looked at his watch; only a minute and fifteen seconds had passed.

"There's a couple of things I forgot." It was Armageddon's voice. Once again it had a defensive sound to it, as if embarrassed that he'd forgotten something in his script.

"Yes, Lars."

The quality of the voice changed abruptly. "And damn it, don't call me Lars all the time."

"All right. What do you want me to call you?"

"Armageddon."

"OK." This was the third time, Ambrose noticed, that Armageddon had changed what he wanted to be called. And in each case, the change followed almost immediately some expression of guilt, or defensiveness, or embarrassment. Ambrose had no quick idea as to what it meant, but thought it significant enough to make a note of it. "OK," Ambrose repeated, using no name at all, "you said you forgot a couple of things."

"That package at Thirty Rockefeller Plaza that's to be picked up. It isn't to be opened; it should go straight to the director. You can rattle it around to see that it's not a bomb if you want, but everything in it is in a very precise order and I don't want some damned clown pawing through it and messing it up. That's one thing. The second thing: Someone is to call the other two networks. Tell them to pick up the telethon from NBC—I want it on all three networks at once—as soon as I give you the order. Got it?"

Ambrose looked helplessly at Goddard; he wasn't even sure it was mechanically possible. Goddard had his head in his hands, trying desperately to figure if he should go along with this request too.

"Are you still there, doctor?" demanded Armageddon.

"Well, I just don't know enough about television to know if what you ask is possible, you see. But I can check—"

The voice was cold and hard. "Don't check, doctor; get it done. I'm no amateur you can kid along. The other networks can pick up the NBC feed off their tielines and that's all there is to it." In the short silence that followed,

189

the men in the room could hear Colonius breathing heavily. It was a potentially dangerous symptom and Ambrose turned in an urgent, silent appeal to Goddard, just as the voice on the phone returned. "Call them and tell them, damn it," Armageddon insisted, his voice rising. "They know how. All I have to do is—"

Goddard nodded a vigorous yes.

"Done," said Ambrose quickly. "We'll take care of it."

"That's better, doc." Armageddon paused and gave his nervous half-giggle again. "Christ, you guys give in easy."

Ambrose very much wanted to relax Armageddon a little, to take the tension off him, if only briefly. The half-giggle was an ominous sign. Gambling, Ambrose decided to try a light twist. "Civic pride," he explained. "We don't want you going around pressing any little red buttons that will blow up Fifty-fourth Street, you see; the mayor wouldn't like it."

This time Armageddon's laugh sounded genuine. "I like you, Doctor Ambrose. You've got class—in spite of what you said about me. You can call me Lars after all."

"Thank you, Lars."

Once again, the buzz of the abruptly hung-up phone seemed so sudden and so loud it startled them all. Ambrose made another note and looked at Goddard.

"I'll call NBC and tell them," Goddard said, "because the Belasco's their theater. But the other networks—that's up to Washington." With a disgusted kick at the table, he picked up the phone, jiggled for the operator, and braced himself for another unpleasant conversation with Eckhardt.

Ambrose looked at his watch: it was nine fourteen. Only twelve minutes had passed since the first phone call, yet he felt as if it were hours. The Armageddon plan had the unique quality of stretching time to its agonizing, outermost limits.

Buzz DiLaco was watching his own reflection in the slanting glass window of the control room when the light on the producer's phone began blinking. He'd directed shows like the telethon before and they were always a damned pain in the ass. This one was no exception. Live shows, though, were hard to come by in New York these days and DiLaco needed the money. But this one—this one he swore would definitely be his last. Too many problems.

So far, none of the celebrities who'd promised to come had showed any sign of even being in town yet. Par for the course. His present emcee was Gumbo Johnson, a black stand-up comic whose chief assets were a dazzling set of perfect white teeth and an endless ability to laugh at his own monologues. For that, Buzz decided, Gumbo should count himself lucky; no one else was.

At the moment Gumbo was struggling his way through an explanation of how the telethon would work—telephone calls from viewers to pledge donations—and was promising them an endless parade of great show-biz names marching across their screens. Buzz smiled grimly at the description. From long experience, he knew the big names, if they turned up at all, would arrive in bunches, and usually far into the small hours of the night. He was prepared for this, and had hired a collection of second- and third-string entertainers to fill in. Looking at the list, he guessed some of the names must be familiar only to their agents and their families.

Momentarily, he was distracted when the light on the producer's phone stopped blinking; he'd almost grown used to it. From behind him, he could hear the producer, Mel Fineman, muttering to someone after he'd answered the phone.

Down on the stage, Gumbo Johnson was jumping around excitedly and pointing at the cardboard mercury of the giant thermometer. "Shove it, friends, let's shove it right up through the old rooferoo!"

Buzz DiLaco winced—both at Gumbo's play on words and because the lights were bouncing off his damned perfect white teeth and causing a big flare on the monitors over his head. DiLaco swore.

Swinging around in his chair beside DiLaco, the TD looked at him in angry resignation. "Jesus Christ, Buzz. Tell him for God's sake to stay on his marks. Every time he wanders around like that we start getting the other cameras in the picture."

DiLaco nodded and began talking through his headset to the floor manager when he heard a voice behind him. "There's a bomb in the theater," it said calmly.

"Sure." DiLaco laughed. "Name of Gumbo Johnson."

He was startled when a hand gripped his upper arm and yanked the swivel chair around. Mel Fineman's face was ashen. "I'm not kidding. Network just called. There's a bomb out there somewhere big enough to blow this place sky high."

From the corner of his eye, DiLaco could see the TD pretending not to hear; through his headset, the TD kept talking to the four cameramen and pressing the different buttons that selected the shot for air, but a small quiver at the edge of his mouth showed he'd heard what Fineman said and was only punching up shots now out of sheer habit.

Mel Fineman had seen the expression, too, and nodded sympathetically at the TD. "Take over, Bob. Buzz and I will fill you in in a minute," he promised, and started pulling DiLaco toward the rear wall of the control room, where they could talk without anyone else hearing. Grimly, the TD looked up at the monitors suspended at an angle above his head, and went back to work; in the bay beyond and below him, more technicians, each one planted in front of his own monitor, were meticulously adjusting the color scales and scanning-speeds of the amplifiers. The lighting director, seated just beyond the TD along the row of stools, looked at DiLaco and Fineman curiously as they moved away. Suddenly, a burst of laughter from the audience crackled through the speakers and filled the booth; involuntarily, DiLaco turned on his way toward the rear wall to see what had caused it. Gumbo, still messing around with the thermometer's cardboard column, had accidentally pulled it loose and was now struggling to get it back in place. The audience loved it. Very funny.

When he turned back, he saw Fineman sagged against the wall. In the producer's hand was some stuff he'd written down during the telephone call from network, and he was visibly having trouble accepting what was there.

One long arm outstretched against the wall to support

himself, DiLaco stared at his shoes for a second and then up at Fineman. "You're sure it isn't a hoax? Don't people call in crazy stuff like that all the time?"

Fineman shook his head. "No hoax. No crackpot. Network says it's this guy whose picture was all over the papers—you read about it—he threatened to knock off the Vice President. So far, he's killed three people they know about—there was a television thing on him, remember? . . . And that mess on Fire Island, too. Now it's us."

"Why?" It was a stupid question and DiLaco knew it. Fineman merely shrugged. DiLaco looked at him and was surprised to see how calm Fineman looked. And wondered if he really felt that calm or was just a good actor.

"Somebody from the FBI's supposed to be here with a package from him. It's got our instructions—some kind of show we put on or he sets off the damned bomb. Nobody's to leave the theater under any circumstances. *Nobody.* He wants two cameras trained on the aisle exits so he can see nobody's trying to. We keep cutting back and forth from one to the other."

"The studio audience. What the hell do we tell *them?*"

Fineman didn't even pause to consider. "The truth. That the studio's been hijacked, and they play ball—or else. You brief the crew in here. And the pages. Tell 'em anybody who tries to leave the theater is to get knocked on the head; maybe they can find a club or something in the box office. First, tell Bob"—he nodded toward the TD's back—"and have him take over for you. He's got to keep the damned thing on the air. Network's going to cover the viewers on it with a voice-over from master control."

Buzz DiLaco's jacket was hanging from a tape hook on the rear wall. He always hung it there when he was working. Now, for some reason, he realized he was carefully pulling it on as though the show were over and he was leaving the studio to go home. The wish-fulfillment it represented was so obvious DiLaco had to laugh and this made Fineman look at him oddly. Then, Fineman saw it too and shook his head with a wondering smile.

"Yeah," Fineman said feelingly, and smiled again. Then

the smile disappeared and his eyes went back to the list. "You ought to get on the headset and brief the camera boys before the audience gets it; also the musical director and the floor manager. I'll go backstage and tell the prop men, the guards, the grips, and"—he paused at an unpleasant prospect—"the talent. The talent. Christ, that'll be a scene."

"Who tells the audience?"

"Me, I guess. *I* do."

DiLaco considered a second. "What if they panic and just start bolting up the aisles?"

"West Fifty-fourth Street gets a new parking lot." Mel Fineman pulled his necktie up tight, adjusted his jacket, and then slipped out the control room door to head down toward the studio floor. These damned converted old theaters made lousy studios. He must remember to speak to someone.

Buzz DiLaco walked back to the control board and rapped on an ashtray standing beside the talkback to get attention. "I got something to say," he announced. The lighting director and the audio man swiveled their heads toward him in surprise; the TD kept looking straight ahead at the monitors, but nodded to show he was listening. "You down there, too, guys," added DiLaco and rapped the ashtray again to let the engineers in the bay below know that he included them as well. They turned around and away from their monitors and their eyes studied him curiously, shocked at this breach of studio etiquette.

DiLaco found his knees were shaking and took a deep breath to steady himself. "We got this little problem," he began.

Chapter Twenty-One

LARS COLONIUS sat planted in front of his three television sets like God watching the Creation—serenely confident of the outcome, but fascinated to watch it unfold. His dress was ritual: the freshly laundered sports shirt with its broad, bold vertical stripes, the tight-fitting white duck trousers, well pressed and gleaming, and the inevitable pair of spotlessly brushed suede shoes. On the table beside his giant overstuffed chair—a set of heavily upholstered Stonehenge slabs—were the wraparound sunglasses. The dark-colored dye had been washed from his hair, leaving it a golden, if thinning blond, and the contact lenses discarded. Everything was back to the beginning; only Einstein and his Brownie were missing, but they were apostles on an urgent mission.

With a slight shudder, Colonius took a small sip from his rum and Coke. He didn't really like the taste of alcohol—even when the Coke managed to bury most of it—but since this was the Advent, it seemed to call for celebration. The glass was put back down on the table beside the telephone and its little black box—Colonius sometimes used the phone freak apparatus in calling Ambrose, sometimes not—and returned his attention to the television sets.

On NBC, Gumbo Johnson was still clowning around with some singer Colonius had never heard of, promising she would sing any moment now. Once every minute, the picture would change to the empty exit aisles, one after the other, and then return to the stage. A page at the head of the aisle was supposed to wave his hands and signal Colonius when the package had been received and its contents understood. By Colonius' count, they were already running late on this. Traffic, possibly.

On the other channels, everything was still running normally. CBS was showing its Wednesday-night movie, ABC a half-hour comedy whose actors were mercifully drowned out by a laugh track most of the time. Abruptly, Colonius' eyes came back to the set with NBC: the shot of the Belasco's left aisle lingered unusually long this time, and he could see a page—Colonius was amazed that the page could look so young and unruffled—step firmly to the head of the aisle and slowly wave his arms back and forth above his head. It was done as mechanically and formally as a football referee signaling a penalty. Package received and understood.

In two steps, Colonius moved over and lowered the sound on CBS and ABC to almost nothing. He picked up the phone—no freak-box this time—and dialed Ambrose's number. "Go. Go *now*," was all he said before he hung up.

On screen, the singer was just about to begin; the camera caught her look of surprise as she saw the conductor suddenly wave the orchestra to a halt midway through her introduction, then yank down his earphones and lean forward to start talking urgently to the nearest musicians. Beside her, Gumbo looked equally baffled as a cue card with instructions was waved quite openly in front of him; DiLaco had decided that if this were going to be his last program, he might as well milk it for documentary drama and let the viewers see such usually forbidden items as lights, cameras, sound booms, etc.

As the words on the cue card sank in, the blood drained from Gumbo's face. Haltingly, he addressed the audience in the Belasco. "There is . . . what I mean to say, folks . . . our producer, Mel Fineman, is coming out here to explain an . . . a situation of emergency . . . if you'll please just stay calm and remain in your seats, please. . . ." He looked off-camera desperately, trying to find Mel Fineman's face in the blinding glare of the strip lights in front of the ancient, gilded proscenium.

The sound coming from the Belasco suddenly went dead, then returned but at a very low level. Over it, from master control, came the quiet but urgent voice of an announcer who explained the situation at the theater, but carefully omitted the Belasco's name to avoid drawing a crowd to it. The voice also asked viewers at home who might think they had friends or relatives in the studio not to call the network; they wanted to keep as many lines open as possible.

Colonius leaned forward with excitement as a small, olive-skinned man—the producer, he assumed—stepped forward and began quietly talking to the audience at the Belasco. "I am forced to give you in the audience some disturbing news, but I first want to assure you that there is no reason for alarm as long as we all do exactly as we are told. . . ."

Colonius had to give this Mr. Fineman a good mark for guts; it must take a lot for him to stand up in front of an audience like that and say that at any moment the building might blow up in their faces, but that they had no option to leave. Like telling passengers on a sinking ship that there aren't any lifeboats, but if they all behaved well a rescue ship might come along and pick them up.

Meanwhile, the director was doing some interesting things with his cameras that fascinated Colonius. The cameras spent only part of the time on Fineman himself, and devoted the balance to shopping the audience for interesting pictures. There was one old lady the director kept coming back to; she was a study in human reactions. First, her look of happy expectancy when Fineman started talking, as if she thought whatever he said was going to be part of some elaborate joke. Then, a confused blinking of her eyes as she realized Fineman wasn't joking, but that something she couldn't quite believe—or didn't want to believe—was happening to her. A handkerchief suddenly appeared and was pressed to her mouth; you got a feeling that she might start crying out that she was old and unwell and it was unfair to subject her to a suggestion of such violence. But then the handkerchief disappeared and her mouth set and she began to look along the seats beside her to see the reactions of others. Next to her, a woman with a little boy looked as if she might fall apart completely and began to clutch protectively at her child, which only frightened him more. Smiling, the old lady leaned down and whispered something to him, finally reaching into her

197

purse and giving him a Life Saver. The calming of the little boy somehow seemed to calm his mother as well. Confidently, the old lady straightened her back and began concentrating on watching the stage intently, as absorbed but calm as if she was watching the late news in her own living room.

The camera briefly paused on a well-dressed lady farther down in the theater who sat pouting in mink. Members of the Colony and the Maidstone would have recognized her as Mrs. Vreeland, vice chairman of the institute, and she looked more angry than anything else; her worst suspicions about PR men, actors, and the theater were all being realized at once.

There were other vignettes to see. A man who seemed to scratch his left shoulder compulsively every thirty seconds. A violin player in the orchestra who leaned far forward and let his head and forearm drop onto the music stand; it was impossible to tell whether he was praying or was just tired from a long day in the studio. And a brief shot of a young blond boy who looked too big for his clothes and wore no expression at all. Only Colonius would have recognized him as the two kilos of plastic that held them all in terror.

A sudden change of sound from the television set carrying CBS caught Colonius' eye. A card with the word "Bulletin" had flashed onto its screen, and an announcer's voice was explaining the situation at the NBC studio. The picture did a lot of flickering and there was some violent static, and then the same shot of the Belasco's interior that was on NBC appeared. ABC followed in a matter of seconds. Colonius nodded in satisfaction, staring hard at the three identical pictures. He was startled when the orchestra began playing—after a second, it occurred to him that this was probably to keep the theater audience calm—and for no reason he found himself wondering what had happened to the praying violinist. On the screen, there seemed to be a great deal of scurrying around on the stage. He knew it was all in preparation for showing the material he had sent them, but the waiting began to get to him. Impatiently, he took another swallow of the rum and Coke and made a face.

The picture—it was strange watching all three screens reacting simultaneously—suddenly cut to Mel Fineman who began speaking directly to the camera.

"Ladies and Gentlemen, this is Mel Fineman again, producer of the telethon that was originally appearing on this channel. By now you are aware of the circumstances under which we are operating at this moment. A man named Lars Colonius has demanded what he calls 'equal time' for his thoughts and the story of his life. And out of consideration for the lives of the six-hundred-plus people in our studio audience, we have been forced to grant it. This presentation was entirely prepared by him, and we are not familiar with what it may contain. There are technical difficulties, particularly in running the sixteen-millimeter film he provided, but we are working to overcome these. I ask that you bear with us." For an instant, Fineman stared directly into the lens. He looked almost embarrassed as he added in a soft whisper: "And I don't think anybody here would object if you prayed a little for us, too."

Quickly, Fineman's eyes moved away from the camera, and another longer shot showed he was again speaking to the audience at the Belasco. "I remind you all here of the necessity of remaining calm and following instructions. I would also like to thank the other networks for their prompt cooperation in carrying this program as Mr. Colonius has demanded. We all owe them a deep debt of gratitude." Fineman applauded and the audience halfheartedly followed suit.

But Colonius was no longer watching. He reached for the phone to call Ambrose; those "technical" difficulties with the sixteen milimeter were easy to solve. As he stood up, Colonius was surprised to discover he was having some equally technical difficulties with his tight-fitting white duck trousers.

Hearing your name on television did things like that to you.

Evan Evans was watching Ambrose carefully, feeling sorry for him, but having to keep prodding him for answers. In the corner of the room, Goddard was on the phone to Washington again, trying to explain. The television set in the room was tuned to ABC, which interrupted the picture portion from the Belasco roughly every five minutes to give a hushed explanation to its audience that they were being eyewitnesses to the first studio hijacking in history. From a small radio on Ambrose's desk you could hear an announcer describing the television picture; spinning the radio dial indicated that other radio stations were either doing the same, or interrupting their musical programming frequently to issue bulletins. (Colonius' estimate of thirty to forty million people as his audience was turning out to be considerably under.)

Realization of the kind of coverage Armageddon was getting only made Ambrose look more miserable. Earlier, Evan Evans had been asking him whether he thought Colonius would actually detonate the bomb once his demands were satisfied; there seemed so little point. Now, he repeated the question again. "What do you think, Carlton?"

Ambrose lifted his head and stared at Evans with a tortured look. "I think I blew it, that's what I think." Abruptly, he hit the top of the desk in anger. "Jesus. All those indications, all those slips and hints he gave me, and I blew it. The sudden show-business language. The emphasis on television people—Carson, Namath, Bernstein, the Jefferson Airplane—even, for Christ's sake—the President. All those obvious symptoms of a man crying out for the world to acknowledge he exists. And what better way than television to get that acknowledgment? Then, the capper, that phrase he begins using: *equal time.* But what do we do? Goddard has police and FBI crawling all over the Capitol and I have them charging around Hollywood Bowl. Goddamn, damn, damn."

Nodding, Evans returned doggedly to his question. "About the bomb. Whether he'll set it off. There are some questions if he could trigger one that powerful by radio, and we're looking into that. But what I'd like to know is whether you think he'll do it. If so—and assuming we find out where he is—we should probably go for broke, break in, and risk his setting it off. There's nothing much to lose. If not, if you don't think he will, the people in

200

that theater would have a better chance just letting him run his course."

Ambrose sighed. "There's no real answer. He's combined the technique of the airline skyjack with the threat of mass assassination—using TV cameras as his eyes—and there's no way to tell how he'll react." Morosely, Ambrose fumbled for a Tijuana 12. "But I somehow have a hard time imagining him surrendering quietly and letting himself be carted off to an asylum." He lit up. "Biblically, Armageddon represented the fight between good and evil. But I'm damned if I can remember whether anybody survived."

One of the men from the police network appeared and handed Evans something. He looked about ready to disagree with the contents when Ambrose's phone rang. The ritual was followed. Goddard lowered his phone. The tape machine was started. The FBI man working the trace operation reached forward to pick up his phone the same instant as Ambrose did.

"Hello," said Ambrose cheerfully. "Well, you seem to be getting very good coverage."

There was nothing cheerful to Armageddon's voice. "I should be."

"You're all over radio, too. I didn't know whether you knew that or not."

"I knew it," snapped Colonius. It was probably a lie and Ambrose rolled his eyes; humoring Armageddon was sometimes a hard act to keep up.

The voice on the phone took on an even more petulant tone. "What's this crap about technical difficulties with the film? If they can't run it there in the studio, you can let one man out and take it to a place where they can. But let me know when. I have men watching both the front and the stage doors, you know."

Evans and Ambrose exchanged glances. Then Evans walked quickly out of the room to start the New York police combing the area around the Belasco for a blond, mentally retarded youth, just in case Colonius was telling the truth.

"Anything else?" asked Ambrose. A signal from the FBI man to try to stretch the conversation for the phone tracers caught his eye. "I mean, is there anything we can get you, or send in to the theater, or—"

A chilling laugh came from Colonius. "What you really mean is keep talking so you can try tracing the call. It's a waste of time, doctor. I told you before—it's impossible." There was a second of silence, then the voice returned. "But it might be a good idea to alert the President. I'll be needing him in about twenty minutes."

A feeling of panic swept Ambrose. There was no way of predicting how the President would react, or what decision he had made. A minor inspiration struck him. "I'm not sure I can," Ambrose told Colonius. "He was operating on the old schedule just the way we were. At this point, getting hold of him may not be easy. Nobody caught the change in date."

"I think you can get hold of him if you want," announced Armageddon dryly. The buzz of the hung-up phone no longer came as a shock.

Goddard looked down at Ambrose wearily. "I suppose I'd better tell Eckhardt about it." He paused on his way to the phone to look back at Ambrose. "What was all that about the film? Is he really going to let somebody out of the studio?"

"I guess. Somebody should call them. Also to find out what else is in that package."

The somebody turned out to be Ambrose himself. He found the director, DiLaco, oddly euphoric, but supposed it was a nervous reaction. It wasn't entirely. In spite of the ever-present threat of being blown up, DiLaco was enjoying himself. After years of directing dogs, he was involved in the making of television history, and an automatic set of reflexes had swung into play that allowed him to concentrate totally on delivering the best damned dramatic coverage of the event he could give it.

Ambrose told him about letting one person—no more —appear at the door and hand the sixteen-millimeter film off to a messenger, who would race it to master control. Hesitantly, he asked DiLaco what was on it.

"Crazy stuff," said DiLaco. "Given the circumstances, it's plain nuts." He called for a couple of shots of a young couple in the front row who seemed determined to spend their last moments on earth happily—they were kissing violently.

"Get off them if they go too far," he snapped into the headset, then added with a laugh: "This is a family-type program." He turned back to the phone and Ambrose. "The film—it's some home movies. Of this guy Colonius. As a baby, as a child, as a teen-ager, and his family. There's a script that goes with it. Pretty terrible." Ambrose could hear him shouting at the TD; the couple had gone overboard. Then his voice came back on the phone. "He's got a lot of other stuff, too, but we can handle it all from here. A tape of himself making an announcement to the world. The tag says it explains everything, why he's doing it, all that crap. Stills of him at high school. Stills of him now. And—would you believe it?—stills of him with Henry Ford, Joe Namath, Johnny Carson, *and* at the White House? A script comes for all that, too." There was a pause while DiLaco swore at somebody named Gumbo, and then a question from him to Ambrose. "Is the President really going to talk to him over the air?"

"I don't know."

There was some more confusion on the other end of the phone and then Ambrose could hear DiLaco was again on the phone, although, for the moment, saying nothing. "How's the audience holding up?" Ambrose asked.

"Pretty good, pretty good," answered DiLaco in his usual machine-gun delivery. "Everybody's doing pretty good, even the talent. They're trying to organize something to keep the audience cheered up until we put this junk on."

"If there's anything you need, just let us know."

DiLaco thought. "How about a medical pass out of here, doctor? Or an excuse from my mother?" he asked, and then laughed.

But Ambrose suspected—and he was right—that the director wouldn't have left the studio just now for an armful of Emmys.

Macon police headquarters looked more as if the bomb had been hidden there than at the Belasco in New York. They had just about gotten the place back to normal after the rooftop sniper at the Ocmulgee Bank, when the new crisis hit them. Down in the first floor, the lobby was jammed with reporters and cameramen. People from the telephone company were rushing in and out with records of toll calls made from pay stations near the Sweet Laurel; these would be taken upstairs, where the FBI was painstakingly checking calls made to all numbers near New York, trying to uncover a place where Armageddon might be holed up. There was, of course, no certainty he was even in New York, but they had to start somewhere and New York seemed logical.

Fun City.

Upstairs, Mrs. Spiers was being grilled. As so often in matters like these, the official's first instinct was to suspect a conspiracy; the FBI could not believe one man could have organized and carried out the plan by himself. Mrs. Spiers was having difficulty explaining why she hadn't at least suspected that her absent-but-paying roomer was Armageddon—certainly, the interrogator pointed out—his picture had been everywhere.

But the most Mrs. Spiers would admit—and it was the truth—was that, yes, the thought had crossed her mind, but the picture wasn't a very good one and Mr. Colonius always paid his bills on time and who was she to go around causing trouble? By this time, a relative had arrived and reluctantly pointed out Mrs. Spiers' daily ration of vodka, and her story began to become more believable. The Macon police did try to get more information from her on Albert, but beyond the fact that he was mentally retarded—"slow," as she put it—Mrs. Spiers seemed to know little. He had just showed up one day, she said, asked for work, and wound up running errands for the tenants. No, she definitely had had no idea that Mr. Colonius might have killed Billy-Joe; she was just as shocked as they were.

By now, Fatback Johnson had also been brought back in and the police were trying to find out if Billy-Joe might have originally been part of the plan. But Fatback was adamant. "Billy-Joe thought the guy was a creep. All he ever did was sell him a piece and tell him where he could pick up some plastic."

On mention of the word "plastic," the FBI landed on Fatback like a ton of bricks. It was, Fatback finally admitted, from him that Billy-Joe had gotten the name of the Algerian—"You know, the guy who got his head blown off reading his morning mail."

"Did the Algerian sell plastic to Colonius?"

"No, this Colonius wanted it in New York. All the Algerian did was give him the name of a supplier there."

"What supplier?"

"I dunno."

But the FBI thought Fatback did. And they were unkind enough to point out that if they could establish that the supplier's name came from *him*—rather than from the Algerian—Fatback could be an accessory before the fact.

"What supplier?" they demanded again.

A call from Fatback to his lawyer changed the answer. Wearily, he named the Algerian's New York supplier for the FBI. He hated himself for it, but the lawyer had told him his friends in the Macon underworld were still very unhappy with him, and that Fatback better get the damned thing over with fast.

And finking on a dead Arab was better than being a dead Baptist.

Chapter Twenty-Two

"WELL, how far *will* the President go?"

Ambrose was on the phone with Eckhardt, trying to prepare himself for his next conversation with Colonius; he was pretty sure Colonius would bring up the President again and he wanted some sort of answer ready. Eckhardt seemed evasive.

"No one can say—I don't believe he can say himself —until we know exactly what Armageddon wants from him. If it's just a private phone call, well, with all those lives involved, I suppose that's one thing. If it's a public one, I don't know yet. I *do* know the President's mad as hell—he's on his way back to the White House now. The last thing I heard him say was that this is what happens when you start giving in to frightened people. He's called off all the extra security, the Vice President's been told to leave the command post in Virginia and go home, and he wants everything to look as if no one was ever even worried."

Ambrose swore. "Does he know there's almost six hundred people in that theater? Well, they're worried all right, damned worried."

"I know, but he has to look at the larger picture. Like who might try it next. How it affects the whole fabric of authority. What it does to the world's picture of us as a nation. Did you know portions of it are being carried by satellite as far away as Russia?"

For the moment, at least, Ambrose could see it was hopeless to argue. There were too many rights and too many wrongs on either side of the argument. And too many unanswered questions about what Colonius expected from the White House.

As Eckhardt put it, "For all we know, Armageddon

may want the President to open up all the jails or sink our own fleet or just about anything."

Grudgingly, Ambrose gave in. It was agreed that on Colonius' next call, he would subtly try to find out exactly what he was after from the President. It was terribly important, Ambrose felt, that any decision be reached before Colonius had publicly committed himself on the air to including the White House in his hijack; from what Ambrose knew of Colonius, this sort of public turndown by a father figure such as the President would be more than enough to make him detonate the bomb.

He hung up and listened to the radio on his desk for a moment. Because radio, unlike television, wasn't locked in to the Belasco, their coverage was a good deal more flexible. They had reporters on the street outside the theater, reporters across the street, reporters in the RCA building, reporters everywhere except inside the theater itself. Radio was free to hold interviews with Colonius' aunt in Buffalo, other people who knew him there (he was repeatedly described as quiet, very quiet; nobody really knew him, the neighbors said), and people who might have known his mother.

Evan Evans got to Ambrose about the same time Goddard did; both of them had news to report. "The New York police just got a call from a man in California who says he's Colonius's father. He'll do anything he can to help," Evans announced.

"Does he know where—have any idea—where his son might be hiding right now?" asked Goddard.

"No, the man says he left the family—deserted them, it sounds like—years ago. But if it'll be any help, the father's willing to talk to him."

"I think he's probably about twenty years too late," said Ambrose sourly. A lot of things about Colonius were clicking into place at once. The father-son thing, for instance. And somewhere in it might be an angle that would help them.

Goddard shrugged and gave his own news. "The FBI has the name of the supplier in New York who probably sold him the plastic for the bomb. They're hoping maybe they'll get some sort of address out of them." Goddard looked at his notes. "And we have some more information on that radio-controlled trigger for the bomb. The experts are having a hard time believing it would be a very reliable system in a studio with so much electronic gear in it; they keep suggesting the plastic may be on a timing device instead."

A man handed Evans a note. "Hold it," said Evans, standing up suddenly, his eyes wide with excitement, "they got a phone number from the pay phone a block away from Colonius' boardinghouse in Macon. A call made to the Regency Hotel here. The date was two days before you gave your television interview, Carlton."

"Check it out with the Regency—" Goddard had started to snap this order at Evans, but before he even got the first few words out, Evans had already disappeared into the room where the police network was.

He returned a few minutes later with the news that the Regency had gotten a call that date from a Dr. Kraus of Macon, Georgia, reserving a suite. He'd turned up the next day with a deaf and dumb patient whose name was not on record. And the doctor fitted the description of an altered Lars Colonius, while the patient's description jibed with that of his accomplice. But, Evans concluded, the Regency said Dr. Kraus had checked out long ago and they had no record of any forwarding address.

"Another Goddamned dead end," groaned Goddard.

Evans wasn't so sure. "The entire staff of that hotel should be questioned—fast. He may have given some hint, even accidentally, of where he was moving to."

Ambrose agreed. The New York police were given the job.

A difference in the sound made them all look suddenly up at the television set. All of them had been so absorbed in the frenzy of the last few minutes that they hadn't noticed, but the program about Lars Colonius had begun. A picture of Armageddon—not any from the past, but apparently a professionally taken studio portrait—was on the screen. The usual impudent smile was missing; he was staring directly at them, his eyes slightly narrowed, wearing a stern expression.

"This is the voice of Armageddon," a tape was playing
208

behind the picture. Although this time "the voice" was not a patched-together tape, but Colonius' own.

"My real name is Lars Colonius," continued the tape, "but Armageddon was the code name I used in dealing with the authorities. And I use it now, again, with you, because it is appropriate.

"Most of you watching tonight considers himself neither rich nor poor, neither success nor failure, neither privileged nor deprived. He has been carefully taught that he is one of the great massed middle and that, in a hungry world, he should count himself lucky for it.

"Well, I don't count him lucky. The arrogant intellectuals have built him a trap, and he has fallen in. They despise the individual, so they keep him too satisfied to rebel, yet too insignificant to matter. If he's hungry, quiet him with food stamps; if he's talented, kill him with taxes. Lull him to sleep with the phony promise of security. Calm him. Destroy him.

"But I, Lars Colonius, have seen and avoided the trap. And it is my destiny to wake you—and the world— from your sleep of safety. To force you to recognize that most uncommon of common men: the individual. To dramatize that any individual with the will can achieve any goal his brain can invent.

"The fact that I am here tonight, in spite of all that was done to prevent me, is proof of this fact. No one could stop me: not the police, not the doctors, not the government.

"Later, when the President of the United States talks to me here by telephone, meeting and executing my demands, you will see further proof of what one individual can effect. . . ."

Ambrose's heart sank. The challenge had been made —and in public. He hit the desk in frustration.

Goddard turned away from the screen in confusion. "What the hell's with this guy? Neo-Fascist? Commie, Populist, or what?"

Ambrose laughed; Goddard was taking Colonius' political pretensions seriously. "No, he's a man without a father. Nothing more."

"What the hell's that supposed to mean?" Goddard looked at Ambrose angrily.

"We know from that California telephone call that his father deserted the family. OK, he's proving how little he needs one, how powerful he is. The same father thing showed up in that telephone conversation with me, where he kept changing what he was to be called: Mr. Colonius/ Lars, adult/child. I suppose even getting the President into the act is part of it."

"Oh, shit." Goddard was in no mood for what sounded like pat psychiatric jargon—or worse.

Evan Evans grunted. "Don't dismiss it too quickly. That phone call from California. When his father called, among other things, he said it was funny about the program his son had picked—a telethon for the blind. He added that the reason he deserted the family was because he couldn't support them; he's damned near blind himself."

This shook Goddard and startled Ambrose. But Goddard recovered quickly. "Is there any way we can use it? The father? Can we use him somehow?"

"Too dangerous, I think," Ambrose considered a moment and then was sure. "Much too dangerous. You don't know how he might react. Nobody does. It doesn't work like in the movies: You can't start probing the emotional hangups of a guy who's got a bomb ticking under six hundred people."

Evans was studying another note just handed to him. Now, he looked up dispiritedly. "Another thing we *can't* do is track him down through the outfit that sold the plastics. They all blew town. The minute they heard what was going on at the Belasco they put that together with one of their customers, I guess."

There was a brief discussion on the chances of the telephone trace and it was dismissed as probably not too fruitful. This left the interviewing of the Regency's staff as the only viable possibility, and no one pretended it was a very firm one.

"For the time being, the thing to worry about is what he wants from the President," Ambrose noted. And as if Colonius were once again reading his mind, the phone on Ambrose's desk began to ring.

Colonius sat in the chair, hugging himself with excitement as he stared at his picture on the screen and listened to the tape of his own voice. The quality of its sound disappointed him, but it always did; it seemed thin and nasal. The mention of the President prodded him into action.

"Hello," he said into the phone.

"Hello, Lars," answered Ambrose. "The shot of you on the screen—it's a much better picture of you than the others."

"I don't like my voice. But I never have."

Ambrose sounded reassuring. "I think everybody feels that way about their own voice. I can't stand mine, for instance; I sound like I have a hell of a bad cold."

Colonius giggled. From the corner of his eye, he saw the film of him as a child begin. An announcer was reading the copy he'd written as the film ran. It annoyed him to be missing it, but making the call now was essential. "Have them stop the film," he ordered. "I want to be able to see it when it's run, but I have to get this out of the way first."

"Just a minute, Lars." Over the phone, Colonius could hear some instructions being given. About thirty seconds later, the film stopped abruptly. Dr. Ambrose's voice returned. "Yes, Lars."

"I want the President to phone the television studio and make a public announcement."

Ambrose's voice sounded confused. "Well, he's in a helicopter somewhere just now. But we'll call him as soon as he lands. Is it a long statement?"

"No, more a promise than a statement."

"Maybe there's something we can do to line up the elements of it for him. What's the promise about?"

Colonius hesitated, wondering if Ambrose was stalling him. "I want him to promise that if I don't blow up the theater, he'll personally guarantee—in public—to fly me out of the country to safety."

Ambrose's voice sounded very far away. "I don't know whether he can do that, Lars. Legally, I mean."

"Remind him of the bomb. And the six hundred people."

A slightly strained laugh came over the phone. "I doubt if he's forgotten."

"And that you know I'll explode the bomb if he doesn't agree."

He could hear Ambrose sigh. "Where do you want to go, Lars? Fly you safely to where?"

Oddly, Colonius hadn't considered this too carefully. But he made a quick decision. "Algeria." He wasn't even sure where it was, but he'd read that it gave asylum to political refugees.

"They may refuse to accept you."

"He can make them. If he really wants to."

"It will take time, Lars. Why don't you think about letting the people out of the theater first, and later we can make the arrangements—"

Colonius began to get angry; it was too transparent. "No, *now*. And don't try stalling me again like this, doctor. Tell them to put the film back on." Colonius hung up abruptly, and stared at the television screens. A large black comedian—Gumbo something or other—was conducting a sing-along to keep the audience busy.

The conversation had, in a way, left both Ambrose and Colonius confused. Ambrose could not imagine that Colonius really expected the President to do what he was asking, or even if he agreed, to keep his promise. And Colonius was too smart to believe something like that.

On the last point, at least, Colonius would have agreed. For even if the President gave in to his demands, Colonius had no way to stop the bomb; the timers in Einstein's pockets were set for precisely ten fifty-five P.M., and there was no way he—or anybody else—could change that. Demanding the plane had originally been planned to cover his own escape, to make sure he could slip safely out of town. While the authorities were wrestling with the international complications involved in letting him escape to Algeria—or wherever—he would quietly disappear. A little later, the theater would go up in smoke and his mission would have been accomplished. But as he had begun to feel the day before, the idea of escape seemed less and less important; it was too much of an anticlimax.

On the three screens, the sing-along was stopped and the

film began again. He watched the movies of himself, about age six, clumsily playing some sort of catch with his father. They were using an enormous, soft-rubber ball, but Colonius was very, very bad at it. Suddenly, he felt infinitely sad and wondered what the hell he, Lars Colonius, was doing in this strange hotel room, watching three television sets at the same time, while movies of him as a child flickered across the screen and a bomb timer ticked relentlessly onward in a theater four and a half blocks away.

As with so many things in his life, Armageddon Day was more fun in the dreaming than in the doing.

On the live monitor above the TD's head, DiLaco could see the film running on and on and winced. An endless parade of undistinguished people walked toward the camera, waved too heartily or hid their faces self-consciously, and then passed out of frame forever. Women on porch railings struck camp poses and laughed silently. Men in bathing suits flexed imaginary muscles. Hamburgers and hot dogs were cooked, Cokes drunk, and cigarettes smoked. A small blond kid appeared frequently—Colonius—although it seemed to DiLaco that no one paid too much attention to him. There was a younger child, damned near a baby, that, especially in the latter parts of the film, seemed to get most of the play. Many of the scenes were shot in the yard of a run-down white clapboard house, although a few were taken on the edge of what was either a river or lake. Whoever was taking the movies was a lousy photographer; it was a typical set of average American home movies—awful.

In the area of Buffalo where the films were mostly shot —and where the Colonius family had lived—they were being greeted with head-shakings and a certain amount of amused shock. The announcer in the studio—reading that awful Colonius boy's own script—was describing his father as an architect, a brilliant man, he said, but distant, self-centered, and completely absorbed in his work; everyone around the neighborhood recalled him as an amiable but not too successful mechanical draftsman. The father got off lightly; the venom was reserved for Colonius' mother. She was painted as an "extraordinarily handsome woman, but a raging nymphomaniac who loathed her children because they intruded into her endless liaisons with wealthy gentlemen; locally, she was fairly well remembered as a fat, usually disheveled and somewhat pathetic lump, who supported her family by grudgingly servicing the local hard-hats along with their shirts, socks, and shorts. Neither this nor the fact of Mr. Colonius' blindness was mentioned; the script explained his move to the coast solely in terms of his needing to continue his brilliant work unencumbered by so insatiable a wife. It was the politest way to describe a man deserting his family anyone in Buffalo could remember.

DiLaco turned his eyes away from the monitor and stared through the glass of the control room at the inside of the theater. The audience was beginning to worry him. Beside him stood Mel Fineman.

DiLaco turned to him. "The audience. It's getting antsy."

Fineman nodded. He'd noticed the same thing on his way from the floor area to the booth, and an idea was trying to take shape inside his head.

"You know," said DiLaco, "it's one thing when you're on a hijacked airplane. There's a guy in the aisle with a gun, you're thirty thousand feet in the air—maybe a little scared of airplanes anyway—and you know what to be afraid of. This—this is so damned unreal."

"And the street is just outside the door. Not six miles down," added Fineman.

"That sing-along helped, but they're beginning to get out of hand. The pages said some people asked if they could go to the can, but if our boy sees that on his screen, he'll think they're trying to get out of the theater. His damned home movies don't help much either." DiLaco looked at some notes on a piece of paper. "Wait until they have to listen to his poetry. Jesus. Somebody's going to make a break for it and there goes the roof."

"I'll go out there after the movies and shake 'em up again." Fineman spoke without conviction; he was preoccupied with his idea.

DiLaco half stood up to see down into the audience better. "Look at that. Some jerk's trying to start them clap-

214

ping and booing." DiLaco spun around in his chair to the sound engineer. "Close the floor mikes, Bert. That's all he needs to hear."

"I'll get out there." Fineman started toward the door of the control room, but stopped and turned around as he reached it. "How long do you think it would take to empty this place?"

DiLaco considered. "Using all exits—stage doors, side doors, even the old mezzanine fire escapes—maybe ten, fifteen minutes." He ran the scene over in his head and stared at Fineman. "But you'd be running one hell of a chance of somebody getting trampled."

"Which is worse? Getting stomped to death or blown up?"

DiLaco didn't have an answer.

"He won't do it and that's all there is to it."

Goddard had just spoken to Eckhardt and was reporting on the President's answer; a very flat—and apparently somewhat violent—no.

"He realizes that no one—absolutely no one in their right mind—would expect him to do anything *but* go back on his guarantee?"

"He realizes."

Sinking into a chair, Ambrose studied the whirling smoke of a Tijuana 12. The answer didn't make sense. Slowly, he took another deep drag and looked up at Goddard. "If he's still worried about his encouraging others, he should know that going back on his word pretty well kills that possibility. It won't be any victory for Armageddon; he'll be in a hospital somewhere—or dead."

"He knows that too."

"Can *I* talk to Eckhardt?"

Goddard grumbled, but agreed. Shortly after he was put through, Ambrose used his most basic argument. "It seems like such a small thing—an empty promise—one that everyone knows won't be kept—to trade for six hundred lives."

Eckhardt sounded apologetic, almost sad. "It's the small givings-in that add up to the really big troubles later. Each one always seems so insignificant. And there's

215

no question, they're always the easier decisions to make. And the more popular ones. But it's the nature of violence, a fact of existing in a violent world, that the easy decisions are almost always the wrong ones."

"Can I speak to him?"

"No."

There was a pause and Ambrose wanted to ask why, but thought he already knew. Eckhardt confirmed it. "He's made the hard decision. The tough one." There was another pause. "And he doesn't feel very good about it."

Chapter Twenty-Three

DıLACO looked at the script in his hand, the pictures flashing on the monitor, and then at Mel Fineman. "You're *sure* you want to go through to the end on this part? Jesus, you know, it's early on the West Coast, there's kids watching, and Christ, that end bit even makes me kind of sick."

"I've already talked to network and they talked to Dr. Ambrose. He's afraid if we don't that nut case is liable to blow his cool and press the button. In other words, there's not one hell of a lot of choice."

They were talking about a section of Colonius' presentation—the one on the monitor over their heads at the moment. This early part of it was no problem; it had the stills showing the first stages of the Armageddon plan—the shots of Colonius at the All-Rite Shopping Center, with Namath, with Bernstein, even the picture of him in the Oval Office (the script, being read by an off-camera announcer, did not point out that this was the Johnson Library replica, not the real thing). Toward the end, though, Colonius got specific about the point he'd made in his introductory tape: how ineffective the authorities, the police, and the government were in trying to stop him. It dealt at some length with Ambrose's interview on television, and the doctor's assurances that Colonius' threat was an empty one.

And there *was* a problem in the material showing Colonius' answer to the interview, which was why DiLaco kept prodding Fineman about showing it.

"I've done everything I can," Fineman said, and appeared to become absorbed in watching the monitors.

They could hear the announcer stumbling manfully through his reading over the shot in the Oval Office as

Fineman reviewed what steps had been taken. "The network has warned the affiliates, but asked them to carry it anyway; nobody knows which part of the country this guy may be watching the thing in. The other networks, well, I don't know about them. Frankly, I'm almost more worried about what the audience here will do."

With a resigned shrug, DiLaco accepted this as a final answer. Scanning the marked-up script he was working from, he looked over at the sound engineer. "Ready tape," he ordered and then turned back toward Fineman. "Well, we're about to find out." His hand clenched, his eyes squeezed almost shut, and he barked out the order: "Roll tape."

On the screen, one after another, appeared the Brownie shots of Tuckerman and the girl from the Princess Grace, taken before, during, and after the "electric orgasm." From the speakers came a section of the same tape that was left behind at the Blue Goose for Ambrose, the groanings and thrashings of Colonius' revenge on Ambrose. Dirty pictures tend to look faintly ridiculous—almost funny—under normal circumstances; there was nothing ridiculous or funny about these photographs with their accompanying sound effects of electric agony. Staring fixedly at them on the line monitor, DiLaco was struck by how much they reminded you of the photographs taken at My Lai or Auschwitz.

The effect on the audience in the theater was a curious one. For the first time in the last half hour, they fell completely silent; the binding sense of sharing a common danger, the fragile camaraderie, the brave attempts at whispered half-jokes vanished. Some averted their eyes completely, others half-covered them with their fingers, frightened but unable not to look, like children seeing a scary movie. A lady near the rear of the theater became totally and suddenly absorbed in her knitting, Madame de Farge with high-voltage needles; the orchestra leader—the musicians had not been called on to play since the sing-along—aimlessly shuffled the score on his music stand, found several sheets of manuscript out of place, and carefully put them back in order. Not a sound came from the audience until almost the very last picture, when you could detect a small sigh rising from them; it was as if for the first time they really understood—and now accepted—the common danger they were in.

In the control room—usually an arena of irreverent banter no matter what was on the screens—there was the same unearthly silence. Only here it was occasionally pierced by muttered commands for moving the cameras, hushed orders to the grips changing the cue cards, and the relentless click-click at the TD pressing the buttons on the control board in front of him. Silently, the last picture of Tuckerman and the girl, their electrocution completed, flashed on the screen, then disappeared.

Abruptly, from the bay below the control panel, down where the technicians sat fiddling endlessly with their shading dials, a sudden, nasal voice piped up loud and clear: "Dissolve in super: 'You can be sure if it's Westinghouse.'"

The control booth exploded into laughter.

It wasn't a very funny joke, but sometimes, when you can't cry, the only way of showing that something matters too much is to laugh too hard.

"And you didn't show the theater aisle like you were supposed to." Colonius was on the phone again to Ambrose, and the room, still recovering from seeing the pictures at the Blue Goose, listened to his voice in angry silence. He suspected, it seemed, that some sort of trick was being played on him. "Maybe," he went on, "you're letting people out of the theater or something. Well, you can't fool me, doctor."

Ambrose nodded at one of the men to call the Belasco right away and give Colonius the quick pictures of both aisles to reassure him. He suspected—and correctly—they had been stunned by the effect of the pictures and the tapes and simply forgot. "We'll take care of it right away. And nobody's trying to fool you, Lars; nobody here's that dumb."

"Have you got an answer from the President yet?"

The question caused Ambrose to redden; stalling Colonius was becoming an increasingly risky business. "Not a firm answer, Lars," he lied. "It's a very tricky thing, you know. More than just the President himself is involved. Algeria won't accept you. The last I heard they were making a phone call to the Portuguese Embassy. To see about Angola. But there's no point getting there and have them not let you get off the plane."

It was a complete lie, and not, Ambrose thought, an overly convincing one. Colonius apparently agreed. "Balls," he said. "I'm getting tired and I'm getting nervous. If Angola won't work, have them take me someplace else. But I want that statement from the President."

"We're doing our best, Lars." Looking around the room, Ambrose reached up and made a tightening gesture around his shirt collar.

There was a pause during which the room amplifier from the phone gave out nothing but the sound of Colonius' breathing, then: "You wouldn't want me to get *too* tired and *too* nervous, would you, doctor?"

Ambrose pretended to ignore the question. "We're doing our best, Lars. Just relax."

Colonius brushed off the reassurance. "And ABC and CBS keep cutting away from the Belasco to their announcers giving voice-over bulletins. It's very hard to hear what they say when they're all saying something different. *That* makes me nervous, too."

"OK, Lars. We'll stop them. Anything else?"

"Yes. You're running out of time."

Ambrose started to answer, but the receiver began buzzing again. Colonius had hung up. Evan Evans, who had taken another call on the other side of the room, hung up his phone and turned to face them. There was a wide grin on his face.

"Carlton—listen, Carlton," he began excitedly. But Ambrose was struggling to understand Colonius' remark about it being hard to listen when the different networks were all saying something different, and held up his hand. There was something significant he was missing in that.

But Evan Evans wouldn't wait. "We know where he is," Evans said in a voice that was strangely calm. "That police check with the staff at the Regency—"

Goddard sprang into life. "Jesus, where? Is it here? In New York?"

"The Hotel Americana. We don't know the room. But the mail clerk at the Regency—"

Phones were picked up all over the room. The FBI regional director—he'd arrived a few minutes before—was on his radiophone to units on the street. Goddard was pulling on his jacket and yelling into another phone to get a car downstairs ready for them. The New York police were being called.

"Hold it!" Ambrose's voice was so loud and commanding that everyone in the room froze in mid-motion, as if they'd been photographed by a high-speed camera. Slowly, Goddard, the FBI regional man, even Evan Evans turned to look at Ambrose curiously.

"Take it easy," said Ambrose in a much quieter tone. "We can't just go barging into that hotel with sirens and all that stuff. He'll hear it. He'll hear it and if he's got a radio-controlled firing thing, he'll use it. And then that's it. And to convince him that nothing's going on, I have to stay in telephone touch, somehow. . . ."

Goddard seemed about ready to move again; once the shock of Ambrose's hollered command had worn off, he was back to acting first and thinking second. "I told you: The experts don't think the plastics are even *on* a radio trigger. They think they must be on timers."

"And your experts could think wrong. So for Christ's sake, no sirens. Meanwhile, maybe I can talk him out of it."

"OK. No sirens. And get the doctor a car with a radio-phone so that nut will still think he's here," commanded Goddard to the room in general as he swept out the door.

"There's one in my car," the regional man from the FBI volunteered to Ambrose.

"How fast can we get there?"

"It depends on traffic."

"One siren in city traffic won't even be noticed," said Ambrose. "I want to get there before anybody else does." The FBI man nodded and they started for the door.

As they pushed through it, Evan Evans turned toward Ambrose with a questioning look. "What the hell are you up to, Carlton?"

Ambrose smiled. "That last telephone talk with Coloni-

221

us. Now I know how to find out exactly what room he's in. And if we can get there before Goddard and that mob of police, maybe we can still get to Armageddon without having him blow up the theater."

The three of them stepped into the elevator. Evan Evans was shaking his head in wonder. "You're in the wrong business, Carlton," he said.

"I manage."

The elevator doors closed behind them with a soft, pneumatic sigh.

With a grunt of displeasure, Colonius mixed himself another rum and Coke. He was beginning to fume. That damned doctor was stalling about the President, he was sure of that. After a swallow of the stuff, Colonius gave the glass a shove across the table, almost upsetting it, and picked up the phone. When he dialed and got the Westbury, he asked for Ambrose's extension; an overly calm operator told him they were having trouble with that line and would he please wait?

Colonius hung up. They were still running the trace, he supposed; Dr. Ambrose wasn't as smart as he'd given him credit for, and for a moment Colonius felt saddened. But possibly, he told himself, it was the police or the FBI and Dr. Ambrose didn't even know about it.

In any case, he'd now have to use the phone-freak box, which only made him madder. He leafed through the list of special numbers you use with the box until he found a toll-free number he hadn't already gone through that night: It was the number of some insurance company with an all-night information service. Once he heard that number answer, he began working tone buttons on the box, electronically routing himself away from the insurance company and out into the telephone system long lines until he was connected with information in Chicago. He pressed another button and routed himself onto an even bigger electronic "loop" of telephone circuits and, once on it, simply dialed the Westbury from a nonexistent number in Chicago. If they tried to trace that, they'd get nowhere.

The same operator at the Westbury gave him the same answer when he asked for Dr. Ambrose's number; there was trouble on that line and he'd have to wait a minute, please. Colonius waited. He reached over for the rum and Coke again, thinking happily of the scramble the call tracers must be going through trying to track his number. Impossible.

Finally, Dr. Ambrose answered.

"Don't you ever learn, doctor?" Colonius asked, tauntingly. "I thought you were smarter than that."

The doctor sounded as if he was clearing his throat in preparation for a long speech.

But Colonius looked at his watch and didn't even wait for an evasive answer. The matter of the President had to be forced right now, or the program would come to a sudden end before the President could publicly humble himself. The timers in Einstein's pockets were set for ten fifty-nine. And it was now ten forty.

Before the phone rang in the FBI car, Evans had been explaining how the New York police had lucked into discovering Armageddon was probably at the Americana.

"It was the mail clerk at the Regency," Evans had noted. "Armageddon left no forwarding address, of course, but asked them to hold any mail that came for him. He never showed up, but the deaf and dumb—the retarded—kid did. The mail clerk remembered because the kid had a note from Dr. Kraus saying it was OK to give him any mail. The hotel doesn't usually do it, but the mail clerk remembered the boy had been a patient of the doctor and gave it to him anyway. He asked him for a forwarding address, but the kid just kept shaking his head like he didn't understand. But when he left, the mail clerk found the boy had laid his room key to the new hotel on the counter while he was waiting, and had to come back from the street to get it. It was a key for the Americana. The clerk thought it was kind of funny they should move from a place like the Regency to a place like the Americana—people in hotels like that are all born snobs, I guess—and that helped him remember the incident, too. Everything but the room number. And you couldn't really expect him to keep that in his head."

Ambrose had smiled. "And I think I know how to get that," was all he said.

It was then that the car phone rang. The FBI man switched off the siren and jammed the car over to the curb. The windows were already closed to keep as much sound out as possible, but he pulled a blanket over Ambrose's head so that any traffic or street noise would be further deadened. Then the FBI man stepped outside to keep away anyone on the street who might find this arrangement curious enough to investigate.

"Hello," said Ambrose again. "I can't hear very well, Lars. There's something crazy with this phone all of a sudden."

"What's crazy is you guys still trying to trace the number," snapped Colonius and then, remembering the time, plowed right ahead. "About the President," he began.

"They're working something out. Really, Lars. Give me five minutes. Ten at the outside."

Colonius hesitated. He couldn't explain that the bombs were on timers, so he couldn't explain that ten minutes was cutting it pretty damned close. "I don't like it. I think you're stalling again."

"Have I ever lied to you, Lars?" Ambrose could say this with confidence; it was a ploy that patients usually responded to.

He could hear Colonius hesitate again, then: "Not *to* me, I guess. But *about* me, plenty. On television. That interview."

Ambrose laughed. "Well, we all know that didn't work, don't we?"

This time the pause was much longer. "OK, doctor. Because I want to trust you. Ten minutes at the outside. But no more. I mean it."

The phones disconnected. Evans waved the FBI man back into the car while Ambrose untangled himself from the receiver and the blanket. With an accelerating groan, the siren started again and they headed for the Americana.

It was now ten forty-three.

Orin Pellar was on the first day of his new job as an NBC studio page. Since that assignment placed him in the

Belasco on the night of the telethon, he would never be able to tell anybody his career didn't begin with a flourish. He stood now, guarding an exit door about two-thirds of the way up the length of the theater; his duty was to keep anybody in his area from standing up or trying to leave the theater. The orders, issued from the control room and relayed through the head page, made this very clear.

But Pellar was probably too bright to make a good page, just as he would have been too bright to make a good soldier; he wasn't the kind who followed orders that didn't make sense to him. And in studying the situation, he'd noticed that the camera sweeps of the aisle, intended to make sure no one was leaving the studio, barely covered the area he was assigned to. Pellar figured that if he grabbed someone from an aisle seat, he could get them out the emergency door he was assigned to guard, and have the door closed again before the camera got back to him.

Twice, he had done this, choosing people who looked either very helpless or very close to cracking; he had to work very quietly in the partially darkened theater so as to avoid other people seeing what he was up to and rushing over to him. His operation ran very contrary to the orders, but if he could save one or two lives by slipping someone out the door, why not? In fact, he was planning the same exit for himself shortly. In the Army, they'd shoot you for something like that; the worst NBC could do was fire him.

Carefully, he watched the camera begin its inspecting sweep toward him; soon it would swing back and search the right center aisle. A little angrily, Orin Pellar wondered whose side the cameramen were really on; but he supposed they had their instructions, too. He saw the red light on the camera blink on, meaning the shot of his area was going out over the air. Then, it went off and the camera turned away.

Pellar moved. He already had his next candidate for escape picked. Once—maybe twice—more he'd help someone else. Then he would slip out himself.

That crap about women and children first was probably an invention of Women's Lib.

At the desk of the Americana, Ambrose was relieved to see they had beaten Goddard and the others. There were some New York police standing around, but they were apparently under orders not to make their move until Goddard arrived.

He pushed the FBI man forward, and he flashed his badge at the clerk.

Shown the pictures of Colonius—along with a Polaroid of his portrait taken off the television screen at the Westbury—the first clerk they talked to merely shook his head. "People check in and out here by the hundreds every day."

A description of the accomplice—Mrs. Spiers of the Sweet Laurel had done her best to give them an accurate one—was answered with the same negative headshake from the clerk—as well as from two others whom the FBI man had rounded up. And no, there was no Dr. Kraus registered at the hotel.

It was exactly as Ambrose had expected—and it meant that Goddard wouldn't get anywhere with the same questions. The FBI man pulled the remaining desk clerk into the conversation, leaving the line of people trying to register milling around in angry confusion. "All right, then," said Ambrose to the rest of the clerks, "please try to remember very hard now. In the last couple of days, has anyone in the hotel asked for—even inquired about—having an extra television set or sets installed in his room?"

Three of the desk clerks replied with more of the same headshakes. The fourth's mouth dropped open. He hesitated as if he didn't want to speak, didn't want himself or the hotel to become involved, but there was no getting around the expression on his face. "*You*," said Ambrose and laid one hand on the man's arm, heavily. "Somebody *did* ask you, didn't they? Can you remember who? Can you find out who? Which room number? Fast?"

Looking shaken, as though he felt he were being accused of having done something illegal himself, the clerk dived into a tray of papers and began thumbing through them frantically. Still wearing an almost guilty expression, he produced a yellow printed form and showed it to Ambrose, Evans, and the FBI man, as if it had been proof of

226

innocence. "Here. Here it is"—the clerk's words tumbled over each other in his desperate effort to be cooperative —"a billing slip from the engineering department. Two extra sets. Color. For Mr. Carlton in—"

Ambrose gave something between a snort and a laugh, making the clerk look up in surprise. *"Carlton?* He called himself *Carlton?"* asked Ambrose, nearly incredulous, and then laughed again. Apparently, Colonius' endless search for a father even extended to the name he'd chosen for himself.

The clerk shoved the paper closer to Ambrose. "See? Right here—'Deliv. immed. to Mr. A. Carlton, Suite 4340.' "

But Evan Evans wasn't pondering the psychological overtones. "Let's go," he said and spun toward the elevator. On the way, the FBI man grabbed the room clerk and a pair of New York policemen and, half-shoving Ambrose ahead of him, commandeered the first elevator with an open door.

Outside, from far away, Ambrose thought he could hear more sirens. Damn Goddard, anyway. The elevator began to rise. Ambrose looked hard at his watch, as if staring intently enough might make the hands move more slowly.

It was now ten forty-nine.

A slight clicking sound in the door was what made Colonius turn around. In one hand he held the phone— he was about to make one last attempt on the President thing, although he realized by now it was probably too damned late—but the strange sound at the door caused him to slip the blunt-nosed thirty-eight from his pocket into his free hand. The clicking, he supposed, was probably the maid slipping her key into the lock, although he'd hung the DO NOT DISTURB sign on the door and she should know better. "Go away," he shouted. The clicking stopped.

Lars Colonius waited a second, then partially turned back toward the phone, the revolver still in his other hand. He wanted to get the call out of the way quickly; on the screen he could see they were about to start reading some

227

of his poems and philosophies. The actor who was to read them—Colonius had missed the name when it was announced—looked familiar, but he was unable to place him precisely. From a television suspense series, he thought. Trying to remember who it was absorbed him so completely for a moment that he was entirely unprepared when his door suddenly crashed open and two policemen tumbled inside. "Freeze!" They both yelled it at the same time so that it sounded more like a child's game than a life or death command. But Colonius froze.

There was some confusion at the door. Two more men appeared and shoved their way into the room. One was the fat little man with the cigar Colonius remembered from the Westbury—his eyes seemed to be racing around the room, searching for something—but the other was totally unfamiliar. Then, struggling his way through between them, Dr. Ambrose appeared.

The two policemen, guns drawn, were moving toward Colonius when Dr. Ambrose stopped them with a shouted order. "Everybody just stay where you are. Until we find out if there's a radio control and where, everybody stay calm, damn it." He turned away from them and spoke to Colonius in a very calm, gentle voice. "Hi, Lars."

"Hello, doctor. I was just about to phone you." Colonius nodded toward the black box. It was a crazy conversation, he thought. Five excited men with pistols pointed at him, yet he and the doctor sounded like two old friends who'd run into each other on a street corner.

"The radio transmitter, Lars," said Dr. Ambrose with a smile. "You don't want to go ahead with that *now*, do you?"

At that point, no one was ever too sure of just what happened. Lars Colonius had frozen, as ordered. But he still had the pistol in his hand. There is some question, since he was standing partly hidden by the wing-backed armchair, whether the policemen even saw it when they first confronted Colonius. Or he may have moved his hands in such a way that they thought he was going to shoot. Everyone was very tense and later no one could say exactly why it happened. A shot came from one of the policemen; Colonius fired back; both missed completely.

The second policeman didn't. Colonius crumpled to the floor.

"You stupid bastard," Ambrose shouted at the cop and raced across the room to Colonius. Gently, he took the pistol from his hand, and then leaned down to him. Colonius was still conscious, his eyes wide with fright, his breathing heavy and irregular. It was a rasping sound, a sound almost lost in the simultaneous reading of his poetry from the three television sets.

"The transmitter, Lars. The radio," he whispered. "Where is it?"

Colonius laughed softly, but this made him cough and he had to struggle to get control of his breathing again. "No radio, doctor. Timers."

"I knew it, I knew it," swore Goddard. He'd come into the room the minute before, and now dived for one of the phones. The control room of the studio answered and Goddard shouted at them to evacuate the theater. He yelled this about half a dozen times, it seemed, and then hung up with a disgusted slam.

Lars Colonius smiled—he would have liked to laugh, but he remembered what had happened when he tried that before—"It's too late, doctor. Much too late. They'll never get the people out of there. What time is it?"

"Ten fifty-five, Lars." Ambrose hesitated a second, then reached down and tried to make him more comfortable. "How much time have they got?" he asked.

"Too late, doctor. Much too late."

A sort of shudder ran through Colonius and he arched his back with a groan. During this, his eyes closed, squeezed tightly shut to ward off the waves of pain. Then it passed and his whole body suddenly relaxed; for a moment Ambrose wasn't sure if he was dead, but slowly the eyes opened again and looked up at him. Ambrose was startled to discover that Colonius was clutching his hand.

"Just lie still, Lars," he said softly. "Relax." Beyond the narrow periphery of his vision, Ambrose could see Goddard pacing and knew that at any second he would come over and start yelling at Colonius; it was no way to get anything out of a wounded man. Speed was necessary if he were to keep Goddard from barreling in and spoiling

229

any chance they had, yet he couldn't move too quickly or Colonius wouldn't give up his secret. "Lie back and relax, Lars. That feels better, doesn't it?" Ambrose gave the situation a second's pause to make Colonius feel he was the real object of their concern. "Now, Lars, consider this carefully," he began again. "If it's too late, why don't you tell us where the bomb, where the plastics, are?"

"No point, no point." His voice had a singsong quality to it, not because Colonius wanted it to, but because he was feeling terribly lightheaded. He seemed to be drifting on some sort of light red haze, floating across the room, drifting in and out of contact. The pain had stopped hurting, which he found odd. The voices in the room were distant and far away, and he thought he could hear music somewhere, which was crazy. Turning his head slightly, he could see pandemonium on the TV screen as the audience at the Belasco, in spite of Mel Fineman's and DiLaco's repeated pleadings over the PA system, all tried to push themselves through the exits at the same time.

It surprised Colonius in a vague, disinterested way, that the cameras were still operating. He had no way of knowing that DiLaco had told the cameramen and the technicians they were free to stay or try to get out, as they wished. But if they stayed, he'd urged them to keep running the equipment. "We're making history, guys," was all he'd said. Looking at the murderous crunch of bodies at the exit doors, most of them were staying. For the moment. So were the technicians, although a few thought they knew of little-used and forgotten exits out of the Belasco and had left to search for them. Part of the orchestra was still there, playing something cheerful and lively—DiLaco thought it was the "March of the Children" from *The King and I*—in the tradition of circus bands who keep playing as the tent burns down around them. Nor did Colonius know that Orin Pellar, the page who'd been granting exit visas to compassionate cases from the audience, was at this moment lying flat and quite dead outside the theater; Pellar was the first to get his exit doors open and the audience simply surged over him as he tried to slow them down. They were too tightly packed together to notice him on the ground or to step over him as they thundered out.

Ambrose's voice brought Colonius' mind back into focus, but all he could repeat were the same words, "Too late, much too late. And you'll never find it. Never, never, never." Some noise inside the room made Colonius turn his head and he saw more police spilling into the room; two of them pushed a rolling stretcher between them and then a doctor was bending beside him doing something he couldn't feel to the wound in his chest.

It was then that Colonius saw Einstein. He was coming through the door. Evan Evans had recognized him immediately from the description and now they had him by the arm and were apparently trying to find out from him where the plastic was. It made no sense that Einstein was here, it was crazy, it was unfair, it was wrong, and a complete act of disobedience. (Actually, it was the disobedience of Orin Pellar, who'd noticed the deaf and dumb boy and chosen him as the last person he let out of the theater before all hell broke loose.)

"You dumb little bastard, Einstein," Colonius groaned, and for the first time Einstein saw him.

Turning, Ambrose signaled the policeman to bring the boy over; maybe some clue about the plastic would come out of a confrontation between him and Colonius.

Looking down, Einstein saw the wound in Colonius and felt his own guilt at leaving the theater. He began to cry. "I'm sorry Mr. Colonius, I'm sorry. But it was those pictures of the people in bed. You didn't tell me they were going to show those pictures, Mr. Colonius. It was wrong what you did to them people, Mr. Colonius. And those pictures, seeing them all blown up like that, I thought I was going to get sick all over the floor. And anyway, the alarm clock in my pocket didn't ring like you said it would, Mr. Colonius, and when the man—"

"Shut up, Einstein, you stupid prick, shut your mouth." The effort of saying this exhausted Colonius and his head, raised slightly to yell at Einstein, fell back on the floor. He felt so awfully tired he almost didn't care. Einstein had spilled the beans and he didn't care; the thought made Colonius smile.

But Evan Evans had caught what the boy said and grabbed Einstein. He and Goddard and a couple of policemen wrestled him to the floor and found the wires and the timers and the plastic. Disconnecting the wires was easy; it had never occurred to Colonius to booby-trap the timers because it never occurred to him that anyone would ever find them. The fishing vest was removed, the suit-jacket torn off him, the trouser pockets ripped open, and along with them most of the trousers themselves. Einstein was sobbing louder now, standing there in his torn trousers and crying, trying to explain to Mr. Colonius and make him understand.

But Colonius was looking directly at Ambrose and saying something, something Ambrose was having a hard time hearing because of all the confusion in the room, particularly Einstein's sobbing and whining. Ambrose turned his head, waving his arm to the police to indicate Einstein should be taken out. He was dragged from the room, screaming and pleading for Mr. Colonius to listen, wrestling with his captors, desperately seeking forgiveness from the bleeding body on the floor.

Impatiently, Ambrose leaned back down. The medical doctor who was handling Colonius hadn't exactly shaken his head the way they do on *Marcus Welby,* but the message was every bit as clear.

Goddard hung up from his call to the studio. There was no longer, he had told them, a bomb in the Belasco. The answer he got from Mel Fineman was so rude that Goddard's face colored. Then, for the first time in some minutes, Goddard looked up at the three television screens. ABC had cut back to its own studios, where an anchorman was holding forth; the CBS picture was coming from a mobile unit on the street outside the Belasco, where firemen, policemen, and emergency units were helping the injured into cars and ambulances. NBC was still showing the interior of the theater, which, with the exception of a few dazed and hurt people in the audience and a man lying in the aisle—he'd had a heart attack during the panic to leave and was being worked over by a hospital emergency crew—appeared almost empty. For some reason, the remainder of the orchestra was still playing, wildly now, in a kind of Dixieland jam session. It sounded, Goddard thought, like "Oh, When the Saints."

Ambrose turned again and angrily shushed the people behind him; Colonius was still trying to say something and Ambrose was still unable to hear him. He wasn't sure himself why hearing it was so important to him, and yet it was, and Ambrose yelled for everybody in the room for Christ's sake to shut up.

One by one the people in the room fell silent. Turning back with a reassuring smile, Ambrose leaned down again to hear whatever it was Colonius had to say. But for Lars Colonius, who had lived so long in silence, the opportunity came too late. The room was silent, everyone was looking at him, his mouth was open, but he could not speak.

Lars Colonius was dead.

"Whatever happens—and I know now that this thing can only end one way for me—I think I won, I still think I won. Because up until all of this, you know, even escape into death was an impossibility for me. It was like that crazy riddle they ask you in school. You know the one: 'If a tree falls in the forest, but nobody's there to see or hear it happen, how can anybody know for sure that the tree really fell?'

Well, that was sort of the way I felt about dying.

After all, how can you die if nobody knows you're alive?"

> —*Closing lines from the journal of Lars Colonius*